THE GIRL FROM JAFFNA

And Other Stories

G. RAJESWARAN THAMPI

INDIA • SINGAPORE • MALAYSIA

ISBN 979-8-88805-441-3

D.T.P. by – Meghnad Thampi and Tejeshwar Thampi
Edited by – Dr. Parvathy Suchindranath

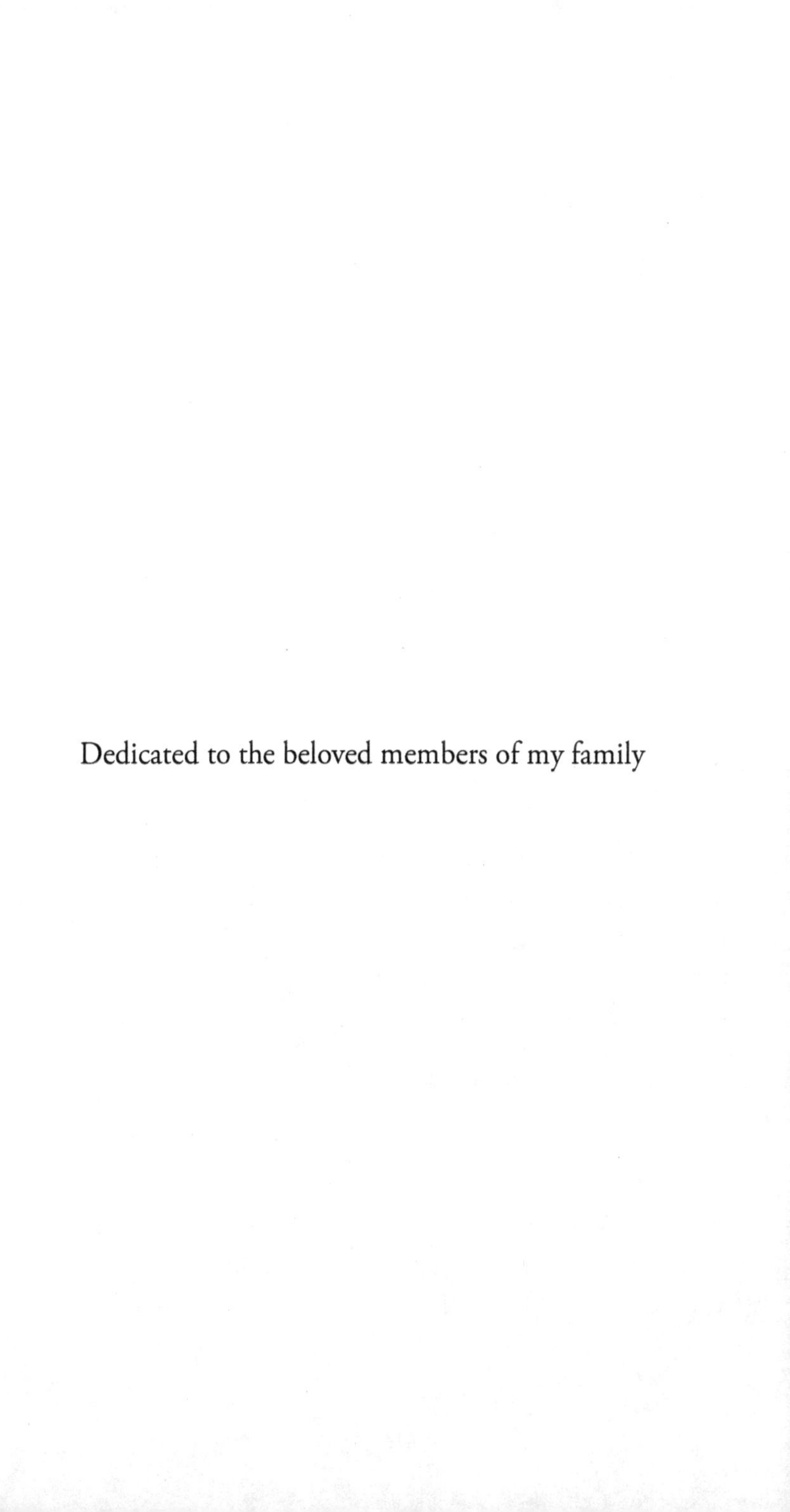

Dedicated to the beloved members of my family

Contents

1. The Girl From Jaffna 7
2. The Loco Pilot 61
3. Ramayee 81
4. Wood and Chisel 103
5. Share of the Church 133
6. The Electrician 151
7. Barn to Home 169
8. Talisman 191
9. The Teacher 235
10. Turmeric and Jasmine 253

1

The Girl From Jaffna

As usual, Nethuni was returning from school along with two of her friends, Santuri and Nihara, living near her home. But today was a different one, a special day for her. They were actually not walking but running, as if they had some urgent work at home. Her friends asked her why she was in a hurry to go home unlike the other days. Santuri, a close friend of Nethuni, commented, "Oh, today you got the first prize in the dance competition, that is why you're just running to your home, to show it to your parents. Is it not?" Giggling all the way, they dispersed on a small junction near the location of her house. "See you tomorrow", said Nihara, "Don't forget to bring sweets."

Nethuni was in class eight in a convent school in Jaffna town. A bright student, she was very dear to her teachers at school. She had an artistic way of talking, walking, and even gestures that reminded many dance movements. Because of her interests in multivarious areas, her art teacher introduced her to a dance centre near the school a couple of years ago and within no time, she mastered most of the dance movements, that adult dancers used to perform. Her first performance was in a municipal auditorium where she received good applause. In the same year, when she was still in class seven, she was selected as a candidate for several competitions. After coming to class eight, she was qualified for the All Sri Lanka Dance Competition in the Junior category. She got the first position and received a number of medals and certificates.

Nethuni's father was a security head in a private tea estate, and her mother used to work in a nearby tea company. After her elder sister was born, her mother stopped working. Her elder sister, Onisha, was now twenty-one-year-old and worked as a teacher in a primary school in the town. Just a couple of years back, she got married. They were a happy family, with Onisha's husband running a shop selling spices and cosmetics. They spoke Tamil at home. Nethuni was well-conversant in English, Tamil, and Sinhalese. Their ancestors, it was said, came from the southern part of India, centuries ago. Most of the Sri Lankan Tamil-speaking people lived in northern and eastern provinces, and also in Colombo. During the early days, a host of Tamil families lived in the central highlands. Nethuni knew that her ancestry goes back to the second century BCE and was mostly Hindus and subsequently, a sizable Christian population also came up. Nethuni believed that she belonged to the so-called Sri Lankan Tamils.

Her friends included Tamil and Sinhalese-speaking Hindus, Christians, Muslims, and very few Buddhists also. As she was an all-rounder in the school, she was loved by one and all. Thus, she enjoyed her school days with plenty of joy and happiness.

On that day, when she came home, the first thing she did was, open the bag, take out the medals and certificates and show it to her mother. Her sister gave her a good hug and blessed her telling her to consider this as the first and an important prize in her life and that she could bring a lot more in the coming days. Her mother made some sweets, especially for her and she celebrated the occasion together with her family members after her father and Murugavel, Onisha's husband, came home, closing the shop.

They sat out for some time on the veranda and chatting, each one telling their day's experiences. During the conversation, Mr Murugavel told that the LTTE cadres were attacking the government installations and creating chaos in the northern areas of the country. When Murugavel told this, there was a chill running through the veins of her father, Koomaraswamy, as he also heard some rumours of government forces might retaliate on Tamils. The cool mother was telling, "Oh, this has been going on for several years…" Onisha said, "both parties are not going to stop, one day or the other, we all will be in trouble."

Suddenly, a heavy wind blew with branches of trees dancing to the monster's tune. Heavy lightning struck the whole area, flashing a flood of light followed by a clap of deafening thunder. They all rushed in, closed all doors and windows and went to retire for the day. It started raining cats and dogs for almost an hour, but by then, all were fast asleep. Outside, there were sounds of people yelling and running out on the road, splashing rainwater. Some were on bikes, shouting broken sentences filled with anxiety and panic. Koomaraswamy got up from the bed and opened the front windows slightly, and peeped outside. He could see nothing in the pitch-black darkness. The electricity was off… Sporadic bike riders could be seen shouting in Tamil asking the people to escape the locality. Sensing trouble, Koomaraswamy was about to alert all the inmates, but before that, he heard sounds of boots and knocking on the doors of several houses including his. By that time, people inside the home were all alerted and ready to get out of the house, via the back exit, which opened out to a small backyard. There was a door in the compound wall through which anyone could reach a small lane leading to the side road. But when they were just about to go, the front door broke open and a few soldiers barged into the house with rifles. No questions asked, they savagely pounced upon the hapless, unarmed people and one soldier pierced his bayonet into the stomach of Onisha who was already carrying a six-month-old baby. Nethuni was in the room and she had to witness this horrible incident. All this happened before she could wake up from her slumber. She felt as if she heard the child pleading to be saved. Nethuni first thought it was all a bad dream but somebody pulled her hands and dragged her towards the backdoor. She escaped from the clutches and ran back to the house. She took the bag containing her ID card, medals, certificates, and some books. She turned towards the back exit door and stumbled upon the body of Onisha, who was bleeding all over and was already dead. With untold remorse and fear, she searched in the dark for her mother, but could not find anybody. In the next room, she heard someone moaning near the door of the bathroom. She went near that place and found out that it was her father. Drenched in blood, he told her in a very feeble voice, to run, and he gave his purse containing a few rupees. She lay there for a while on the bloodstained body of her father. The moaning had also stopped. She could not find her mother or Murugavel. When again torchlights flashed here and there, she ran outside with her bag sobbing and shivering with fear. It was now drizzling, and she could finally make out a silhouette of a soldier at the back exit. All drenched in the rain, she hid between the thick jasmine bushes and the wall of the well and sat on the mud for a few minutes, till she heard the sound of starting of a vehicle outside the front door. Still, there were gunshots, noises, shouting and crying that could be heard clearly.

After ensuring that there were no soldiers at home, she got up from the mud, clutching her bag against her chest and shivering, due to the rain and drenching. She ventured inside the house again and took the small torch Murugavel used to keep among the *pooja* items below an array of pictures of gods and goddesses. Now she hated all these figures and asked herself why all these figures were daily worshipped, why all this had happened. The front door was ajar. A few stray dogs were running along the road, howling, as she had never heard previously. She dared to get out through the front door but could not see anything clearly because of the darkness. On the veranda, where they used to sit, a body of an elderly man was lying. She flashed her torch and found that the old man was shot in the neck and a lot of blood was lost. She went inside again and searched every nook and corner of the house. She could not find anybody, either dead or alive. She inferred that the monsters would have taken the body in their vehicles. She looked at the clock, it was two a.m. Now the rain had almost stopped and occasional drops of water falling from the trees could be heard whenever the wind blew.

Sobbing heavily, with swollen eyes, she cursed the entire humanity and all the gods she knew. Why was this happening, when they were called the protectors, saviours, etc.? Her father, mother, brother, sister, brother-in-law… No one did any harm to anybody, so far. But still, alas… That little thing inside Onisha's womb, did it do any harm to those monstrous soldiers? No, just for nothing, they shot everybody. It was their pleasure, but did these gods also join hands in this cruelty? She went to the kitchen and drank a glass of cold water, washed in the bathroom, and changed her muddy and drenched clothes. Dried her long, black and thick flowing hair with a towel and sat on a chair near the window. Now the initial fear was gone. She was looking out and thinking about what to do further. It seemed to her that everything outside was near normal. Only sounds of dogs howling near and far could be heard. Occasionally, some night birds were also fearlessly flying and searching for food in the nearby trees and bushes. Now Nethuni wanted to see the night birds but as it was pitch dark, she could hear only sounds. One or two bikes sped away on the road. The sound of water flowing from the street into the gutters was clearly heard, which resounded some music to her ears.

Nethuni got up from the chair and inspected the back exit door latch which was fastened and the front door was broken and one-half of it was on the floor. She once again searched for her people but none were there. As she had determined some future course of action, she took a small leather bag and filled it with necessary clothes, for changing if needed and kept a small bag containing her belongings also. She took another glass of water as she was thirsty and again sat on the same chair, looking outside through the window. As on a television screen, she could visualise the horrible massacre which had just happened in her home. She could not believe what had happened and cursed her gods several times. The clock was showing three a.m. when she looked at it flashing the torch. A visibly tired Nethuni sat on the chair again and just dozed off for a few minutes.

Suddenly, the sound of a heavy truck woke her up. Now it was only twenty minutes past four am. She got up, went to the toilet, washed, and took her airbag. Also, she ate some leftover sweets along with a few slices of bread. The rest of the food packets were pushed into the bag which was already bulging. She looked around her favourite place once more. The laughing and smiling figures in the framed pictures on the wall, the clock she had been watching since her childhood, the newly purchased television set, the dancing doll from Tamil Nadu that was gifted to her by her friend, Tarushi… and of course, the images of gods and goddesses. When her sight fell on these pictures, she pulled herself away and looked at the picture of her father and mother. She touched that photo and kissed it several times and bid goodbye. Carefully, she got out, for a long journey. The destination of the journey was unknown to her.

Stepping out on the muddy road, she walked towards the city. On the way, she looked at familiar houses, somewere opened ajar, doors and windows were broken, some were found locked and yet, a few others had inmates for faint lights of chimneys could be seen through the glass windows. Aimlessly, she walked through the main road, side road, lanes and by-lanes. There were plenty of people like Nethuni. Mostly old, children and invalids. She could see them wandering on the road in the twilight. The day was just breaking and some buildings could be seen. By the time drizzling also stopped, the town seemed normal. The milk vendors, newspaper boys, fish sellers, and bread sellers were seen speeding in bicycles and motorbikes in both directions. The sellers were, as usual, shouting in peculiar voices to attract the households. Nethuni had come a long way from her home; she had walked for more than two hours. Exhausted, she needed some water. She remembered her filling up the bottle yet failing to bring it due to the lack of space in her bag. She spotted a small house on the roadside where a lady was cleaning the veranda. She asked for water from the lady. With a suspicious look, the lady brought water in an old bottle and asked her to take it and clear the place immediately.

Cursing her fate, she again walked and walked. A vegetable vendor came behind her in a motorbike and asked her, "Where are you going at this time of the day? Can I drop you?"

He spoke Sinhalese. Nethuni stopped and did not answer for some time. The stranger told in a warning tone, "You're a small kid. Do not walk alone like this. It is not safe." This time, he spoke in Tamil. "It is a danger zone for Tamilians. You might get attacked by some vandals. You're a Tamilian as well, aren't you? Come, ride behind me. I am trying to help you only because you look like my daughter. Hence, this offer." Nethuni hesitantly came near the vehicle. She decided to avail of the offer and jumped on the pillion. She put her bag in between him and her. Though it was very difficult to sit like that, she adjusted herself. The man started the vehicle and left the place with Nethuni. The bike was running with a lot of noise. Again, he asked, "What is your name? Where are you going?" She sobbed. He turned back and saw her moist eyes. "Don't cry, tell me, what help do you need? Are you one of those affected by the last night's carnage?" The conversation was in Tamil. Nethuni replied, "Yes."

"Where is your home?"

"Navakuli Street near the church".

As he seemed to be genuine, she answered all her questions.

"Now, where do you want to go? We are nearing Jaffna railway station. Now you are more than ten miles away from your home. Do you have any safe place to go? Any known places? Friends? Family? Relations? I can drop you there."

She sobbed and said, "No," and started crying.

"It is all right. I understand."

Within a short distance ahead of the railway station, on Candy Road, there was a by-lane. He stopped, "Be seated, I am coming."

A kind of fear grew in her mind. First, she thought of getting down and running away. But by then, he came out of a big house nearby along with a hefty lady in her fifties, wearing a nightgown. She looked at Nethuni and gestured for her to follow. Nethuni's heart pounding fast and visibly gripped in fear, she slowly approached the lady. The man blessed her in the name of Jesus and said goodbye to her. Before he left, he told Nethuni that this lady would take care of her.

The lady got into the house and asked Nethuni to come to the backyard, via a side lane within the compound of this fairly big house. When Nethuni reached at the backyard the lady also came to the rear side and opened the door. She asked Nethuni to sit on a willow chair lying outside and offered a glass full of tea. She enjoyed the beverage as she desperately needed some hot drinks, though she had no habit of taking tea or coffee. As she had a very long walk in the morning, which she never undertook ever before in her life.

The lady, named Christina also sat opposite her in the open yard in another chair. The yard looked like a mini garden with a gravelled floor, grass patches and flowering bushes, etc. that were neatly maintained and an array of trees, both flowering and fruit-bearing, including a few neem trees were also seen. In that fine climate without rain or shine and with a little breeze, Nethuni got a kind of relief to her physique and mind. She really enjoyed that serenity and wished she could continue this forever or at least for some time. But at present, she wished to be alone for some time.

Christina was observing Nethuni silently and studying her physical features. Breaking the silence, she asked, "What's your name?"

"Nethuni," she trembled.

"You go to temple?"

"Yes."

"Tamil?"

"Yeah."

"What language do you speak normally?"

"I speak Tamil, Sinhalese and English."

"Very good."

"Do you go to school?"

"Yes, Navakuli Christian School."

"Your grade?"

"I am in the eighth standard."

"Did you go to school yesterday?"

"Yes."

"Your parents?"

Nethuni told her the names of her parents, sister, and brother-in-law.

"Ok, ok. The vegetable vendor Fernando talked about what happened to your home and family. A lot of houses were attacked, but nobody knew what happened to them. What to do? All this is part of fate."

After a brief silence, Christina continued.

"Now what is your idea? I don't think you will have any specific proposal… Then what about your relatives? Your father's people, your mother's people…?"

Nethuni told in a low voice, "I don't know their whereabouts. All I know is that they're all in the Central Highlands and are dispersed somewhere in Candy, Colombo, Kilinochchi, etc."

"Ok, any address or phone number?"

"No, I don't have any."

"Anyway," Christina continues, "For your information, I'll tell you that many Tamil families were attacked. Therefore, it is not safe for you to continue here. It is a miracle that you have escaped from this carnage. Let my husband come. He is on duty nowadays and he comes late at night only."

"Ma'am, where is he working?"

"He is a high-ranking engineer. He may come by another hour or so. You freshen up and change your clothes. Have you got any dry clothes with you? Or should I give?"

"No, I do have some…"

Christina, pointing out a room along the outer wall, said, "Well, go to that bathroom complex."

She was shown the complex near the outer wall on the left and Christina went inside and closed her door.

After a few minutes, Nethuni came out in another skirt and blouse and dried her hair in the early morning sun. With a towel in hand, she sat as still as a statue, with the memories of the previous horrible night. The very thought of the brutal happenings drained all her energy through her feet to the ground. Those bloody soldiers did not seem to have any sisters, mothers, or children. The very sight of the bayonet piercing Onisha's stomach... Even if she did not want to think about it, it automatically came into her mind.

She thought of her family's belongings. There might not be much cash but some jewellery of mother and Onisha could be there. She had seen them keeping it in the safe in her mother's bedroom. Then she came to the conclusion that those brutes would have taken it with them. She thought in these lines because something similar happened with one of Onisha's friends a couple of years back in Jaffna. These beasts had looted all their valuables after killing each one of them, including two small children... Horrible!

She woke up from her bloody thoughts when somebody took the towel from her hand. She immediately stood up and looked blankly at the person. It was Maria, Christina's housemaid. She seemed to be about thirty years old. She held Nethuni's hands and invited her to have breakfast. She spoke Sinhalese. Maria ushered her to an anteroom adjacent to the kitchen which looked like Maria's, where a small table and a chair were available with a wooden double bench in the wall with bedrolls. Nethuni was seated in that chair and a plate of bread and omelette was served. A starving Nethuni quickly finished the items on the plate, and Maria offered a cup of tea as well.

When Nethuni was trying to go out of the room, Maria told her to stay back and she also sat on the floor, leaning against the wall, stretching her legs. Maria asked, with a friendly smile, "Ma'am told your name is Nethuni. Good name. Hindu-Tamil?"

Nethuni nodded her head affirmatively.

"Have you gone to school?"

"Yes, till yesterday."

"In which class are you studying?"

Nethuni said, "Eighth."

"Oh eighth?" With a feeling of despair and guilt, "I had never gone to school," said Maria.

Nethuni asked eagerly, "Where is Ma'am?"

"She is in the bathroom, taking a shower."

Nethuni was anxious to know who the master of the house was and what work he engaged in. She quietly asked Maria, "What is Ma'am's husband's name?"

"Mr Mascarenhas, he is a big construction engineer. He is expected any time."

Nethuni was just relieved to hear this. He was not a police officer. Because she saw a khaki uniform hanging from a coat stand in a corner near the kitchen. Nethuni asked, "Is he an engineer?"

"Yes, very rich. That is why he is employing guards, drivers, etc. Didn't you see?"

"No."

"Maybe they're off to their morning ablutions. They may come back quickly. The master is also expected before nine. Immediately upon coming, he will have his shower, take a quick breakfast and leave for work again. He is a very busy man."

On hearing the cluttering of plates and cups, Maria stood up and told, "It seems Ma'am is ready for breakfast. Let me go and see."

She left the room, asking Nethuni to take a rest if she needed any. Nethuni was dead tired, due to last night's sleeplessness and the morning walk, her eyelids were drooping. But she tried to be awake so that she could ask Ma'am what she had decided to do with her.

Within a few minutes, more voices could be heard from inside the home. She listened carefully and came to the conclusion that the master had come. After half an hour or so, she was summoned to the front hall where the engineer Mascarenhas was sitting. Nethuni entered the hall with a soft walk and her eyes resembled those of a deer in the cage of a tiger. Mr Mascarenhas asked her several questions in the same way as Mr Christina did, to which Nethuni answered convincingly. When he asked for some sort of identification, to prove her identity, she gave the school ID, medals and certificates received yesterday. Looking at the certificate asked her, "Nethuni? You don't recognize me? I was the person who presided over your school function yesterday. Don't you remember me?"

Nethuni exclaimed, "Oh! Yes, sir!"

"Then why didn't you tell me earlier?"

Nethuni put her head down, "Er…That is, sir…"

Christina intervened, "How could this poor child recognise you with your *lungi* and *banyan* attire? Yesterday you were in your full suit with a cap covering your bald head."

It seemed that Nethuni enjoyed the satire.

Mr Mascarenhas said, "Nethuni, now you go to your room and take a rest." Thinking for a while, he phoned up someone and asked him to come to his residence. Nethuni retired to her room and was relieved to see the behaviour of the master. But she thought again, about the call, who was the person he had phoned? Could he be a police officer? Slowly she fell asleep on the bare wooden bench.

She was woken by Maria and was served a decent lunch around two pm. After lunch, he was again asked to go to the front hall where, apart from Mascarenhas, another person was also present.

"Nethuni, I can keep you in this house for some time more and it is not safe here for people like you. I hope you understand the present situation here which is so turbulent that any time anything can happen. I have to keep my dignity and loyalty to the government. Now tell me whether you want to go to any of your relatives you know or any intimate family friend who would be able to take care of you. If so, give me their phone numbers and addresses."

Christina intervened, "She doesn't have anyone. If there is some clue we can trace it out but that would take a hell of a time. And moreover, the government forces, if they find her on the road… I don't know what would happen". Mascarenhas finally said, "Therefore it would be better that she is left to flee, like many people who are currently fleeing out of the country for their safety. Both Elam fighters and the government forces are equally dreaded. Therefore, she can never spend a day more here".

Turning to Mr Kani, Mascarenhas asked, "What do you say, Mr Kani?" Mr Kani a middle-aged man who looked like a businessman said in a remorse-filled tone, "Near about a hundred households in her locality were severely affected in the last night's programme by the forces".

Nethuni asked him, "Uncle what happened to my neighbours?" Her eyes were red and it seemed that the tear glands of Nethuni had already dried up, "all the people in the area?".

Kani replied, "Two or three streets, including yours, entirely wiped off the people from both sides of the streets. Most of them, men, women, elders, kids, babies every one fled. Mostly towards the north. Many perished in the ambush. By now the authorities must have removed all bodies including the cattle! Some people were captured, very innocent people who didn't have any connection with the liberation fighters. Even children, some grown-up students all were taken in trucks and driven away."

Nethuni, "To where?"

"Nobody knows."

Mascarenhas asked, "Do you know any of your neighbours?"

Nethuni replied, "There are many—my friends, schoolmates and classmates, Santhuri, Nihara, Fathima, Jeyson, Rasangi and quite a lot."

Mascarenhas replied, "But trying to trace them would be a suicidal attempt". Christina asked her husband Mascarenhas, "Now tell me what are you going to do with the girl?" Her husband was sympathetically looking at Nethuni. His thoughts were somewhere else.

Mr Kani told firmly, "My definite opinion is we must send her to India along with some other persons or family going as refugees to India by boat. Of course, it is a discrete operation, but we haven't got any other way. I can find a place in Abdul's boat going to Rameswaram". Mascarenhas woke up from his thoughts and let out a deep sigh.

"As of now, I think this would be the only way to save this hopeless child."

Christina said, "But they will demand a large sum of money. Nethuni may not have money to pay for the boat".

Mascarenhas said, "I can meet all her expenses till she reaches Rameswaram."

Christina asked, "What do you say Nethuni?"

Nethuni simply wept, and then she said, "I don't have any idea whatsoever. I am totally at your mercy. You may decide anything which you think is right for me at this moment of turmoil."

"Smart girl," Mascarenhas commented.

"She is a good dancer also". He looked at Nethuni and told, "Even after you go to India continue practising dancing. You will become a renowned dancer one day." Nethuni blankly looked at everyone and she pointed her eyes towards Christina as if she was seeking asylum at Christina's house forever.

But Christina could not face her. Her eyes were pointed towards the picture of Jesus behind the burning candle which destroyed itself while giving light to everyone.

Nethuni finally came to know that she would never get asylum in that mansion because of the explosive situation in the city. She understood fully well this fact by intruding into the minds of everyone there. She began mentally preparing for the long journey into the unknown and unfamiliar dark area ahead.

Understanding the turbulence in her mind, Mascarenhas tried to pacify her by telling her many things and finally, he revealed his travel plans to her.

"Now, my child, listen carefully. As early as possible, you will have to leave this place, and you will be accommodated in a boat, maybe a catamaran, a country boat with or without the outboard engine, or a motorized fishing boat, a trawler or any type of vessel that sails in shallow waters. Your co-passengers could range from children to the aged ones, would be fleeing to India as refugees."

"You know who are refugees?"

Nethuni, "Yes I have learned in detail about them."

Mascarenhas continued, "In India or elsewhere also they are known as Sri Lankan refugees as you are going to another country clandestinely without any passport or travel documents. On arrival at their port, all these people would be taken out by the marine police or other government security agencies and put in a camp specially set up for these people and mind you, you must never step out of the camp without the permission of authorities. If you do so, you will be arrested," he paused for some time and asked her again, "have you got any money with you?".

She showed a purse that her father gave along with other things. Mascarenhas examined her school certificates, medals, identity card, etc. On seeing those documents, he said, "Very smart! Even in such a trying situation you could gather all these things. This will greatly support you in your camp life. I give you some extra money in India rupees," he turned towards Mr Kani and said, "Kani, hurry up. No time to waste. As early as possible, you should put her in the first boat that might leave Sri Lankan shores this night. It is your responsibility to take her to the jetty or some fishing village from where the boat leaves."

Kani said, "I will do it in Abdu's boat tonight itself."

He hesitatingly said, "Sir, you may arrange a safe vehicle from here, so that I can take her to Abdu safely. If it is done right now it would be convenient for me to reach Abdu before evening. And by the time I would ask him to reserve a seat for her." Mascarenhas intervened, "To reach Thalaimannar shore or jetty it would take at least three hours from here. Therefore, if you start from around seven pm you can reach by ten pm. Normally as you know, the boats could leave before midnight and the boat journey also takes around three-four hours or even more. They would reach the mainland by dawn, covering near about fifty nautical miles." Kani Said," I learned that the Navy here has increased patrolling. They are firing at any boat and our coastguard has also stepped up vigilance."

Mascarenhas said peacefully, "Don't worry, that part of the job would be intelligently handled by Abdu as he has men in all these agencies and the money works wonders everywhere. You have to be cautious only from here to Thalaimannar during the road journey. Once you reach Mannar province, you need not worry much. Because Abdu has deployed agents everywhere.

Mascarenhas went inside and came back with a bundle of Indian currency notes, divided it and gave one part to Nethuni and the other to Kani and said, "Hope this would suffice for all your needs till she is landed in Rameswaram. It includes your fees as well as boat charges for Abdu. Okay? Now you can leave and come by seven pm with a good vehicle which would not make any trouble on the way."

When Kani departed, Mascarenhas turned towards Nethuni and told her, "Nethuni, now I think everything is clear. Don't worry, you will be safe there. I can't give any guarantee, but if you stay here, it will be bad for us also. Anything may happen at any time. Maybe worse than whatever happened so far, such is the situation here. So get mentally and physically ready for the journey. I am leaving now. We will meet this evening."

Nethuni prostrated before them with tears and they blessed her in the name of Jesus. She went to her allotted room at the back of the house to watch the trees and birds.

When Nethuni came back and sat on the bench, Maria was busy in the kitchen preparing lunch. She came out of the kitchen and said," You are a lucky girl."

"Lucky girl?" Nethuni asked with surprise, "yesterday, all my loved ones were brutally murdered and I do not know if my other near and dear ones are alive or maimed or dead. Now, I am forced to run away from my motherland full of agony, anxiety and uncertainty... Still, how can I be described as a lucky one?" she asked Maria angrily.

Nethuni lowered her voice and asked, "What made these good souls help me? I don't have any relation with them. I have seen them for the first time, and that too by accident. Moreover, he is a senior government engineer... he is taking that much of risk."

Maria replied, "Now you should know one thing... if they are doing this for a hapeless Srilankan girl, this means that something must have induced them to do so. They had a daughter. She must be your age. A year ago, that sweet poor girl was killed in a road accident. She even resembled you to a great extent. She was very dear to them as she was their only child and was born quite a few years after their marriage. Maybe on seeing you, they found their daughter in you. For fear of action from the government, they are sending you to India, otherwise, I am sure, they would have kept you as their adopted daughter."

When Maria left, Nethuni went out and began to stroll in the backyard for some time when she squatted on the grass patch under the mango tree and started thinking about her dark, bleak and unknown destination.

On that day itself, Mr Mascarenhas sent his men to clean Nethuni's home and repaired the doors and windows that were badly damaged by the rummaging soldiers. This was done keeping in its mind that whenever Nethuni comes back after this turmoil she could use it.

On that night around ten pm, a dark-coloured vehicle came and stopped in front of the big mansion where Nethuni was ready with an airbag presented by Ms Christiana with all the travelling essentials and foodstuffs enough for two days. Both Mr and Mrs blessed her from inside the gate with Maria behind them. They bid goodbye to Nethuni and closed the gate.

It was a pre-war *Jonga* van that could carry nine persons excluding the driver, but already thirteen persons were seated tightly in the two long seats. Nethuni was accommodated along with Kani who was on the wheel in the front seat comfortably. The van started with a jerk and entered the main road and started running.

Nethuni looked back, but she could see nothing as it was dark. Suddenly, she felt a kind of fear and started trembling with tearful eyes. Noticing this, Kani, while driving, told her to gather courage. "Nethuni, now you are alone. Gather enough courage and set your mind to confront anything in life. Okay?"

"Try to sleep for some time, it may take at least three hours if there is no rain."

She stared at the road and she could see the worn-out black topped road with a lot of potholes.

The faint yellowish light falling on the road did not give her any idea what was on both sides but in the pitch dark, a few houses on the roadside mostly tiled could be seen with bright lights in the closed windows that sported artistic coloured glasses. When crossing the city limits there was a police checkpoint, and a couple of policemen flashed torch lights on the vehicle. Mr Kani immediately stopped the vehicle and gave some papers and an envelope. On seeing the signs in the envelope, the men in uniform waved their hands to go and after half an hour's drive again the vehicle was stopped.

Nethuni, who was sleeping clutching the airbag, suddenly opened her eyes and looked around. Here she found again Kani talking to security personnel but did not give any papers or cover. The police officer smiled at him and told him to proceed. Kani took the vehicle a little further on the left of the road and talked to the passengers.

"Friends, I am Kani. Abdu's friend. You may not know me or Abdu because all of you came to me through your agents only. Now it is another two hours run from here to Mannar. You may sleep if you want. If I stop the vehicle on the road, do not get out or do not talk to anyone through the windows. There would be more check posts like this further. Don't panic, it is common these days."

He started the vehicle which began to show its pulling power as if to please Kani. Many checkpoints were crossed, but the vehicle was not stopped upon seeing the number plates. Nethuni was fast asleep with both hands on the bag. Driver Kani took special care of Nethuni as per the instructions from Mr Mascarenhas. The other passengers in the vehicle also noticed this special consideration towards that girl. The boy sitting nearest to the long seat behind Nethuni, near the door started giving occasional glances at Nethuni. He seemed definitely longing to talk to her, but the grim-faced driver kept his mouth shut and concentrated on driving.

At about one pm in the dead of the night, they were offloaded from the van and taken to an isolated building not far away from the main road. Kani announced that they were free to use the washrooms available in the building. After having rest for an hour, the passengers were given sweetened black tea and biscuits available in one of the rooms.

Kani said, "You may not get anything to eat hereafter till we reach the shores. You may be having some items with you. But if you want to have more, you can purchase some biscuits or bread from this place and keep it with you. You can also carry water from this place in cans kept over there at some price."

Everyone had water with them in their luggage including Nethuni except that boy. When they started again, Kani asked that boy to come to the front seat.

Kani said, "I saw several times you were about to fall from the edge of the seat. Now come and sit here, between me and that girl and I forgot your name?"

"Velavan," said the boy.

He looked around fifteen years old only. He was happy that now he could talk to Nethuni. He was from a lower middle-class family from Jaffna and was a school dropout helping his parents in their family business of running a small eatery near the Murugan Temple. His only sister got married to a Sinhalese a few years back and they were living in Batticaloa. But in the holocaust of last night, his hotel was burnt down, his father beaten to death and his mother captured by the forces and taken away while he ran out. He was helped to escape from the area by a known taxi driver who came to the hotel just a few minutes before the grotesquery. He was given some money and was asked to run along with the people running in screaming but before they packed and were about to leave the place, those brutes rained in along with the few local Sinhalese whom his father knew well and who used to visit his shop frequently. Still, they had joined in the heinous crime of beating and killing innocence around that area simply because they happened to be of Tamil origin. Nobody could predict the insanity that the human mind possessed.

Sitting side by side, Velavan and Nethuni exchanged their tale of woes, of course not in their entirety. The sudden change in their life did bring them a kind of courage in their tender minds to face whatever calamities that might happen in the future. Looking at the closeness of Velavan and Nethuni, Mr Kani requested Velavan to give company to Nethuni as a protector in the boat as well as in the camp, if required.

The *jonga* was speeding up on the pitch-dark road other than natural light there was darkness all over. No houses could be seen on either side of the road. The vehicle took an easterly direction into a small gravelled road and was moving at a slow pace. From a small junction, another bike rider also joined as a pilot to lead them to the shores and after a few minutes, the signs of the shores could be seen. Apart from the dark trunks of palm trees, there were a few Baobab trees were also seen. The vehicle slowly stopped near a thatched hut that housed bundles of fishnets. The passengers arrived at the hut. Inside it was dark; nobody uttered a word and only the sounds of tides and the hustles of palm leaves could be heard relentlessly. Within no time a dark, slim man brought an engine to be fitted onto a country boat which was tied with a long rope to a palm tree stump on the shore. The boat was dangerously tilting due to the monsoon tides and wind.

Not only Nethuni but all the passengers got a terrible sense of fear when they thought that they were going to the sea in this old country boat with an outboard engine. The Yamaha engine was fitted hurriedly and all the passengers were hustled into the boat. The clothes of the passengers were wet below the thighs. The dark, slim man, Mr Justin, cautioned them to sit properly on the watery floor of the boat. They all, including some families who were already waiting in the shed, jumped into the boat braving the troubled waters and the cold easterly wind. They were physically helped by Kani and Justin to get them into the boat. Justin untied the ropes and along with Kani jumped into the boat and told the passengers that they would be taken to a large vessel waiting at a distance pointing to a small light shining in the sea above the dark waters. Justin started the engine and the boat began moving towards the larger vessel. It was an improvised trawler in which a few persons were already waiting. When the country boat neared the trawler, the boat was fastened to the trawler by a rope. One by one all the persons were physically lifted by Justin and Mr Wills safely to the trawler. There were only a few seats on the open-air trawler on which the elders and ladies with children were seated and others were sitting on the wet iron floor of the trawler. When everyone got in Kani and Justin returned to the country boat and to the shores. He did not forget to introduce Nethuni to Abdu as the person sent by Mr Mascarenhas whom he respected very much. Therefore, Abdu asked Nethuni to come to the engine room so that she could get some heat from the engine to escape from the cold wind and aerosols from the waves dashing against the walls of the vessel. First, she was reluctant to go to the engine room. Then understanding her unwillingness, he allowed Velavan also into the small cabin. This time she readily accepted. Both of them sat on a toolbox kept to the rear of the driver. Velavan commented, "The trawler is overcrowded, Nethuni". Nethuni said, "Yes. But better than that country boat. It was going to capsize many times, I felt. But by God's grace we all safely came to this trawler." Velavan said, "All your clothes were wet." Abdu intervened, "It does not matter whether your clothes are wet or dry. Pray to your Gods that you reach the Rameswaram shores safely and do not ponder on your wet dresses and the crowded vessel.

Then both of them kept quiet for some time. Nethuni could see the dark waters all around with stars shining above. In some places, the sky was over-cast. Nethuni's eyes were not free of fear. After some time, she felt drowsy but tried not to sleep. But the warmth of the engine room induced sleep though the diesel smell was nauseating.

A few minutes later they could see the high beam from the lighthouse, and also small and big light sources from the shores at a distance. Mr Wills came and told them that the vessel could reach the shore in just thirty minutes and they were asked to prepare to alight. Soon the trawler was surrounded by a set of two coast guard boats which escorted the trawler to the Jetty. This time they were not required to jump into the choppy waters but jumped off from the trawler to the shallow knee-deep waters near the jetty. Immediately after emptying the passengers, the trawler sailed back. All the passengers were directed to proceed to a temporary shed near the Jetty. They were asked to sit on the available places on the floor, benches and a few chairs. The bewildered new arrivals were in total confusion and they were searching for somebody who might direct them to the next step. But in their faces, there was that visible joy and satisfaction in the knowledge that they escaped the definite danger had they continued on the island. They sat on the floor in family groups and newfound friendship groups.

Nethuni was now clear in her mind that she had to get along with the new and unfamiliar environment alone. She gathered enough courage to face the things that were going to happen whatever they might be. She was searching for Velavan because she could not talk to him after embarking on the trawler. They were asked to sit in one place and not to go out of the shed. Moreover, there were enough security men from the local police, Port security, Marine police, etc. who were guarding them. The scene was tense but fascinating also for Nethuni. After a few minutes, Velavan spotted Nethuni and came near her when the security personnel announced that they may form groups, family groups, etc. so that in the future it would help them. There were a number of similar sheds full of refugees which suggested that the arrivals were on for some days and still continuing. Everyone was searching the crowd to find at least one or two known persons or their own relatives. Of course, many of them found someone somewhere from the assembly. Later, they were lined up and brought to a hall near the shed where enumeration was going on. They were again segregated as per their own wishes according to families, singles, couples, orphans, etc. Now it was dawn and yellow sunlight was peeping into the hall through the windows. Nethuni could see clearly that there were a few more buildings and some coconut and palm trees within the enclosed area. Soon after the preliminary enumeration was over, they were given a cup of tea and bun each.

Velavan and Nethuni formed two-person group photographs, and thumb impressions and signatures were taken. The officers were very jovial and friendly. They were helpful and caring but at the same time very strict and vigilant also. They assured them that they would be taken to a camp nearby where they would get facilities for their stay and that free food would also be served for a few days till they set up their cooking arrangements on their own. They would be given some rationed rice, wheat flour, cooking oil, kerosene and such items including some money as monthly allowances.

Time went and soon it was past eight in the morning. The babies and young children started asking for food. Somewhere else, people were in need of going to the restroom. Altogether an increase in tension and resulting commotion could be noticed. One of the officers came and announced that they can go group by group to the washroom available at the far end of the ground. Sensing the emerging rush Nethuni and Velavan quickly went to the washroom area and came out soon refreshed. Now they were free in the open area but within the compound wall always watched by an array of security personnel.

By the time their identity tags were prepared and given to them, it was nearing lunch time. They were served some rice preparations with vegetable curry before they were taken to e nearby police camp. Each one was interrogated for several hours and was carried in a bus to a British-built refugee camp at a place called *mandapam.* They were given some petty amount and a ration card that entitled them to weekly rations. Many in the group never thought that they would get their many facilities. They were really happy to have all these basic facilities because they had heard on their island that they would be suffering a lot in the camp.

These refugees had the option to go to their relatives and live with them. But this was permitted only after a few days of verification. They would be called non-camped refugees living with relatives or known persons but under strict surveillance. These non-camped refugees later were scattered in several places in Tamil Nādu, Kerala and Andhra Pradesh. But they will be losing their monthly allowances ration etc. A week later a few persons including Nethuni and Velavan were shifted from the "mandapam" transit camp to another camp in a village near Ramanathapuram. The facilities at this camp were not as good as those at the mandapam camp. Nethuni started feeling discomforts of all sorts within a week. She needed an urgent shift from that place to a better one.

One day at noon time, Velavan and Nethuni were sitting on a low-lying branch of a cashew tree which gives shade to a large area and were remembering the past when a couple came there and sat near them on the same trunk. The man opened the conversation by looking at Nethuni.

"What is your name?"

"Nethuni."

"Yours?" He asked the boy.

'Velavan."

"Sister and brother?"

Velavan said, "Oh, no. We met each other in the van which brought us from Jaffna to the shore."

"Hailing from Jaffna?"

Nethuni said, "Yes."

Velavan said, "Same area."

The lady accompanying the man said, "We are also from Jaffna, near St. Mary's cathedral on Press Road."

"What about your people over there?" the lady enquired.

Nethuni and Velavan kept quiet for some time looking at the branches and leaves dancing in the strong wind. As the wind was blowing in the afternoon, it did not feel very hot.

Velavan said, "Both my people are gone," he could not resist weeping.

"What about you Nethuni?" she anxiously enquired.

Nethuni just sobbed looking at the lady.

The man said, "We two were the only occupants in that rented house. Actually, we hail from Anuradhapura."

"Sensing some trouble outside we slipped from the house and came to the cathedral in the evening along with a few other people like us. Thus, we escaped from a large-scale holocaust. I used to run a textile shop in the town near Bairavar temple."

The lady introduced herself as Nihara and her husband Ashokan and said, "We are recently married and we don't know anything about people in Anuradhapura. I hear that lot of them had left for India. Some have even gone to the UK, Australia, and Canada. But they had enough time to plan their exit unlike us. Here we had to leave suddenly. First, we were homeless in our motherland and now refugees in India."

Nethuni asked her, "Should we continue here like this forever or would they allow us to go to school?"

Asokan said, "We can opt for non-camp refugee status provided we have somebody, relative or friends, who would be willing to take us."

"You mean outside the camp?" Nethuni asked with wide eyes.

"Yes, there is a provision but you have to produce strong evidence. Then the authorities would take you there, but you will be under strict watch."

Asokan continued, "I have a family, a distant relative. But I can never beg them. They know me and my family very well. They are living somewhere in Madurai. Now, they are engaged in the grain business for a long time. They came to India as a refugee back in the 1948 holocaust and settled down in Madurai. I have their address. Only today, I wrote to them. If they invite us, we may go to Madurai."

"You can escape. But what about us?" Nethuni asked them anxiously.

Nihara said, "After we reach Madurai, we would surely ask them for some way out for you."

Asokan continued, "Here the authorities would release us only if those people come to camp and sign a set of papers. The government will obtain an undertaking from both parties. After verification, if they are convinced, they will take some favourable action."

On that night, all four resolved to go to Madurai somehow. After a few days, Mayuran and Valli, relatives of Asokan came to the camp and signed a set of papers in front of the authorities vouching for all four. A few days after, when the verifications were over and the government approvals were received they came to take the tour. They bid goodbye to the camp and sped away in a car to Madurai. Before entering Madurai city, Mayuran stopped his car in front of his godown-cum-office.

Valli said, "This is our office."

Looking at the big facility, Velavan told Nethuni, "They seem to be wealthy people". When they entered a hotel for lunch, Nethuni asked Valli."

"Madam, what about your children?"

"What to say, Nethuni? We had a daughter. We educated her, got her engineering degree and she got a good job also in Bangalore. But one day she phoned me to say that she was going to marry a colleague, a Punjabi, and was going to settle in Delhi. We would have accepted him. But there was staunch protest from his people and without telling anybody, they got married with the help of their friends and finally settled somewhere in Delhi, antagonizing both parents. All fate. What to do?"

By evening, they reached their Madurai home, which was on the outskirts of the city where new buildings were coming up. It was a fairly large house, having several rooms with all amenities and well enough for a large family. There was a sprawling garden also in front of the house.

Mayuran led Velavan to one of the first-floor rooms for his stay and Nethuni was given a room adjacent to their bedroom on the ground floor.

The next morning, Mayuran took Velavan to his office and asked him to learn certain jobs in the godown.

As Velavan had a working knowledge of English and Tamil, he was given some office work also. Mayuran was impressed with the work done by Velavan, both in the office as well as in the warehouse management.

At home, Valli was planning the future of Nethuni who expressed her strong desire to go to school. One of these days, Nethuni asked Valli, "Valli auntie, I do not know if I can get admission in any school here. Could you please tell when Uncle comes?"

But for a few days, Mayuran didn't attempt a school admission which was a great disappointment for Nethuni. She joined in the household activities along with Valli and the maid Gomathy. Except for the kitchen work, all other jobs were attended by Nethuni. She loved the well-laid-out garden in front of the house and spent her leisure time in the garden doing sundry things. After Nethuni took up the gardening work, the place looked more enchanting to the Mayuran and Valli.

One evening when Nethuni was doing some work in the garden, Mayuran asked her, "Nethuni, you said you were studying in class eighth in Jaffna, didn't you?" Don't you think you should study further?"

Nethuni enthusiastically said, "Yes, certainly. Once I sounded Valli aunty also."

Mayuran, after thinking for a while, said, "No problem, I will enquire with the Sister in the nearby convent on the formalities to be completed for your continuing education."

Nethuni was very happy on hearing this. "Thank you, Uncle," she said gleamingly.

A few days later, Mayuran got some papers from the convent. Then in the next month on most of the days, he went behind these papers visiting the convent and education department and finally, she got admission when a certification came from Jaffna and vouched by the local education department in Madurai.

By the time it was next school year and Nethuni was admitted to the eighth standard in the convent.

The principal of the school, Fr. Jacob was gladdened to see the achievements of Nethuni back in Jaffna. After looking at the testimonials He said she would be an asset to the school.

By this time, Asokan and Nihara settled in a small rented house near his textile shop set up by him with the help of Mayuran on south masi street. Sales were much better than at his Anuradhapura shop. He was looking for a larger area for setting up a bigger shop. Occasionally they used to come to Valli's house and enquired about the well-being of Nethuni and Velavan. They often felt happy that they could help these children to have a better life with Mayuran and Valli.

Velavan has become a well-experienced and much-trusted employee of Mayuran, supervising several departments and handling them intelligently to the surprise of Mayuran and Valli.

Time went fast and Nethuni excelled in all classes. She has passed the twelfth standard in the school with flying colours. She also stood first in most of the extra-curricular activities, especially in the dance sector. She equalled any grown-up dancers in the city who were well-trained. But Nethuni was merely self-trained. During every performance in the school, she got excellent appreciation. Mayuran's drawing room was mainly decorated with several pieces of medals, cups, mementos and certificates. St. Theresa's convent in Madurai had never seen a Bharatanatyam performance like the numbers done by Nethuni during the cultural festival in the school.

Now Mayuran and Valli were planning to send her for higher education. They were aiming for Medicine or Engineering. But from the detailed discussion with Nethuni involving her class teacher, sister Jesuntha, they came to the conclusion that Nethuni was not at all interested in medicine or Engineering, but very much inclined to art subjects. Therefore, as per the advice of the class teacher, Nethuni was placed in the local college taking up history as the main.

During the vacation, one evening, a lady Mrs Mudhra Srinivasan came to Mayuran to request him to send Nethuni for advanced training in her dance school. When Mrs Mudhra came to the house and pressed the calling bell, Nethuni was there to open the gate.

Soon after entering the compound Mudhra got hold of Nethuni's hands and walked along the granite stone paved walkway, appreciating the well-laid-out garden. She behaved like a long-time acquaintance and family friend but Mayuran knew her by face only as she was a renowned dancer in the city. Having performed in several events during the last twenty-five years in most of the cities in India and abroad. Her face was familiar in the known circles and among the dance connoisseurs. Mayuran was surprised to see Mudra unexpectedly in his home. He welcomed her and introduced her to Valli. They exchanged pleasantries and after conversing for a few minutes, another girl who accompanied Mudra revealed the purpose of their abrupt visit.

She explained, "Last week we happened to witness a fantastic performance by Nethuni, this wonderful girl in her school. Madam got much interest and would like to impart advanced training in Bharatanatyam".

Mudra explained," Exactly". That is the main purpose of our visit. I have a dance school where I have been imparting training to several girls from all over the country. Most of them come in search of me, but today I have come in search of Nethuni as I could see a great dancer in this wonderful little girl who already knew and executed beautifully the intricacies of Bharatanatyam with ease. Even some of the *bhavas* and *abhinayas* which only the experienced dancers perform with much turbulence. But Nethuni simply does it without any effort at all. This extraordinary talent had brought me here. Therefore, I would request you to kindly send her to me if she desires.

Let her come only on holidays so that her studies are not disturbed".

Looking at Nethuni Mudra asked, "Nethuni, what do you say?"

Nethuni simply looked at Mayuran and smiled.

Mayuran said immediately, "I am lucky that a renowned dancer coming to my house and requesting something which I had never expected even in dreams. Though we are not that crazy in cinemas and theatres, we did attend some of your programmes in the city. If Nethuni wants, we are okay. Don't you think, Valli? And what about you Nethuni? with a large smile on her face, Nethuni gladly accepted and immediately rushed to Mudra and touched her feet. Mayuran said, "Now madam, you can consider Nethuni as one of your students. She would be at your place from this Sunday."

They departed after having coffee and snacks.

On that night, Nethuni seemed exceptionally happy that she was going to be trained by an internationally well-known dancer. She would never believe this sudden development after so many days she slept with a lighter heart. Even in that condition, her eyes filled with tears when she thought "if my people are present now!"

From the next Sunday onwards, Nethuni became one of the many students in Mudra's institute. Within a year, she mastered most of the *mudras*, *bhavas*, *abhinayas*, and movements including composition and choreography.

Mudra, a multi-faceted, illustrious exponent of not only Bharatanatyam but also other dance forms like Kuchipudi, Odissi and Mohini *attam* was simply awestruck by the excellent performance by Nethuni. She was specifically appreciative of her innate ability to compose Jathis. Even when watering plants or cleaning musical instruments her rendering of Jathi with vigour vitality and clarity, at the same time, her simplified precision was highly notable. Nethuni also excelled in the Nattuvangan which was feisty and joyous and the audiences were enthralled in several performances in the city under Mudra's supervision.

The power and clarity in rendering the "*solkattu*" gave her a high reputation in the circles where some masters praised her for her grasp of rhythmic intricacies. Nethuni was a perfectionist who used to say that perfection could never be complete. According to her, nobody had ever done a perfect performance as done by Lord Nataraja and goddess Parvathy. Perhaps even they would have quarrelled by finding fault with each other's so-called perfect performance. During the discussions on the subject, she used to say," What he can do is only try to do perfection and not to complete perfection because perfection is never accomplished by anyone in any art or craft or action." Nethuni's husky voice and the sweet reverberating low voiced laugh in the dance halls greatly attracted the students, professionals and the audience alike.

Nethuni has finished her graduation and wanted to go for PG in art History, but there were no colleges in

Madurai offering that subject. Therefore, Mayuran let her go to Madras, and take the subject. During the last three years, she read a lot of books on Indian dance forms from Mudra's collections.

In Madras, she had umpteen opportunities in her subject and profession. Every evening she used to talk to someone practising Bharatanatyam, Kuchipudi, or Mohiniattam. She took membership in several *sabhas* having cultural activities round the year. Soon, she became a well-known figure in these places with performances during the music and dance festival conducted in Madras and other cities.

One day Mr Rajamanickam Pillai, one of the renowned dance exponents in the city contacted her and suggested she start a dance troupe when she was in the second year of the PG degree course. She politely rejected telling him that she had to concentrate on her studies. Her goal was to take a PhD in her subject from Madras University.

But the Idea of the dance troupe was deep in her mind that one day after finishing her final examinations she contacted Rajamanika Pillai and revived his idea of the troupe. When she consulted Mudra in Madurai, She said, "It is a good opportunity, you could become a very popular figure in Madras within no time".

She thought for several days and consulted many people including Mayuran, Valli and Mudra and also a few friends in Madurai regarding her career. Finally, she selected dancing as the future career that would give her a way out of living.

After a few days, she formed a dance troupe under the name of "Madras Dance Academy" where apart from organising performances around the country, she took classes for young dancers There was a team of dance instructors to teach young girls. While doing research work she used to roam about the cities performing dances Within a year her academy became one of the best sought-after troupes in the city.

Her bank balance swelled to several lakhs, yet she was not happy with the aspect of earnings alone as she was not able to spend for her parents and people and when their thoughts came to her mind this bank balance seemed to equal to the sands of the marina.

During this time, when she was finalizing her research papers somebody approached her with an offer in a film with a story of a dancer. At first, she refused, but because of the pressure from all sides, she had to accept it and acted in it which had about seven dances including Bharatanatyam and Kuchipudi. It was a grand success. But she straight away refused when further offers came in search of her. The reason told was that she didn't like the filmdom for various reasons. She could earn crores in a very short time but she considered her dancing career a pure form of art dedicated to Lord Shiva. She purchased a large house with a garden for running the school. Mayuran and Valli along with Velavan used to visit her at least once in three months. They were happy to see the rise of Nethuni in all her endeavours. But she gradually lost contact with Asokan and Nihara.

One day, Mayuran called her to say that he was coming to the madras to meet her on some important matter. She wondered what would be the important matter.

A couple of days after, Mayuran came to her house along with Asokan and Valli. They sat in the garden and started a discussion on various matters including that of Nethuni.

Mayuran came to the subject, "Don't you think it is the right time for Nethuni to get married. She must be crossing thirty. If she goes on like this what would be her future life?".

Valli said, "Nethuni says she is already married to dance. Several times, I spoke to her on phone over this for the last few years."

Mayuran said, "Maybe she is shy about telling something regarding her own marriage".

Valli said, "She was firm in that decision. I don't think she would budge."

Nethuni was silently going around the garden but at the same time listening to their conversations.

Mayuran said, in a louder voice, "Nethuni is not a child to obey us. She knows many things which we may not be aware of. Therefore, we have to accept whatever she decides. But there is no harm in giving little pressure to her in this matter".

Asokan finally said, "Okay, we call her and discuss things."

They called Nethuni to sit with them for the discussion.

Mayuran asked her, "Nethuni, I think you must have heard what we discussed. What do you say?"

She, nonchalantly said, "Please leave that matter, for now, I will let you know later."

These people were disappointed by her reply, so they didn't go further regarding the matter.

As they realised that no amount of pressure would change her attitude in this matter, they left for Madurai.

But in the meantime, something unpleasant happened in the life of Nethuni in Madras. One day, after a performance, when she came to the school late at night a stranger came to her dance school introducing himself as Kadhiresan, an uncle of a student learning Kuchipudi. Nethuni received him with due respect and gave him a seat in the office room and asked him politely, "Yes, sir. What can I do for you?"

Mr Kadhiresan responded, "Madam, I have come here on behalf of my factory workers. We are sponsoring a cultural program in a famous temple near my factory in the city. This year we would like you to perform with your troupe. Can you agree? Please honour us."

Nethuni replied, "I will confirm it in a couple of days. Please leave your contact number."

Mr Kadhiresan and the accompanying person left the place after profusely thanking Nethuni for accepting the proposal and reiterating that there was no dearth of money.

After consulting her secretary Nethuni confirmed a program for a particular day. But before the programme, Kadhiresan came to Nethuni several times in his Mercedes, on one or other pretext and finally the programme was done beautifully well. Dr Nethuni's dance was appreciated by one and all. She was presented with a purse having, fairly a large amount, on the stage itself by Mr Kadhiresan.

In her reply speech, she thanked Kadhiresan's industry and the temple authorities for allowing a dance programme in the temple. She also announced that the purse received by her was being donated to the temple.

A week later, Kadhiresan came again to meet Nethuni when she was discussing something on the phone in her office room. Nethuni said, "Please come, sir."

Kadhiresan said, "Yes, thank you, Dr Nethuni, many thanks, this visit was specially to thank you personally for taking my proposal in the right spirit. They talked many things about the industry and the temple. It was getting late for Nethuni."

After a pause, Kadhiresan looked left and right and in a low voice told her, "I wanted to tell you something… rather a request and it is purely personal and confidential too."

Nethuni realised something fishy in his approach, she called the vice principal of the school Ms Sneha to the office room but before Sneha came to the room, Kadhiresan opened his mouth, "I like you. I want to marry you. Please don't say no."

When Sneha arrived, he got up and said, "Madam, I will come again tomorrow, expecting a favourable reply."

He hastily stepped out with an awkward smile.

A startled Nethuni was just blinking at Sneha. Unaware of what had happened there, Sneha asked, "What madam? Another offer for performance?"

Nethuni told her what had happened just before her arrival.

Sneha replied, "Madam, only last week my father was telling me about this Kadhiresan. According to my father, Mr Kadhiresan is a filthy rich fellow and a known fraud. Already, he has two wives officially. He…"

Nethuni intervened, "Okay, I don't want to hear anything about him anymore. This type of incident has happened to me many times. Sometimes, things had gone worse than this. That was the sole reason that I rejected several lucrative offers from the film industry. These filthy rich men… I don't want to talk about them anymore… I'm fed up with this city! I tried my very best to get a passport, but due to my refugee status, I am not getting one. So many dignitaries are showering praises on me but nobody is ready to help me to get a passport. If I get an Indian passport I can simply leave Madras and have a global tour as some other dancers are doing. As they don't have any refugee status, they are going around the world for performances."

Sneha said, "Why don't you go back to Sri Lanka and apply for a Srilankan passport, then you can go on tour to many countries? If you go on like that, I can come and join you in any third country for a performance with a few students."

Nethuni said, "My dear Sneha, I had thought of this several times, But I don't know if I would be successful. Okay, let us try."

A couple of days later, when Kadhiresan came to the office, he was stopped by the security at the gate itself and turned away. He frowned and murmured something and got in his car and sped away.

As promised, when she came to Madurai after a few days, she explained these bad experiences to Mayuran, Asokan, Valli and Nihara. Upon hearing this, Mayuran immediately said, "That is why we wanted you to marry somebody soon."

Valli said in a chiding tone, "How many times have I told you? You never bother!"

Reminding an incident, she continued, "Didn't I propose that Thenkasi boy? He was also doing some research work on a similar subject which you have done. But you never cared."

Nethuni squatted on the grass, held everybody's hands and asked them to listen to her, "My dear auntie and uncle, you know I earned enough money for a few generations and my fame in the city is also known to you. Without you people, I would not have been able to make it… starting from the vegetable vendor who picked me up from the wet muddy road to a lot of great souls, specially Mascarenhas sir, Mayuran uncle, and Valli aunty, Asokan uncle and Nihara aunty, everyone… I thank everyone."

Mayuran interrupted, "Now, what are you up to? Tell us your plans."

Nethuni continued, "I am sure you must be aware of my frequent visits to Madhurai lately and frantically running to government offices. I have been busy getting our official documents so that we could return to our motherland."

"Wait, wait," Mayuran intervened. "You said our papers… Who are the others?"

Nethuni replied, "You will come to know later."

Everyone blinked at each other. Asokan asked, "Are you joking?"

Nethuni said, "I am not kidding, believe me. I have already made arrangements to start a dance academy in Jaffna and I planned to entrust the administration of the school to Asokan Uncle and Nihara Aunty."

Asokan said, "No, thank you for your offer. We are well settled here. Why do you go back? Even now we presume that we have no safety over there. We don't want you to willingly jump into the sea where sharks rule the waters".

Nethuni contested, "But I have to go. I have done everything. Only tickets are left."

"Then what about the Madras school?" asked Ashokan.

"I am leaving that to you people. Anyone can operate that school from here. Ms Sneha, a very talented dancer, is the vice principal over there. She can manage things single-handedly.".

Now that Nethuni had firmly decided everything, Mayuran and the party simply kept quiet as approval for her plans. They also wondered, why she didn't utter a single word about Velavan. They talked about him among themselves after Nethuni left.

Nethuni came to Chennai and completed all arrangements and entrusted the academy to Ms Sneha. Her ticket was from Trichy next week and therefore she came to Madurai for a final goodbye. She had asked Mayuran to call Asokan, Nihạra and Valli.

She touched the feet of one and all and set out to Trichy airport. Others also accompanied and Asokan was on the wheels. He phoned up Velavan, but could not get connected. Nethuni seemed fully contented and was having a placid face and talked jovially. Asokan has never seen her in this mood.

They all alighted from the car and walked to the airport. To the surprise of everyone, except Nethuni, Velavan was there with a suitcase waiting for these people. On seeing them, he came running to the awestruck couples. As they were wondering what was happening, Velavan pleaded, "I beg your pardon. Please allow me to also go with Nethuni." He told several lame excuses for not telling the facts to Asokan or Mayuran.

Valli commented, "Finally, Nethuni has executed her plan beautifully. Smart girl!"

Before clearing security, Nethuni and Velavan waved their hands. The right hand of Velavan held the left hand of Nethuni. They lost sight among the passengers.

Back in the car, Mayuran said, "It is good that finally, Nethuni decided to marry."

Asokan, in anger, said, "Bloody fellow! At least Velavan could have told me!"

Valli commented, "Anyway, they make a good match."

Nihara told, "Marriage could have been done here."

Valli, "Maybe Nethuni didn't want any publicity. Anyway, she got a life partner. God bless them."

The vehicle sped towards Madurai.

2

The Loco Pilot

From his primary school days, Sarasan was fascinated by train engines and had a dream to become an engine driver. Every day, as he went to school, he had to pass through a railway crossing near his house. He and some of his friends would always wait for the train to pass when the gate was closed. But he saw that many people didn't wait for the train to cross but, they went below the red iron pipe and ran to the other side. Sarasan never liked that. He always wanted to see how the driver was working inside the engine room. But he could never see him working only putting his head out and looking onto the track where people waited at the crossing. Sometimes, he would acknowledge someone who knew him among the waiters behind the STOP bar.

One day, Sarasan also raised his hand and waved at the driver who reciprocated. Sarasan was overwhelmed with joy and told all his fellow students that the train driver said hello to him and smiled at him. When this was told at home, his mother didn't believe him and asked him not to repeat the same again in the future. Who knew what was the intention of the driver? Hearing this, Sarasan's friends also started waving at the driver. They enjoyed doing that. But after a few days, that smiling person was not to be found and another man with a big moustache was sitting. He never bothered to look at these children. Thereafter, the practice of this "Hi" business was stopped. Moreover, the man in the engine room never looked at the people waiting. So gradually, the children forgot this practice of waving.

But Sarasan had some kind of attachment with the engine, tracks, the sound it made, the wheels and the engine driver. In short, he enjoyed most of it. When he reached high school, he told his father that he wanted to become an engine driver. The poor father who was a daily wager clearing the green growth after the rains in somebody's coconut farm and getting a paltry sum as wages couldn't think of making his son an engine driver. He just wanted him to pass the tenth standard level and immediately join him for the work so that income could be doubled to run the home. But his mother was very much for her son that he must become an engine driver. She vowed to work for that and started to save some money every month out of the salary she got from the small hotel where she worked near the railway station. She gathered information on all the formalities required for the post. Accordingly, after completing the twelfth standard, he was admitted to a government-run ITI centre with automobile engineering as a subject. He fared well in the final exam and with the assistance and guidance from the local station master Mr Philipos, necessary forms were brought and the application was prepared with all copies of certificates and waited for the results.

To the astonishment of Sarasan's father, one day, the postman delivered a call later regarding a written test from the railways. Joyfully, Sarasan went to the exam centre and found that there were thousands of candidates who had come to write the exam. He never expected this much of a crowd. Still, without losing hope, he attempted the exam to his fullest satisfaction. After about six months, the results were declared and he was on the selection list. His joy knew no bounds. He quickly ran home to inform his parents. They were very happy. His mother was telling him that she knew he would get it. Earlier, his father had some negative opinions about the result, but when he knew that he got it, he was happy that his son was going to become an engine driver in Indian Railways. Very soon, a call letter arrived for joining. Sarasan took the call letter to Mr Philipos and came to know many things he had to do in the future. As this work was an operational one, he had to undergo rigorous training for six months which included classroom sessions, and field training followed by a test of competence before deployment in any working post. The first phase of computer-based training was successfully done. Then there were more computer-based aptitude tests which he attempted at several places.

As the medical examination was very stringent, and no margin of error was allowed for the Loco pilot, Sarasan was very careful and fortunately, he came out successful in the medical test also. He was sent for a six-month training course at Avadi in Madras. He felt elated with all arrangements like a hostel, food, medical care, etc. which he had never imagined. He completed the training to the best satisfaction of his superiors. He was asked to report to the Trivandrum Divisional Manager. Accordingly, he reported to the Divisional Office on an auspicious day and joined duty. He was posted as Assistant Loco Pilot and assigned duty on the Kollam–Kanyakumari section. He was happy that he could drive the engine through the very railway crossing where once, he waited to see the engine driver on most of his school days. He enjoyed his driving on the route Kollam–Kanyakumari. On his duty days, his mother would wait at the station to hand him his lunch or dinner. On most days, his father would also see him at the railway crossing. One day, his mother told the gateman that she never dreamt of his son driving an engine this way.

A few years passed. Sarasan was occasionally shifted from passenger trains to long-distance trains. Sometimes, even goods trains crossing more than two or three states were also given to him. So, his presence in his parent route had become rare. Whenever he got a chance, he preferred to work on the Kollam–Kanyakumari route. During these years of service, he had seen several accidents on the tracks, mostly suicides, by people for various reasons.

So far, more than a dozen lives lost crashing against this engine. Every time it happened, he was saddened, and wouldn't talk to anybody that day. He used to think why these people were doing such things. How could they do it? Simply jumping in front of a speeding train… Moreover, many cows, calves, buffaloes, donkeys, and dogs... He used to think that his job was a killer job—licensed to kill anyone who came dashing his engine. But he was never punished for such "murders". It was strange how people did not care about their animals. The owners of the animals should be punished. But nothing like that happened. He wondered if this was his account for seven or eight years, what would be the total for the entire Indian Railways!

Every day, he used to see the old man sitting in that familiar shop near the tracks, when he passed that way. In that shop, nothing much was stored—four or five glass jars containing candies and other low-cost sweets, a few packets of cigarettes and *beedis*, betel leaves and *supari* and a bunch of bananas. These were all the things you could purchase from there. Most of the time, no customers would be there. Though he was very familiar with that shop, he never had any interaction with that old man. The bald-headed man sat there chewing betel leaves. Occasionally, a few school children, from the nearby primary school, flocked to the shop during the lunch break for buying candies and some salted mangoes, gooseberries, etc. brought by a grand old lady living nearby. She made around Rs ten every day as profit.

A few regulars come for bananas for emergency use. In the evenings, *beedi*, cigarettes and betel leaf would be sold on most days in the shop. Every day, Sarasan used to see that old man during morning and evening trips. A bit of nighty or skirt could also be seen from the anteroom. But the visitors would not be able to see the person wearing it.

Sarasan was curious to know who the owner of the cloth was. But how to ask, whom to ask! He wondered a lot about it. Always, it was the man chewing betel leaves and spitting mouthfuls of the thick red solution on the lush green vegetation outside the shop.

One day the old man was standing outside the shop and when the train arrived he looked at the driver. Sarasan also looked at him and waved his hand in a friendly gesture. A smile bloomed on the old man's face, for otherwise, he looked grim every time. They exchanged pleasantries and when the guard signalled, he moved the already running engine. He did not forget to look inside the shop for a bit of pink or yellow clothes. Ever since he started looking at the shop he could see only these pink or yellow ones. He inferred that one or in addition another person was also available in the side room. Nowadays daily he used to wave his hands at the old man. A few weeks after, when the engine stopped near the shop he could not find anyone in the shop. At that time, an old lady came to purchase something and made sounds in the shop. No one came and as the train started moving suddenly there appeared a young lady of around 25 in a pink nighty from the room and was asking something about the old lady. As the engine was moving he could see only a glimpse of the lady and immediately the view was marred by the tree trunks. Just a little away on the railway approach road he also saw the old man bringing a new bunch of bananas and a cardboard box. The man was on his old rusty bicycle and was pedalling slowly. Sarasan concentrated on the tracks and the engine started picking up speed.

At home, Sarasan's parents started looking for a girl for marriage in and around the place, but, even after much searching, they could not find anyone. Whenever they approached any family for a suitable girl, they simply turned their face away. Sarasan's mother Thangamani one night asked her husband, "Why are the people not entertaining us? Our son has a decent job, is well-mannered, with very good habits. There's no complaint of any kind whatsoever. But then why is this happening?". His father, Thankayyan, did not reply for some time. He simply enjoyed his beedi and was looking at the dark paddy fields with a number of fireflies flying around across the road. Again, Thangamani asked, "Tell me why..." this time she asked with a tone filled with anger and remorse. She shook Thankayyan's head. Thankayyan threw the beedi butt and replied in a calm and low voice, "Look, who would give a girl to your son. Though young and healthy, he's darker than me with a bony face, having two large eyes bulging out, below which a hammer-beaten nose is positioned and he can never close his lips because of the protruding incisors. Then, who would like to marry him? If it were you, would you have agreed?" Thangamani kept mum. She stared at him with tears in her eyes. She thought to herself, "Is it my mistake? Didn't I like you even though you were not having any notable physical features with one polio-affected leg?" She spurned her experience which led to her marriage when nobody wanted her as a bride, for no fault of hers, and this Thankayyan was ready to marry her because he was not getting any girl.

Thangamani was not beautiful either, but not mediocre. She hailed from a very poor family, so poor that all jewellery during her marriage was bought by her father for a paltry sum from a fancy shop. The glittering silk sari on the day of the marriage was loaned to her by one of her friends. She didn't have enough clothes to wear. Moreover, the family was staying in a thatched shed on the roadside on *poramboke land.* Many boys came to see her, but none were ready to tie the knot, and finally, she herself had found Thankayyan who had come to work for a week in a farmland near her house. She remembered the day when Thankayyan came to her dwelling and asked for drinking water. At that time, her parents were away at work. Thangamani was about to pour out the boiled rice-water in the backyard when Thankayyan came. On seeing Thangamani, Thankayyan asked for water. "Do you want this hot rice-water or just plain water?" Thangamani asked. He opted for the rice water and Thangamani gave it in an aluminium vessel, and he did not hesitate to ask for a pickle if any. She went inside and brought some mango pickles on a piece of banana leaf.

Thankayyan gulped down the rice water all the while licking the mango pickle. Thereafter, he sat on the low mud veranda and asked her if there wasn't anyone at home. Thangamani answered from inside, "Appa and Amma have gone to work in the school compound."

He continued his query, "What work do they do?"

"Masonry."

"Oh nice, they must be getting good money."

Thangamani was a little afraid as she was talking to a stranger when no one was at home. If somebody came to know of it, they would have different thoughts. While going inside, she looked around and when she was about to close the door, Thankayyan asked her name. She said, "Thangamani." Thankayyan stood up and went to resume his work at the coconut farm. Before entering the farm, he looked back at the closed door but did not see anything. Thangamani noticed him getting into the coconut farm through the cracked wooden doors.

The following day also, at the same time, he came from the farm and asked for water. This time, her mother was also there. She saw him and identified him. Her mother asked, "Thankayyan, were you working here? I didn't see you yesterday." "I was a bit late yesterday," replied Thankayyan, "And sister, did you know, yesterday

I got tasty rice-water from here." She turned towards Thangamani and asked her if she gave him the water. Thangamani, with a sense of guilt, said, "Yes". Her mother stood up and went into the kitchen and asked her in detail about what had happened yesterday. Thangamani narrated the whole story. Her mother came out along with a vessel full of rice-water and pickles.

All the while when Thankayyan was relishing the rice-water, something was brewing in the mind of Thangamani's mother. She thought that Thankayyan would make a good match for Thangamani. If possible, the matter can be settled in consultation with Thangamani's father.

At night, Thangamani's father and mother discussed the matter among themselves. Her father cautioned her mother.

"Don't ask anything about this to Thankayyan. I knew this fellow for a long time. Although he doesn't look smart, he is a good type. Let us wait… if he shows any interest in our daughter, we make a move, okay? Don't tell this to Thangamani either."

A couple of days later, Thangamani's father happened to be at home when Thankayyan came for water. They had a few minutes of talk on matters other than that of Thangamani. He even invited Thankayyan for having lunch at their home. Thankayyan readily accepted, and after lunch, they strolled around the coconut farm where Thankayyan worked. In the course of the conversation, Thankayyan indirectly showed his interest in Thangamani, and several subsequent visits ended up in their marriage.

Like on a cinema screen, Thangamani remembered each event that led to the marriage. She woke up from her journey through the memories, and silently went to the bed, unrolling a grass mat and positioning a stone-like pillow below her head. Thankayyan continued to sit on the steps, enjoying his *beedi*.

While going to sleep, Thangamani wished that something like that would happen in her son's life soon, because Sarasan was getting older, and may not get married. After a few weeks, Sarasan was given a special duty on a goods train going out of the state for a few days. He returned to his old route and on another day, it so happened that after the arrival of the train at the station there was no signal to proceed further even after five minutes. Sarasan got down and walked to the station and within minutes he returned to the engine and stood outside.

The old man asked, "What is the problem, sir?"

"Oh, just a signal problem. It will be over in an hour. People have come to rectify it," Sarasan replied.

Drawing an old dancing wooden chair from the shop, Paramu said with respect, "You can sit here, sir."

The shade of the big mango tree and the gentle breeze blowing from the west were soothing for Sarasan, so he sat on the chair, arms of which were full of lime paste used by Paramu for his relentless betel sessions.

"Your name, sir?" Paramu asked.

"Sarasan," Loco Pilot said with a smile.

"Oh! You are that Thankayyan's son? I know. I know."

"Would you like to have some bananas?" Paramu offered.

"No thanks," Sarasan replied.

"What is your name?" Sarasan asked.

"My name is Paramupillai. People call me Paramu," Paramu replied.

"I have been seeing you since my childhood".

Sarasan continued, "Do you get enough money from this shop?"

Paramu said, "Oh yes, we are only two here. All we want is three times food. What else!"

Then Sarasan asked, "Your wife and children?"

Clearing his throat, Paramu said, "No, sir. I don't have any children. I am not married."

Sarasan, "Never?"

Paramu with a smile, "Never, sir"

"Your other relatives?"

"I don't have any."

"Then who is the other one apart from you?"

"Oh, that's my adopted daughter."

Sarasan asked again, "Your adopted daughter? Oh, that small girl I used to see a few years ago?"

"Yes, exactly," Paramu replied.

"From where did you adopt her?" Sarasan asked and said, "I had seen her coming along with you to the market. But I didn't know much about you both…"

"No official adoption or something like that. One day, long back, when I was returning from the market, a girl of around five years caught hold of my *dhoti* and asked for alms."

Sarasan asked, "Was there anybody with her?"

Paramu said, "I asked her who was there with her. Only then did I come to know that she was dumb. She could only answer with gestures. From the market, I brought this girl to this place and ever since, she has been with me as an assistant."

"You didn't send her to school?"

"Yes, I did. I sent her to the nearby government school but she could not cope with the atmosphere. Even then, she was there for three or four years. A teacher offered me to take her to a special school but who will take her to the city and back every day? Many people around here told me that you cannot keep a girl like this here. The matter was to be reported to the police. But I didn't budge. The police station is nearby only. The matter is known to everybody. Now it has been over twenty years. She must be around twenty-five now. Somehow, I managed to enter her name in my ration card and got a voter ID card also!" He smiled jubilantly.

He went inside the shop and called out, "Mini, come here." Mini came out of the anteroom dressed in a pink nighty. By look, she was not a local. Sarasan asked a few questions but only a blunt smile or some positive and negative nods came from her. Paramu said, "She can hear and understand everything. She does all the work here." Paramu gestured for her to go inside when the signal man came there to tell them something. Sarasan spoke to the station master through wireless and boarded the engine telling goodbye to Paramu. He did see Mini look at him from the window with a friendly smile. After seeing her and knowing about her, was he giving his mind to that girl? "No, it should not be so. She was such a fair and beautiful one. How can I think of any such thing?" But again and again, the thoughts about her were increasingly pounding his mind. The following few weeks, he found himself always thinking about her.

During this time, he again got further training for three months in Guntakkal Division for operating long-distance express trains and a new version of diesel and electric locomotives. He was reluctant to go for the training because of his involvement with Mini mentally. As it was his service matter, there was no other way except to go for the training. After completion of the training, he was posted in his parent division and was assigned the express train on the route which did not stop at the local stations where the passenger train stopped. Therefore, he could only have a glimpse of his favourite shop. For a few days, he had been noticing that the shop used to be closed. And sometimes, Mini was sitting near the cash box. The shop got improved a little as it sold a few more items. One day, he even saw a lot of youngsters flocking to the shop smoking and gossiping.

Suddenly, on a fine morning, the railway authorities came and asked her to close the shop by giving one month's notice. The old man was not to be seen for a few days, and there was some railway notice pasted on the closed shop, Sarasan, on an off-duty day, came to the place on his bike and enquired. He came to know that the old man had expired due to some age-related illness. The shop was run by Mini for some time on behalf of the advice of many locals. She purchased more items for sale. Simultaneously, she had been getting into a lot of trouble with the local youth also. Since she was staying alone, she was much vulnerable and several attempts had been thwarted by her and a few neighbours. As she had nowhere to go, she continued to stay there only. Sarasan came to know from a local man that during the previous week, the railway authorities came and gave another notice to vacate the place. As the land belonged to the railways, and a parallel line was also being constructed, the action was unavoidable. Sarasan met her inside the house along with a few local people. All had sympathy for her, but none were offering any kind of help. Sarasan had in his mind to ask her to go with him, but he didn't express his feeling, fearing the local reaction. She looked at him as if she begged his sympathy but at that juncture, he was not in a position to express any feelings. After a few minutes, he said that he would try to find out some solution and assured her that she would not be harmed in the future by the railway authority and that he would come again soon.

She wiped the tears rolling down her cheeks with a towel stained with kitchen soot. The wipe left a mark on her cheeks with charcoal. He yearned to wipe those cheeks with his hand towel, but for the few people around him, he controlled his emotions and tried to hide his tears-filled eyes.

On that day, Sarasan went home and told everything to his mother and said that if Mini would agree, definitely he could bring her home provided his parents agreed. A few days later, Sarasan's parents set out to see the girl. When they reached the shop, they found it closed. They knocked at the side door. Mini opened the door and asked what they wanted. They said that they had come to buy some items for the house. Thankayyan and Thangamani were very happy to see the girl. Even though they knew she was dumb, they didn't disqualify her. Mini wondered why they had come and they were looking at her curiously and analysing her from head to foot and they had also asked some questions for which she told yes or no with gestures.

They returned home and happily told Sarasan that if she agreed to come with him, he could bring her home. Thankayyan asked Sarasan anxiously, "Will she come with you?"

"I think so," Sarasan replied. "But she is very beautiful, then how can she come with me?"

Thankayyan said, "I don't know. But if she comes with you tomorrow, we will definitely welcome her. We will have a simple marriage ceremony here, with a handful of locals."

Sarasan was elated. His joy knew no bounds. He was trying to meet her as early as possible but duty came as an impediment every time he tried to meet her. Thus, a month passed. On a rainy day, he was on duty in an express train and when the engine approached the shop, it was closed and there were no lights inside the adjacent room. It was nearing seven in the evening and was raining heavily. The assistant pilot was also in the cabin. They reduced the speed to twenty kmph to negotiate a curve before the bridge. Suddenly, the assistant pilot shouted at Sarasan, "Sarasan, see! Somebody is running on the track."

Sarasan looked at the track and found someone, but in the heavy rains and poor light, it was not clear. The only available light was that of the engine. Nothing was visible clearly. The loco pilot applied the brakes. The figure was fast approaching the engine. Sarasan yelled, "IT IS MINI, the shopkeeper. I know her!" At this juncture, they could not do anything except distress hooting. In a minute something happened. There was a THUD sound and some shrieks. The train halted at a little distance away. A few people got out from the compartments, drenching themselves in the rain, and ran towards the spot. The assistant loco pilot and Sarasan along with the guard ran to the spot with a flashlight in hand. People were looking among the bushes. First, Sarasan saw a curved horn of a buffalo on the cowcatcher with some pieces of its head. Somebody in the crowd said, "It was a buffalo! See the body parts." But the pilot and Sarasan wondered where that figure coming towards the engine had gone. Undoubtedly, they heard human shrieks, not of an animal. To Sarasan's knowledge, it was Mini who got hit. Yet another passenger called out from near the carcass of the buffalo. "A lady is also there. She seems to be dead". Everybody surrounded that place and found a lady lying over the thick bush with a lot of bruises and blood all over her clothes. One of her ears got torn but her hands and legs were intact.

The assistant pilot examined her breath. He said, "She is breathing. Lift her." At that time, two or three people together took her to the guard's compartment. Someone said, "Inform the police." But Sarasan intervened, "We cannot wait for the police now. We will have to take to the next station and admit her to a hospital."

In the meantime, the driver told the next station to call the police. When the train reached the station, the police received her and immediately shifted her to the nearest hospital. After having all formalities, the train left for its destination.

The next day, Sarasan took leave from duty and reached the hospital where Mini was admitted the previous day. She was out of danger and the doctors said that it would take a couple of weeks for the wounds to heal completely. She was almost okay when Sarasan met her. By gestures, she explained what happened on the track. She wanted to die, therefore, she walked towards the engine. At that time, the heavy rain started. When the engine was approaching her, a buffalo came running from somewhere and it tried to cross the track, hitting her aside. In the impact, she was thrown off and the buffalo was hit by the cowcatcher. She believed that the buffalo came in the guise of God and thwarted her suicide attempt and saved her.

After two weeks, Sarasan came and got her discharged from the hospital and took her to his home without asking her anything. She also did not utter a single word and followed him obediently with a bent head. When they reached his home, she, with folded hands, touched Sarasan's parents' feet.

3

Ramayee

Ramayee took her lunch brought from the Mani mess next street and was just taking a rest on the small veranda in her rented house. The house was situated strategically at the end of the street in a junction. Opposite her house, was a small school, where tiny tots played and studied. On the right, across the road, was a small Ganesh temple. Left to the temple, there was a vegetable retail shop next to the Kannan provision stores. In front of the shop, a public tap stood, which was very rarely used, because most of the house owners in the street had water connections at home. So, very few people like Ramayee used to come to the tap, in addition to some stray dogs. The street had a mosaic of people which was once occupied entirely by Brahmins. As time went by, the original dwellers sold their houses to various people and went too far off cities and even abroad. The house occupied by Ramayee was one-third of an original Agraharam house. The siblings of the original owner got the ownership and divided the house among themselves. In one of these parts, Ramayee was living. The width of the house was only fourteen feet but the length, runs into more than one-hundred and fifty feet, including an open area as a backyard. Having two coconut trees, a lemon tree, a neem tree and a flowering Parijatham tree near a well that was not in use as the water level was very deep and the motor got repaired long ago. Ramayee did not use the well water as she got fresh water from the public tap. She lived alone in the house and did household work in three-four houses in the vicinity. Normally, she got around Rs three thousand on average from each home. Sometimes, she used to get breakfast and lunch from the houses that she worked for. Only dinner was to be cooked at home. For emergency purposes, "Mani mess" was already there on the next street.

She sat on the warm granite steps resting her head and back against the old paint-less wooden pillar and was looking around aimlessly. There was no one on the street at this time. People must be sleeping indoors. The school was also open till one pm. Two sparrows were sitting on the branch of the neem tree on the school premises. A lone sparrow was sitting on another branch and was chirping relentlessly. A recently married couple went past her. It seemed to her that they just had their visit to one of their relatives. The saree draped by the lady was shining in the afternoon Sun.

Normally she would not take a nap at this time of the day, moreover, she had work to do at Rukmani's house. Her job was to clean the utensils and sweep the floor. Again, at four, she would have to attend to Mrs Padma to clean the entire house. Then came Latha madam's home. There, she would spend most of the time because she had full freedom there. When Madam came from the college after five in the evening, she would go to her room and take rest and the uncle would come only at night. She was allowed to see TV programs, she could use the kitchen for making coffee, tea, etc. Madam seldom came downstairs before seven. Therefore, the home was under the full control of Ramayee, including the white Pomeranian. The only thing she hated was the hair of the dog found all over the house. Because of that, she often had sneezing when cleaning.

Often, Sudha aunty of the next door asked her several questions about her past but she never revealed anything. One day, after having dinner, she was sitting outside on the veranda of her home with a little transistor radio. Then Sudha Aunty came and invited her to sit with her on her veranda. She switched off the radio and went to the next door. She also sat on the stone slab, by Sudha's side. Sudha's husband worked in an office in the town. Every day, he would come home very late as he worked in a private insurance firm. Sudha started the conversation.

"Ramayee, you have been here for two years. I haven't seen anyone coming to see you, or you going to your native. I always wanted to ask you about your native place, and about your relatives. Will you tell me about your past?"

Ramayee, smilingly asked, "What would you do with this information, aunty?"

"Because I have seen you several times with that Nithya doctor, going in her car. I presume you worked at her home," Sudha replied.

"Yes aunty, I was there with Nithya madam for some time."

"Now, tell me which is your native place, your relations, etc."

Ramayee looked at the stars shining through the leaves of the neem tree and did not reply. Bluntly, she looked straight into Sudha's eyes. Both of them did not speak for a while. Most of the houses in the streets were closed. Only a few had lights beaming out on the tiled street. A few night birds shrieked and flew away breaking the silence. Tired after the day's work, the vegetable vendor had just closed his shop and retired on the open platform in front of the temple. It seemed that he was fast asleep. Sudha was not willing to let Ramayee go. She repeated her question, "Tell me, Ramayee, as your elder sister, I ask you, just out of curiosity. Once, my husband also enquired about you." After a few minutes of stargazing, Ramayee opened her mouth. Looking at the stars, she told, "My native place is Rameswaram. I do not know who my parents are. I was with an old lady selling flowers on Sannadhi street near the temple. She said that she got me as a child of six or seven years. I was found by her on the beach wandering alone. All the traders and temple employees knew me well. I used to get enough food and money by begging the tourists who came to the temple specially, the Hindi-speaking people used to give me currency notes and not small coins. So, I used to go to those persons only. Many times, I was chased by some employees in the temple, and even the police, but they never did any harm to me. When this old lady called Katachi Patti found me, she took me, held my hand and asked me to go with her."

Curiously, Sudha asked, "Who took you? You said some Katachi Patti…"

"Yes, Katachi Patti. I never knew her real name. But everyone called her Katachi Paati, probably because she was very short in stature."

"Wait, wait," Sudha intervened, "who told you your name is Ramayee?"

"I don't actually know. Since my early days, people called me Ramayee."

"Before finding Katachi Paatti, where did you sleep at night? And who took care of you?" Sudha asked.

"I don't know, I never had any memory of living in a home, with parents or family."

"My God! Very sad indeed. Poor thing! Have you finished your dinner?"

"Yes."

"Then tell me, after Patti took you to her home, what happened?"

"It was not home. She lived on a veranda-like thing, but large enough and facing the road. The house was locked and nobody lived there. I was with her for more than five-six years. Yet, no one ever opened the heavy door."

"During the rainy season?"

"One of Paatti's relations had made a front cover with an old tarpaulin brought from his truck company where he worked as a driver. Once in a while, he came to Patti's place and gave some money to her. That uncle even bought me a doll from the city once."

Sudha asked, "Okay, during the day, you went to beg?"

"No, no, no," Ramayee replied. "Patti refused me to go to beg. And told me to be always with her, selling flowers near the temple. We had a brisk business with the flower selling. But you know, by begging, I had more money than what we both earned by selling flowers!"

Now, Sudha asked, "What did you do with the money you got by begging?"

"The only thing I wanted was food. After buying food, the rest of the money was used to give it to my fellow beggars, mostly old and invalids. I never kept anything for me as savings."

"Did your Patti cook? How did you take your food after coming to Patti?"

"Every day, Paati brought food from some place, and we shared it every day and the leftover was given to Raju."

"Raju? Who was Raju?"

"Oh! He was my dear friend, a brown dog. He slept just below our veranda."

"Oh. Nice. Then how did you come to this town? Rameswaram is very far from this place. And what did make you come here?"

Ramayee heaved a sigh and started again with more fervour. "One day, when I was selling the flowers, I was almost fourteen years at that time, one family that seemed to be rich people, came to buy flowers from me. Patti was away at that time. The couple had a boy of around seven years with them. This couple bought flowers for Rs. twenty and gave me a fifty-rupee note. When I gave back Rs thirty to the lady, she didn't accept and told me to keep it with me. I could not understand what was happening. I was simply blinking at her. She touched my cheek and bid goodbye and entered the temple. After a couple of hours, when they came back and were about to proceed to the beach, I told Patti that it was this family that asked me to keep Rs thirty. Patti stood up, went to the lady, and gave back the same. They turned back and came to the flower stand and said that this amount was willingly given to me by that lady. Then at a distance from me, they were talking about something serious and were looking at me very often.

"Ok, then what happened?"

"Nothing happened after that. They did not accept the money. Patti came and started her business as usual. On that night, when we were preparing to sleep, Paati called me and asked me whether I was happy with her. And said that I was growing fast and within a couple of years, I would be a big girl. So, she was afraid of not giving her shelter. She urged that we had to find out a safe house to live in. But I told her that with our meager income, we could not go to a rented house. Patti did not reply. She was looking at the street and thinking about something else.

"I saw she was not at all happy. She was reluctant to eat her normal quota of *idli*. That night, Raju got more than he wanted. She was seen as stressful also. I didn't know when I slept. When I woke up, Patti was not to be seen anywhere. Patti had gone to the wholesale flower dealer's house where we used to have morning ablutions. She finished her *rangoli* on the frontage of some of the houses in the street from which she used to get some money. She finished everything before six am. When she came back, I was sitting on the granite steps. She told me to go and come back early. I asked her the reason as it was quite early. And moreover, the wholesale flower dealer wouldn't give me flowers now. Usually, after seven only we used to go and get the flowers. Patti left the place without saying anything.

"Paati came back with tea. We shared the tea and she asked me to go and come immediately. I rushed up to the bathroom at the back of the flower seller's house, took bath and came back. Paati opened her trunk and gave me a frock which she kept there to give me for the festival.

I asked Paati why was she giving it now because the festival was two months away. What happened? Patti talked with a sense of love and affection, as a real grandmother, and reminded me of her talk yesterday about her growing up. Then I asked, 'Why? Are you sending me away?' To that, Patti replied, 'No, my child. Do you remember the couple yesterday? They asked me whether you can go to the city with them. They said they will take good care of you. They will give you a separate room with a cot and bed. You will get all the good food. You won't have to go to the market. They will give you a lot of money as well. They can provide a lot of things your Patti cannot.' I asked, 'Why would they do all that? In return, what should I do? And Patti, are you selling me for Rs thirty?' With tears in her eyes, Patti said, 'No. I am giving you a good life which is surely safe for you.'

"'Patti, you also come. We will go together.'

"'No child, I cannot come. I belong to this soil and if God willing, I will have a few more years and perish here only.'

"After a moment of silence, I started sobbing. Finally, she made me accept the proposal. Then Patti went to a hotel at the end of the street and met the couple where they were staying.

"Immediately around nine in the morning, the couple vacated the hotel and came to the temple in their car. When they came out from the temple, they asked us to enter the car. We all sat in the car, and the lady asked me,

'Did Patti tell you everything? We are taking you as a house maid. You have to do very simple work at home. Okay? Not much work. Already one lady comes there and does most of the kitchen work and cleaning job. You have to look after the home during the day and keep it nice and clean. My uncle will go to work in the morning. Sekhar will also be coming with us to his school. We will come back only around eight pm or even later. Sekhar will come early from school. Dinner will be prepared by the other lady for all and she would leave by six in the evening. Okay? You will like it.' Then Patti said, 'It would be very good for you, my child. Don't *hesitate*. Accompany them happily.' After telling this, Patti got down from the car. Shankar sir started the car while the lady opened her purse, took out some rupee notes and handed it to Patti. Patti immediately refused it and moved a little away from the car and said, 'If at all you want to give money, you may open an account in the bank and deposit it in Ramayee's name. Even the monthly salary you mentioned, also may be deposited. If possible, we will meet again. Goodbye Ramayee.'

"Patti departed, wiping her eyes, and waved her hand. Before getting into the car, I did hug her tightly, but now I felt that was not enough. I felt very sad to leave the only soul who loved me.

Ramayee told all this with tears in their eyes. After heaving a sigh, Ramayee said, "It is time for your husband to come. I am leaving." Sudha said, "No Ramayee, there's still time. You first finish your story. But you never told me how you landed in this small place. That was what I wanted to know."

"Okay, I will tell you," then Ramayee continued. "Shankar sir was driving. Sekhar was beside him. Madam and I were at the back. It was my first car ride. You may not believe it! When I was very small, an auto uncle, Babu, would take me for a ride around the temple, and streets just for fun.

"Here, in the car, I was thrilled and felt happy but a kind of unknown fear also gripped me. I was thinking about Patti and I didn't talk anything on the way. They stopped the car somewhere on the highway and took me to a hotel for breakfast. Aunty asked me to choose whatever I wanted. For the first time, I had tasty food from that hotel. After several hours, in the afternoon, we reached their house in a good locality in Madurai City. From the point of entry onwards, my work started. The work I had never done. Aunty asked me to take the luggage from the car and keep it on the veranda. It was heavy and too large. I could not lift the box from the car. Noticing this, Shankar sir came and helped me. So, we together took all the luggage and kept it in the hall. I had no baggage of any kind except a small handbag. Aunty gave me some clothes in an old suitcase to keep in my room. It was like a hotel room having all facilities. I wished I could bring Patti also. I continued there for about seven years. During that time, many things happened to me and the inmates of the house. By this time, I had complete control of the house. Both Shankar sir and Sandhya aunty were very busy and well-known doctors in the city. They went out early morning and came late in the evening. Vasantha *Akka* normally used to come early and prepare food for all of us. On certain days, Shankar sir and Sandhya aunty came for lunch. Otherwise, most days, they packed their lunch. Sekhar grew up and was time for him to go to Chennai for higher studies. He was a very good boy and always addressed me as 'Ramakka' with sisterly love. He felt very happy in my presence. I learnt many things from him like playing chess, caroms, and speaking and writing English. Now I know English very well. He was so nice that he treated me as his own sister. I was also very fond of him because of his good manners and behaviour."

There was silence for a few minutes and Sudha asked, "Why did you stop? Continue."

"Oh no. I just had a thought of Murugan, a frail boy, a friend of Sekhar who used to come home for combined study. I really disliked him for his approach to me, which was not encouraging. He looked at me not as his elder one, but as a tool for entertainment. Because of his repelling behaviour, I sounded Sandhya ma'am also and he started visiting less frequently.

"But again, when Sekhar went to some engineering college in Chennai, one day this Murugan, who was in Madurai only and doing some technical job, came to our house. Whenever Sekhar came on leave, this fellow would also come home and his approach towards me became increasingly intolerable. This time, I told Sankar, sir, about this and told him that if it continued, I would go back to Rameswaram. It resulted in a quarrel between Sekhar and Murugan, and Murugan could not be seen for a long time."

Now Sudha impatiently asked Ramayee, "But you never told that how you landed up here." Ramayee said, "I am coming to that, aunty. Why are you in a hurry? By that time, the phone bell rang inside the house. Sudha went and attended the call. On returning, she told Ramayee that her husband was coming in five minutes. Sudha hurriedly said, "We will continue your story tomorrow". Saying this, she went inside the house. Ramayee also returned to her house and locked the door. She looked out through the window. The vegetable vendor, Govindan, was still on the temple platform, fast asleep but visibly disturbed by mosquitoes. The street was empty and she heard the noise of the next-door uncle's scooter. Ramayee made her bed and cuddled the events that brought her to this place and slowly fell asleep.

The next day, after all the work was completed, she waited for Sudha aunty to come out. But even after eight in the night, she did not show up. Ramayee was an urge to tell all her woeful and sweet memories to Sudha. After some time, she stepped down and saw Sudha's door locked. A disheartened Ramayee came back and again sat on her stone slab. She looked at the temple platform. Govindan was also not there. As the power went out all of a sudden, there was total darkness in the street but she could hear the sound of the closing of doors from other houses. But even then, she continued to sit there unperturbed by the situation. Gazing at the stars through the branches of the neem tree, she sat resting against the pillar. One or two bikes and cycles passed flashing lights and breaking the silence. She felt it was going to be raining as the cold wind blew from the west. The wind became strong in a few minutes and the tree branches were dancing heavily. She looked at the street. Nothing was to be seen outside. Disgusted by Sudha *akka's* absence, she retired inside, closing the doors and the rain also started lashing. Now she decided to go to bed and as she was preparing for her retirement for the day, she heard the sound of next door uncle's scooter. She looked through the window and found Sudha aunty sitting as a pillion rider totally drenched. Now Ramayee realised that Sudha wouldn't be coming tonight. Again, she looked through the window and found the temple platform damp and empty. She searched for Govindan, but in vain. Moreover, how could she find him in this darkness and rain? She remembered what Sudha said a few days ago while they both were in Govindan's shop. He had gone inside to bring out a sack of onions. Sudha had commented, "Poor fellow, I have been observing him for several years now. Nobody is there for him to help. At least he could have married so that his wife would be of help to him. Moreover, he is not that old. Sudha looked at Ramayee and told, "You also have nobody here. I haven't seen anyone so far." Saying this, she smiled at her meaningfully. And on another day, Sudha praised Govindan for his good health, conduct and character. She even suggested, "You are not that old to be alone. It is high time you married. Now that you are healthy and young, marriage will be easy. If you don't do it now, when you get old, you will have to repent. I don't know how you spent all these prime years in your life without any company. I could not even think of that." Ramayee answered in a cool tone, "Akka, it depends on one's fate."

"But don't leave everything to fate, Ramayee," Sudha replied, "we have to work for the goal."

In reply, she only had a deep breath and looked at the nearby tree where two *mynahs* were sitting close to each other.

All these thoughts passed through her mind as she slowly drifted to sleep.

The next morning, she went to Govindan's shop and purchased some vegetables. On that day only, she had a close watch on his facial features and his well-built physique. Though she had been there several times over the last two years, some kind of feeling flowed in her nerves. After having the transaction, she looked at him for some more time, and when other buyers came to the shop, she left the place. Before going, she turned and smilingly told him, "I know your name is Govindan.

Where do you come from? I haven't seen anybody visiting you so far." Govindan, throwing a surprised look at her, said, "I don't have anybody."

She didn't leave. She again asked, "Your family, your parents, your relatives?"

Govindan said, "I don't know if there are people like that for me".

He gave her an uninteresting look. "OK, you got the balance? Now you go home. Other people are coming. Don't disturb my business."

This curt reply left Ramayee a little disappointed, but still, she liked the way he talked. Slowly, she started to like him for some unknown reason. She even started to purchase vegetables for all the homes where she went for work. Also, she started advertising to other people and other new settlers on the streets. She used to say, "Govindan's vegetables are best. Fresh and prices are also very low. I will get it for you, aunty."

After a couple of days, she got a chance to sit with Sudha in the evening. They started their conversation with Ramayee's life story. This time, it was on the insistence of Ramayee who volunteered to tell the story. She asked, "Where did I leave the story on that day?" Recollecting the previous conversations, Sudha told, "You stopped at Murugan."

"Yes, yes." Ramayee started. "Whenever he came, I used to go out in the garden and pretend to be watering the plants. He would call me in again and again. The aunty in the kitchen also had a very bad opinion of Murugan. Therefore, she warned me not to go near him. After experiencing severe resistance from me coupled with auntie's rebuke, Murugan stopped coming.

"It was a happy life for me, as there was not much work at home, but plenty of conveniences and a lot of money. Every month, Sandhya ma'am deposited an amount in the bank and she used to give me receipts from the bank. The money in the bank grew into a large amount and I was also growing up. Once Sandhya Ma'am told her husband to find out a suitable boy for me so that he could also be accommodated in this house and she would not have to worry much about me. He took it lightly and nothing happed thereafter."

Sudha asked again, "But what brought you here? That's what I have been asking you."

Ramayee said smilingly, "Don't be in a hurry, aunty. I am coming to the point. Be patient".

"After a few years, Sekhar got to study for some higher course at a university abroad and he left. During those days, some hectic activities were going on at home. After coming from the hospital duty, both husband and wife were very much engaged and busy with the computer. On a Sunday, I was invited to have lunch with them at the dining table. First, I refused, because I had never taken food along with them to the dining table. When I said no, they insisted that I must. Therefore, I also sat down and enjoyed dinner. After the dinner, Sandhya ma'am told me seriously, 'Look Ramayee, your stay with us is going to be over by this weekend, that is up to next Sunday only. We both are going away to Dubai and nobody will be staying here. We will engage a watchman outside, and the house will be locked.' Shankar sir said, 'Ramayee, we should thank you for all the service you sincerely did for us, but it is time now, for you to go back to your place.' I was shocked to hear the sudden decision, but I knew that one day or the other, I would have to leave them. But this was just like a bolt from the blue. Ma'am went inside and gave me a lot of new clothes and a pair of gold bangles. Which I am wearing now, see? She also did not forget to give me my bank passbook. I was shocked to see that there was a staggering amount of ten lakhs plus in my balance". Handing over the passbook, Ma'am said, 'This is your savings from the very first month since you came here. Moreover, we plan to visit Rameswaram, you can come with us and we will hand you over to your Patti. Okay? Get ready.' I just bluntly looked at them. They had nothing else to say as I was totally awe-struck."

Sudha asked anxiously, "Did you go to Rameswaram?"

"Yes *Akka*, what else could I do?"

After a moment of silence, she continued, "On that designated day, we set out early in the morning, and reached Rameswaram around noon. They wanted to take lunch at a hotel. Rameswaram was all changed. With big hotels and lodges, shops. All the old houses were changed to modern ones, rarely, some tiled houses could be seen. After lunch, we went to Paati's dwelling place. To our dismay, there was no Patti, veranda, or old locked house. Instead, there stood a tall four-storeyed building with a name board Vastala Lodge. Then I suggested we would go to the flower-dealers house to find out Patti. Luckily, the flower dealer was present in the same old place. When we enquired, he informed us that Kattachi Paati expired four years ago. I got a big shock and looked at Aunty and Uncle, who were looking at the temple tower where pigeons were flocking around. As the flower dealer was turning away from us, I asked him, 'Brother, you recognise me?' He said, "No". 'I am your old Ramayee.' He gazed at me as if seeing some strange animal. Then he exclaimed, 'You are Kattachi Patti's Ramayee? I thought you were their daughter.' Looking at Uncle and Aunty, we purchased some flowers from this person and entered the temple. After having *darshan*, when we were walking in the *prakara*, I felt that the uncle and aunty were somewhat disturbed mentally and they discussed many things about me among themselves. Then we sat on a stone bench on the beach and Sandhya ma'am asked me whether I was willing to go to her sister's house in Trichy. She told details about her sister Radha, who was staying in Trichy with her family. Actually, we planned to stay in Rameswaram for a day but now we went back to Madurai the same day. At night, they asked again about my going to Radha's house. As I had no other place to go, I accepted it immediately.

Later that night, they phoned Radha aunty to come to Madurai and take me.

"Radha aunty was not rich and or placed like Sandhya ma'am. Her husband was a clerk in a government office and she was a teacher in a local school. Sandhya ma'am said, 'Radha *Akka* won't be able to give you this much money, but she would take care of you.'

"The very next day, Radha *Akka* came and they had a very long discussion. From their talks, I could understand that she had two small children going to primary classes whom I should take care of. Radha *Akka* called and asked me to sit near the dining table. When I hesitated, she told me, 'From today, you have to obey me. Okay?' I replied, 'Ok, Aunty.' She continued, 'You won't be getting all the facilities or money like you are enjoying here. Okay?' 'Yes,' I replied. 'I can give you only Rs three thousand per month. Okay?' I replied again, 'Ok.'

'Yes, you have to assist me in the kitchen also, ok?'

'Yes.'

'There is no separate bedroom for you, so you will have to adjust in the kitchen. Okay?'

'Ok.'

'Another important thing is that I will see your performance for a month, and then I will decide accordingly.'

"As I had no other choice, I said okay. So, she seemed to be very strict and very different from Sandhya Ma'am. In the afternoon, before leaving the home, Sandhya Ma'am called me, hugged me and said, 'As there is no other choice, I am leaving you to my younger sister. I hope you would adjust to the surroundings. In case we return from abroad, surely we will take you with me.'

"In the afternoon, we were brought to the Madurai bus stop and then, from there, we reached Trichy by bus and yet by another bus to this place. Now, you understand who is Radha?"

"Oh, that Radha? Working in the school and staying in the newly built house near the village office?"

"Yes, yes. Now you know how I came to this place."

"But you didn't tell me how you reached this house."

"Ok, I will continue. I worked for a month or two, but for some reason, Radha and her husband quarrelled once resulting in Radha aunty telling me that I would have to go in a rented house. You can come to this house in the morning hours only, and do whatever work you can. After that, you can work in any other house, for which I can help you. Thus, she took this house for a monthly rent of Rs one thousand and also introduced me to a few more houses including Nithya Aunty where I could go for work. This is my full story."

"But why did Radha decide to send you out of her house?"

"God only knows. And anyway, I am happy this way."

All this time, Ramayee was watching Govindan's shop. But he was nowhere to be seen.

After a few weeks, Radha and Sudha came to her home at dusk and asked her directly, "Ramayee, if Govindan accepts you, will you marry him?"

"But, Aunty..."

"We have talked to him already," said Sudha. "He is fine with it. Now you cannot stay here alone. You are crossing thirty years, but you look very young, not more than twenty-five. Do you know three-four boys are hovering around you after dusk?"

Radha said, "How can she know? She does not think that way."

They sat for one or two hours and talked about a lot of things. They advised her that since she had a hefty amount in her bank, she could purchase a second-hand home, and settle here with Govindan after marriage. On South End Street, there was a good old house that could be purchased with the money in my bank. For that, they would make all the arrangements.

A few weeks later, her marriage was solemnized in the main temple with a few important people from the village witnessing the event. At that moment, Ramayee wished that Kattachi Patti, Sandhya Aunty, and all the others should have been present there. From the temple, Govindan and Ramayee entered the new house.

4

Wood and Chisel

Selvam was an average woodcarver. He carved beautiful images of gods and goddesses. He also did, on-demand, some floral motifs on the doors and panels in new buildings of the affluent people in the nearby town. He was an expert in carving teak wood and rosewood on which his great-grandfather excelled. His grandfather was an expert in carving panels to be fixed in the temple chariots which were sometimes thirty-forty feet high and weighing several tonnes. When his father's time came, there was not much demand for the temple chariots but he continued carving the same panels depicting celestial beings with fine ornamentation. These carved panels were sold through the government and private shops in the country to be adorned in the homes of the rich. These panels were also brought by craft exporters in the big cities and exported at prohibitive prices to foreign countries. Selvam also continued the same work but was getting not even enough money to make both ends meet. His family consisted of only four members including himself. His wife, Seetalakshmi, was a simple village woman who had never gone beyond the borders of her district, they lived with whatever income they had. Their two children were in high school. The elder one was a boy, Ramkumar—an average student of class twelfth; and the younger daughter called Ramya was four years junior to him and pursuing studies in a smaller class.

They lived in the old dilapidated ancestral house on a narrow street in the village with just two rooms and a kitchen with a side thatched shed which was used as the workshop, locally called *Pattarai*. On the old soot-coated walls, there were a few yellowed certificates given by the erstwhile kingdom, the government of the state and even a photo with a certificate given by the President of India. Those were the rare inheritance by Selvam along with the house. He was happy that he got the legacy of his ancestors in the field and was proud as well. The village bank had loaned Selvam a sizable amount. Whenever he got cheques as payments for his carvings sold to the exporters and shops, he would repay it in instalments and a very small amount was brought home for daily expenses which were just near sufficient. Everything was going on smoothly until his boy passed his twelfth standard exam. Ramkumar was insisting that he be allowed to study further but Selvam had other designs. He wanted Selvam to induct him into his profession. One day there was a heated argument between the father, mother, and son. Ramya was the mute spectator. Ramkumar said gleefully, "Appa, I am sure I will pass this exam colourfully! I would like to go to engineering college and pursue my B.tech."

"Son, what are you saying? Can I send you to an engineering college? Look at my financial status. First of all, you need very good marks in your twelfth standard. Then you should pass the competitive exams. If that is also done, you will have to get admission. I know, but that demands a lot of money. No, it's not possible at all. Moreover, after my time is up, who will carry on our woodcarving? Should not our legacy continue? I have only one boy. Therefore, listen to what I say. You stop your studies after this and train yourself in woodcarving. In our district, most of the carvers are gone either to some distant places or stopped working. Their children have gone to some other job-oriented studies. If I also do the same, what would happen to our woodcarving industry here?"

Selvam sat on a bench and stared at the pictures of his forefathers. A minute passed. Ramkumar angrily said, "Why have they gone to the job-oriented studies, Appa? Because there is no demand for the carvings like it used to be earlier. The cost of wood has increased enormously. Machines have come now. When you take a month to finish one door carving by hand, that Muthu Anna in the next street does the same in three days with machines."

Selvam threw a smile and said, "Ram, those machine carvings are used only for doors and not for figures. That's why I am continuing this hand carving. Those who use machines, let them. I am getting my dues from the market as usual."

In this way, Selvam tried to pacify Ramkumar. But Ramkumar was not at all ready to budge. He shouted at his father, "Are you selling as many items as you used to do earlier? No. Why? Because there is lesser demand as the cost of wood has increased, machine carvings have come to rule. Even fibre moulds come at a cheaper price. Naturally, demand has dwindled. Therefore, understand the present trend and let me study further."

At this juncture, his mother Seeta, intervened, "Son, don't get angry or disgusted. Whatever you say might be correct, but see our situation here. Your father is already in a lot of debt, in this situation, how can we send you for higher studies? Moreover, you are the only son we have to continue our traditional work," she looked at her husband in an assuring way.

"Traditional work? What traditional work?" Ramkumar retorted, "Amma, times are changing. You cannot go on like this… our future is in machines and computers and not in your hammer and chisel. He is not getting a lot of orders like he used to get. Why don't you people understand?"

Seeta lamented, "Ram, in a few years, your sister will be ready for marriage. If you also start earning by carving wood, it would be of great help to our family. Don't you know how much people ask for dowry these days? Do you think that with the meagre amount earned by your father, and with small savings, we can marry off your sister? Impossible. So don't be silly. Obey what your Appa says."

After a moment of silence, he started again, "Appa, could you ever build a new house? At least a small house with your income? See Ramakrishnan uncle from the next street, he is also working in wood. But he sent his son to college and now he is earning a lot of money as a teacher. Are you listening to me, Appa?" After this much yelling, he murmured to himself, "Tradition, hereditary, legacy… and what not?"

Selvam was quite stunned after hearing all this. He never expected such a demonstration from his son. Staring at Ram's face, Selvam asked, "How can I send you to college? That needs a huge sum of money?"

"Take a loan from the bank," retorted Ramkumar.

"But how will I ever repay it?"

"Don't worry, as per the regulations, I can repay the loan after my education."

In the next room, his sister was sitting in front of the school notes and was listening to all of this, which greatly disturbed her. She called Amma and said, "I would learn wood carving now and stop going to school. Let Ram anna go to college."

Thereafter, the discussion came to an end.

That night, Selvam could not sleep. He was thinking of several ways and means to find funds but in vain. In the dead of night, he stood up from the mat and sat on a rickety chair near the window. He totalled all his loan amount and he also totalled the money that he was to be received from his customers. He was stunned when he found that the loan amount was just double the amount to be received. Moreover, every month, the interest on the loan amount was also added. Besides, the amount taken from the Marwari in the town at a higher rate of interest also threateningly stared at him. His head was swirling and he was sweating all over. He took two glasses full of water and after some time, he dropped himself on the mat and he didn't know when he fell asleep.

The next day, both the husband and wife discussed a lot of things regarding their son's determination to reject traditional work. After a series of sessions, with even their well-wishers and neighbours, they could not find any solution. A week later, they decided that Ramkumar should go to the engineering college at any cost. To discuss this, Selvam went to the local bank and told everything sincerely to the manager. After hearing him out, the manager assured him there was no hitch in giving him the loan. Selvam doubted, "Sir, what about the repayment?"

"You don't worry about that. After his studies are over and he gets a job, he can repay it. The loan will be in his name only."

"But what about guarantee?"

"No, as it's under a new scheme of an education loan, you have to produce papers like certificates, admission letters from the college, some undertakings, etc. That I'll discuss with your son. Send him tomorrow, okay?"

Selvam was really relieved that the repayment was not his job. Jubilantly, he returned home and narrated what all happened in the bank. But still, he had doubt in his mind. Would all these things really happen? Hefty loan, interest on the loan, son becoming an engineer, daughter getting married... Both of them spent several days thinking about and discussing these aspects and finally recoiled to themselves, "Lord Murugan would take care of everything." After a few days, Ramkumar's results were announced and it turned out that he passed the twelfth standard with really good marks. As per the discussion with the manager the other day, he went to the bank and learnt all the procedures for availing of the loan. The confidence which was shining in Ramkumar's eyes was very much appreciated by the manager. During those days, admission into a city college for a boy from a village was something very special. And from his community, there was not even a single person studying in any engineering college in the village. His contemporaries had even left the traditional carvings and left for other jobs without any further higher studies.

A month later, Ramkumar received an admission letter from an engineering college in the city and he promised his parents that he would study well and become an engineer and get a good job so that his father would not have to fight with the wood and chisels. His words, although indigestible to Selvam, made him happy that his son would become an engineer in a few years and bring a lot of money home so that all his woes would end including the marriage of his daughter. Now, his joy knew no bounds when he thought of himself as the father of the only engineer in the village. He called Seeta and asked, "Seeta, don't you think you are going to be a proud mother of an engineer?" Seeta although overwhelmed with joy, marring his feelings said in a low voice, "Don't tell such things now. Your own evil eyes should not fall on him. Take your toolbox and go to the shed. Did you finish the order given by the government emporium in Kerala?"

"Yes, yes, I forgot to finish the work in the melee of admission. At least I may get half of the total bill if I supply that order. Get me a coffee in my shed. I am going." Uttering these words, Selvam stepped out to the shed with his toolbox which he always kept on the floor in front of an oil lamp and an array of pictures of gods and goddesses.

A month had passed. No customers had sent him any payments. He ran out of money. Seeta was asking for money for various urgent needs. He very well knew that Seeta never asked for money unless it was for the utmost necessary things. Only for immediate wants, she used to ask him because she knew how hard Selvam worked to run the home including children's educational needs.

A peculiar characteristic of Seeta was that she would never ask money for to buy groceries and vegetables. Somehow, she would manage things. If she had no milk, she would give everyone black tea or coffee. If there was no tea or coffee powder, she would give them a concoction of palm jaggery and coriander seeds. If there is not enough rice and vegetables in the house, she would prepare gruel with millet and green grams with a lot of water. The side dish would be dried pickles made of mango or citrus. She used to make these pickles in plenty because that would help her largely when there was no money to buy vegetables. These are the indicators that there were no provisions at home. Understanding the situation, Selvam would go out and get some small loans even from his fellow carvers. The condition of the majority of woodcarvers was more or less similar.

One day, Selvam packed all his carved panels ordered by the government shop in Kerala and set out for delivering the goods. Ramkumar accompanied him to the bus stop in the village and loaded the boxes containing the carvings. He had another cloth bag that contained his lunch, a bottle full of water and a diary having all the details of recent supplies and receipts of cheques, the balance amount to be received, etc. When the bus moved, Ramkumar left for home. Sitting on the bus, Selvam was thinking about whether he would get the payment today or not. Sometimes, they would say, "Leave the goods here, you will get the payment by cheque within two weeks." But usually, that would not happen. Because of the rushing cool wind on the bus, gradually he went to sleep. After a few minutes, when the bus arrived at a check post near the state border, the passengers were told by the conductor that the bus would not move further because of the lightning strike by some political party in Kerala. The sudden incident upset Selvam. Nobody knew when they would withdraw the strike and the roads would be clear. It was eight in the morning, and the conductor announced that all the passengers must come down immediately. The bus was parked at the extreme left of the road near a tea shop. Some of the passengers were seen getting into the bus and preparing for a nap. A few were waiting with the hope that the talks between the government and the strikers would be successful and the bus would continue its journey. Time went by, and it was noon. Selvam saw vehicles plying from Kerala's side and crossing the check-post. A bike rider was announcing that the strike was over as the talk was favourable to the worker's union.

The driver and the conductor along with a few passengers of the bus were sitting and having their lunch in the tea shop. Selvam approached them and asked whether the bus would start soon. But the conductor told him that as soon as the message came from their depot, they could go. Selvam also took out his lunch packet from his bag and started having it with tea from the shop. After around two pm, the bus started from the border and reached the bus terminal at Trivandrum an hour later. He hurriedly got out of the bus with the intention of off-loading the box somehow. But Lo! The boxes had been off-loaded already and a hefty fellow in the uniform of a union and another slender man with a *beedi* called out.

"Whose box is this?"

"It is mine," replied Selvam.

"Give me Rs two hundred."

Selvam was astonished. He asked, "Why should I pay you Rs two hundred?"

"It is our coolie," he plainly said.

Selvam asked him with a smile, "Who told you to off-load my boxes?"

"Why should anyone say? It is our right.

Selvam again said with ease, "Who are you to touch my boxes without my permission?"

The guy with the *beedi* angrily came forward as if he was going to hit Selvam and said, "We don't need anyone to say. Take out the money and simply get off!"

The people gathered. There were heated exchanges between them. Finally, a policeman, who was watching all this drama, from a distance appeared at the site.

"What is going on here?" he asked authoritatively.

Selvam told, "Sir, without asking me, these fellows off-loaded my package from the bus and are demanding Rs two hundred! How can I give?"

The policeman suspiciously looked at him and asked, "What is there inside the package?"

Selvam politely said, "Woodcarving."

Neither the policeman nor the union fellows understood.

"What is it?" again the policeman asked.

"Woodcarving panels."

Again there was confusion among the crowd. He demanded to see what was inside. Enthusiasm grew in the crowd to see what was inside. Selvam sat down on the footpath near the terminal and unpacked the box and took out one of the panels. On seeing the things inside, the policeman said, "Oh, dolls made of wood? Okay, close it." Then Selvam repacked the box.

"Where are you taking them?"

"Sir, I am a woodcarver. I do the work on wood and sell these types of panels to shops. I have brought similar pieces several times. This time, as it happened to be a bigger box, it caught the attention of these people. I only get a meagre sum by doing this. Not a hefty amount as these people who simply climb up the bus and come down."

"Which people?"

Looking at the union people, he said, "These people. They just climb up, take the box, come down and now are demanding Rs two hundred, but I get Rs two hundred if I do a day's work from morning till evening. See this."

Selvam opened his diary and took a letter from the government shop, asking him to deliver the goods.

As the letter was in English, the policeman took a long time to digest the contents of the letter. Then he said, "Now they've done their job for you. Therefore, you just give Rs fifty to them." Selvam took Rs fifty from his pocket and said, "See, I have only Rs fifty which will be required for my return journey." After a while when the policeman was thinking, he finally said, "Give Rs ten to him, and get away from here." After receiving the Rs ten, the fellow murmured, "In the morning itself, these beggars come with large boxes with no money for paying coolie." On hearing this, Selvam told, "Hello? I didn't beg you. You were the one who begged for Rs two hundred." One of the onlookers commented, "Even if you had off-loaded the boxes, these fellows would have demanded money from you!"

Anyway, Selvam left the place in an auto-rickshaw along with the boxes. Only when he needs money urgently, he would carry the goods personally. Otherwise, he would send parcels by transport services. Now he decided that he would never carry goods personally whatever may come.

On reaching the emporium, he saw the purchase manager was locking his office. On seeing Selvam's plight, he accepted the consignment and recommended payment only on the next day as most of the staff members had left the office. He took a cup of tea from the canteen and returned with the receipts given by the purchase manager and sat on a cement bench on the lawns of the emporium. Though he had taken tea, he was feeling tired and hungry. He counted the money available in his pocket. There were a few rupees just below a hundred and some small changes. He decided to take one more tea along with snacks to fill up his stomach. Again, he came down to the bench, sat down and immersed himself in a variety of good and bad thoughts. Time was running out and the emporium was to be closed at seven pm. The security came and asked him to vacate the place as he was going to lock the gate.

Selvam got up with a guilt feeling and started walking towards the bus terminals. He reached home at around ten pm and found himself very much exhausted. After freshening himself he took some food that Seeta gave him and went to bed. Seeta did not ask anything about the trip and the payment. She knew that if they had given payment, he would have handed it to her along with a packet of sweets for children immediately on arrival.

The next day, in the morning itself, he set out to the emporium and met the purchase manager, quality control inspector, accounts officer, etc. and after a lot of requests and arguments, he could get only fifty percent of the total bill amount and that too by cheque. As there was no other way, he accepted the cheque as he was confident that the manager of the local bank would give him an overdraft. And thus, by afternoon, after having a quick lunch at the canteen, he bid goodbye to the manager and returned home by evening. Unfortunately for him, the next day was Sunday and he could get cash only on

Monday from the bank. During the night, after dinner, Selvam and Seeta used to sit on the granite block under the neem tree near his work shed and talk about various subjects starting from the marriage of next-street Radhika who defied her parents and went with a boy of the same village, rains in Kerala, the likelihood of MGR coming to rule the state, latest Tamil films to even what Indira Gandhi thought about MGR. That day also, they started their night dialogue. Seeta opened up, "How much did they give? I mean the payment from the emporium?"

Selva, in a low voice, told her, "fifty percent of the bill."

"That's all?" A dismayed Seeta muttered something about the emporium.

Then Selva started explaining all the experiences he had meted out during these two days and told with a sigh of relief. "At least they gave this much. Otherwise, they would have sent the cheque after many days..."

"Lazy lots. They should know how we craft workers suffer all day and night to eke out a living," Seeta harshly said.

"It is okay, now leave it. It is our fate. Why do you curse them? Everywhere the same thing happens, almost to everybody in this field."

Seeta with a widened eye, said, "At least our son escaped from this kind of suffering."

"Though he's not interested in our traditional job, it was his adamant nature that drove us to take such a decision."

"Anyway, I think it's for good," appreciating his decision, Seeta said, "All that is okay, now I'm worried about my girl."

Pacifying Seeta, Selvam said, "Don't worry about her. There are plenty of boys in our own community."

A startled Seeta asked, "Our own community?"

"Yes," Selvam said assertively.

An annoyed Seeta asked him, "Why do you insist that we should find boys only from our community?"

With a calm smiling face, Selvam said, "That has been our tradition."

"What tradition? What have you ever earned from your tradition?" Seeta noted with disgust, "You, your father, your grandfather… everyone stuck to the tradition and got nothing. As Ram asked you, could you build a new house for us? Just like your forefathers, you are also living with us in this dilapidated century-old house."

Silence prevailed for some time.

Selvam got annoyed, "What is the problem with this house? From time to time, I am getting this house repaired."

"So will it be there for another hundred years? Don't dream that Ram Kumar and his family would ever want to live in this house," Seeta told sarcastically.

Selvam did not speak for a while. Seeta knew that her words hit him hard. With some pacifying words, Seeta came closer to him and said in a loving tone, "Have I said anything wrong? If you think so, please pardon me. But what I told you are only facts. Now think about it. Within two-three years we have to settle our daughter's marriage. Therefore, do not hurry and get into the trap of your relatives."

"What trap?" Selvam asked.

"Ram Kumar may be snatched away soon after his studies. Hope you understand what I say."

Conclusively, Seeta said, "Okay, what I'm coming to tell you is you do not give word to your family members. That is all I say now."

Selvam stood up. "Okay, we will see later. Now you go to sleep and let me sit alone for some time."

Seeta held his hand and said, "No, cool wind is blowing. Get in. It is time to sleep."

Somehow, the years rolled by. Ram Kumar finished his course and also had a selection in the campus interview. The offer was from a multi-national company and the workplace was Bangalore. While the entire family Selvam was celebrating the event, something bad happened in his sister's family. His brother-in-law Senthil died in a scooter accident. They had only one daughter, Nisha, who was undergoing a degree course. Senthil was a machinist in an engineering company in Coimbatore producing machine parts for motor-based industries.

They were living in Coimbatore ever since Selvam's sister, Shanthi got married. They had even purchased a small plot of land on the outskirts of the city near the airport and constructed a budget house.

Now Selvam had to leave for Coimbatore immediately. He took the night bus and reached Coimbatore by the next morning. By that time, most of the relatives had assembled and were busy carrying out various duties assigned to them. By evening, everything related to the cremation was over and very few of them stayed back in the house though there was no place to accommodate everyone. Somehow, they spent their night there and by the next morning, they started leaving the place. By noon, there were only Selvam, Shanthi, Nisha and one or two relatives of Senthil. There seemed a distinctive separation among the people assembled there which clearly indicated that Senthil's people were in a hurry to go. They were not even discussing the future course of action to be taken in this family but Mr Muthu, brother of Senthil came to the front room and asked Selvam, "Brother, now what?"

Selvam said in a tone filled with melancholy, "I don't know what to do. What do you think?"

Muthu replied, "Now after the ten-day function here, Shanthi and Nisha may not be able to stay here without anybody's help. Shanthi doesn't have any job also. Nisha is still in college." He stopped for a while and expected a reply from Selvam. All this time, Nisha who was in the next room, came out and told him that she had to continue her studies.

"Mama, this is my third year. Now, only six months are left for the final exam. Till that time, I and mother will continue to stay here." Muthu intervened, "So you are going to stay alone here with your mother?" Selvam noded his head in disagreement and replied, "That cannot happen."

"Then you tell a better solution," Muthu said assertively. "Let us consult others as well," Selvam said. But nobody had any tangible solution. There was utter confusion about the future stay of Shanthi and Nisha. It seemed that nobody was willing to arrive at a solution or take guarantee of these two persons. They postponed the discussion for another day.

On the tenth day of the function, many people assembled including Seeta and Ram Kumar. Lunch was served and many of them left. Muthu opened up the discussion when there were a dozen people sitting in plastic chairs outside the house. Now that all of us are available here, we should take a decision on the future of our girls here. Some were smoking, some were having a mouthful of betel leaves yet others had in between their fingers, a pinch of snuff to be inhaled which nobody could say when they do it. Sometimes, for several minutes, they would hold the snuff between their fingers and look out for the auspicious time for using it. All of a sudden, they inhale it in different fashions which would be of much amusement for the onlookers.

Sivamoni, the eldest in the family, told in an authoritative voice, "Let them continue here until the girl gets a job. Another Mr Ganeshan questioned, "If they continue here, who will give the required finance? Will you give?" Eagerly, everybody looked at the elderly man. He got angry got up with a volte-face and said, Then I do not have anything to state in this matter. You solve it. I am leaving."

Then Selvam got up and pacified him and made him sit again and told, "Brother, you are the eldest in our family now, and if you say like this, what will others do?" Sivamoni sat again silently for some time and then said, "Ok, the child has six months more to complete the course. They haven't got any resources to spend a few more months here. The company in which Senthil was working would give them some amount but it may take some time. But till then, we cannot wait. So, what I suggest is, we all contribute some amount till they get the payment from the company. What do you say?" He looked at everyone's faces with a smile. Ganeshan said, "I am ready. Let us decide now itself who should give how much?" But the true faces of some people came out explaining that they were not in for parting money. On seeing this, Selvam intervened, "No, we cannot force anybody to give this much or that much. It is left to them." Ganeshan was miserly in this matter, but he was a well-to-do man also in the clan and he owned a gold jewellery shop also. On hearing this, he kept quiet and looked at the sky and trees to avoid faces fearing he might have to give a lion's share.

"Okay," Sivamoni told. "I suggest that each one may contribute whatever they can consider their capacity and cash reserve." He meaningfully looked at Ganeshan. But Ganeshan was busy looking at a squirrel carrying a nut to its nest in the nearby tamarind tree. The youngest in the assembly, Velu who was a carpenter, opined, "Okay, now money is collected and the amount from the company is also received. Her exams were also over, then what next? Should they again continue? Don't they have a permanent solution? Anyway, they cannot continue forever. Nisha has to get a job, and has to be married, how will all these things happen? And who will take care of them?" Everybody was in silent mode for several minutes. All this time, inside the house, the ladies were listening to their conservations and were discussing among themselves regarding their continuing in Coimbatore. The majority of them told that they should be left in the care of Selvam. A few others did not open their mouths fearing the responsibility might come upon them. A few among the gents were also of a similar opinïon. When the discussion was going on, their attention was on the next compound, trees and sky as if they had nothing to do in this matter.

Seeta was, all the while watching, listening and analysing all the blabbering inside and outside. In her heart of hearts, she was just thinking why should she suffer here in Coimbatore among these people? Why didn't Selvam take her to his house along with her Nisha? She looked at Selvam through the window and immediately came out and took Selvam to the corner of the compound behind a tree, and started discussing. Even while discussing with Selvam, Shanti was brimming with tension thinking about what would happen Now she was not able to act or say on her own. She had to depend on these people only. All she had wanted was that Nisha's future should be secured. She should get a good job and a good boy as a husband. She was not at all concerned about herself. Shanthi stood near the window for more than an hour. Only when Selvam and Seetha disappeared from behind the tree, she came to the bench where Nisha and her friends were sitting.

Nisha said, "Ma, you look very tired. Now you need some rest. Go and have a good nap."

But Shanthi was not in the mood to go to the bedroom. She prayed to all the gods, that her brother should take a decision favourable to them.

The assembly outside was still not in a position to arrive at a final decision. Each and everyone was interested in leaving the place as early as possible throwing all the responsibility to Sivamoni and Selvam. Some even started leaving the place, excusing themselves with one or other imaginary reasons. The ladies inside had also taken leave saying that their husbands outside were calling them as they were in a haste to go.

Now it was evening and only Sivamoni, his wife, Thanamma, Selvam, and Seetha were available for taking any decision. Thanamma was also pestering Sivamoni to leave early as there wouldn't be any bus after seven pm to their village.

A calm and undisturbed Selvam was pacifying Shanthi and Nisha by telling simple jokes. This made Sivamoni angry. He shouted at Selvam, "Selvam! This is not the time to have your jokes here! Don't act like a clown. Now we are getting late. Don't you want to say anything about the future course of action?"

Selvam, unperturbed by Sivamoni's angry tone, said in a calm voice, "Brother, I have already taken a decision that we would be here in this house till Shanthi gets all the benefits from the company. Tomorrow, I would be going to the company along with Shanthi and applying for her dues. As all of you have nothing to say in this matter and most of them have left also, leaving these people in the lurch, I have taken this decision. I will leave Seetha here for their company till Nisha completes her exam. Then I will take them to my home. Rest we will see later.

Upon hearing this, Sivamoni and Thanamma were greatly relieved. Turing towards Selvam, they joyfully said, "Then what? Selvam, you are doing a very good job. Now can we go?" Within a short time, they also left. A couple of days later, Selvam and Ram Kumar also left for home leaving Seetha with Shanthi and Nisha. Before leaving Coimbatore, Selvam ensured that Shanthi got all the dues from the company and that the amount was deposited in her bank account.

Back in Selvam's house, the girl Ramya somehow survived with the neighbours' help during all these days. After a couple of weeks, a call letter was received by Ram Kumar from a company in Bangalore. Thus, shortly after that, Ram Kumar left his village for joining the company as a trainee engineer.

On that night, Ramya asked, "Daddy, for how many days would Mother be at Shanthi auntie's home? I suffered much here during these days to manage to have my food. The aunty in the next house was very helpful and we together looked after the kitchen. That is why I could at least complete my homework."

Selvam replied, "She will be there for about six months, till Nisha's exam."

"What! Six months!?" exclaimed Ramya. "Up to that time, I have to work in the kitchen?"

Selvam said smilingly, "Don't worry, I will also help in the kitchen."

"Beware, it is not as easy as chiselling wood. Do you have any idea about cooking? We have to eat every day. So, we have to work every day carefully in the kitchen. But you have to go the work-shed also."

This sarcastic remark induced Selvam to say, "You have to go to school also. So, we will manage somehow, don't worry."

Once a month, Selvam visited Coimbatore and saw personally the well-being of everyone there. Now it had become his duty to look for a boy for Nisha. It was a great job. He pacified himself. Everything would be alright with the grace of God. Now the problem was, how to find resources for two more people. Already it was insufficient. He hoped Shanthi would spend from her sources. All her money was intact in the bank. Definitely, she would share the household expenses. The almighty will see everything. So, he needn't worry. During the journey home and back, he always thought of these things on the bus. He restarted his daily work of carving images of gods and goddesses. In between the work, he also made some jokes on contemporary matters to his assistants working in the shed. Every day, Selvam had to give wages to them. There were at least ten craftsmen regularly coming to work for him. But nowadays, that number had dwindled to just two craftsmen. Others had gone to some other work like mechanics in automobile workshops. A few went as assistants to senior carpenters. One person had even gone to Dubai, whose wife was one-day boasting that he earned a very good salary. A couple of them had become masons where they could earn double their wages. Thus, the production in Selvam's shed has greatly reduced. All these boys were looking for any other work other than woodcarving. Although they knew woodcarving very well, trained by Selvam, they were interested in shifting to artistic carpentry or some architectural work where they could get more wages. Naturally, the number of woodcarvers in the village had reduced to very few in number including Selvam.

Selvam felt happy that his son became an engineer, which he never thought even in his dreams. He would not suffer like Selvam in the future. His wife and children would be having a happy and contented life. Now, he understood why Ram Kumar was vehemently opposing his tradition of wood carving. If he had not gone to the engineering classes, he would be sitting here along with these boys doing some carving work for me, which would fetch him a few more rupees. But with his big salary, he was sure that he would transform his house into a new one. But it should be done, as Seeta once told before he married any girl. Who knew what type of girl he would bring?

Exams were over for his daughter, and there in Coimbatore, Nisha's exams also had come to an end. Now he had to bring them over here. Would they come? Or change their mind? No, that could not happen. Seeta was already there and she would manage things.

At the end of the month, Selvam went to Coimbatore, to bring all of them to the village. He travelled by bus and reached the very next morning. After tea, that evening, they left Coimbatore and arrived at the village the next day. Here, Seeta was more at home, than in a newly built house in Coimbatore. The walls, the bed, the familiar smell of the house, everything mesmerised her in her own village. The tree branches were seen waving at her and she felt as if they were asking her, "Where have you been? We have missed you." She looked around and entered the house happily.

But Nisha was not able to accommodate herself in her uncle's home. She asked Shanthi as soon as they went inside the house, "When will we go back to Coimbatore?" She asked her mother, looking around at the smoky walls, old tiles with cobwebs and smell of teakwood, etc. Understanding Nisha's feelings, Shanthi told, "We have come just now. I think we will have to continue here for a long time."

A worried Nisha asked again, "Long time means?"

"It depends on your mama," Shanthi replied.

When they were having this conversation, Selvam entered the front room. "What happened Nisha? Are you tired?" Nisha replied, "No mama, I was just asking my mom when will we go back…"

"Go back! What are you talking about? You have come here not to go back."

"What do you mean?"

Mama told in a strict voice, "Your leaving this house depends on your marriage."

"My marriage? But I don't want to marry now."

"Don't say like that. Now you are not a child. Anyway, you have to go from this house to your husband's place. Only time will tell you, my child. Now don't worry and spend your time with the inmates here.

A week later, news came that Ram Kumar was coming on leave for a few days. They were expecting him by bus, but on a Saturday morning, Ram Kumar was involved in a bus accident and his left leg was fractured. Selvam rushed to the medical college in the city where Ram Kumar was admitted. He was compelled to stay there for a couple of weeks looking after Ram Kumar. After the discharge from the hospital, they arrived at the village by taxi. Ram Kumar was advised to rest for a month.

During that one month, Seetha and Nisha were in-charge of taking care of Ram Kumar. Nisha was looking after Ram Kumar with the utmost care, and slowly the wounds started healing. He was ready to go back to work. As most of the time, Nisha was looking after him in the room and it lead to some kind of nearness and on several occasions, their eyes met and talked in silence but meaningfully.

Meanwhile, Seeta also started liking Nisha as she was behaving in a very civilized manner and doing most of the household work. All the time she was seen working on something or the other. She had changed the house into a very orderly one, which Seeta had never been able to do. Her way of talking approached people with an interest in housekeeping and almost every action of hers attracted Seeta. One day, she discussed in detail her exceptional qualities and humble behaviour with Selvam. Selvam asked in an exclamatory tone, "What happened to you Seeta? Nowadays you have too much appreciation for Nisha. Last week also told me Nisha is wonderful." Seeta said shyly, "Nothing, I just like her, she's a smart girl. She is crossing twenty years now and already behaving like a seasoned housewife. In fact, she is behaving better than our Ramya."

Selvam paused for a while. He was trying to read Seeta's mind which he had done several times before.

Selvam asked her, "So are you indirectly telling me to fix her for Ram Kumar?"

Seetha said, with wide eyes, "How did you know what I was thinking?"

Selvam replied in a loving tone, "I know you for the past twenty-five years."

They stopped the conversation when somebody came from outside.

A couple of days later, they put up the matter with Shanthi who readily agreed and then Ram Kumar was asked his opinion, as a good boy, he just smiled at his parents and went off to see what Nisha was doing. He ran to Nisha at the side of the house under a neem tree and informed her about what was going on at home. She didn't say anything but kept her face down on the sand-covered side yard and she had a glance at him with a mesmerising smile and went to the kitchen. Now it was Seeta's turn to ask Nisha about the matter. There were no different opinions and Ramya was also happy to have Nisha as her sister-in-law. The marriage was organized after three months and the couple went to Bangalore to start a new life. Before leaving, Ram Kumar told his father, "Do not find a woodcarver for my sister. Find out a good boy with a good job and inform me. We will come and arrange the marriage. You need not worry at all regarding marriage expenses and also find out an engineer to remake our house." On hearing these words, Ramya came running and objected to his words, and said, "I don't want to get married now."

Ram Kumar said, "Okay, my dear, your marriage will be conducted only after finishing your studies and getting into some job. You concentrate only on studies now."

Everyone vouched for Ram Kumar's words. Although Selvam liked everything that Ram Kumar promised, in his heart of hearts, he was not happy, not happy because there wouldn't be any successor to carry on this traditional work in this family. After they left, Seetha and Selvam sat in privacy but didn't talk much. Finally, Seeta said, "Don't worry about woodcarving. I know that you are thinking about that only. Anyway, we cannot ask Ram Kumar to learn woodcarving and train his children in woodcarving. We have to change according to the times."

In reply, Selvam was simply staring at the semi-carved panels and the tools, and of course, the unpaid bills from his customers.

5

Share of the Church

The Mangalam family members were very proud that they had been considered the descendants of the Royal family. To prove that point they had a large expanse of estates not far from the erstwhile king's capital city. These landed properties, from time to time divided among the family members for generations. And finally, one section of the Mangalam family got a share of about twelve acres of agricultural land. The present head of the family Mr Raman Nair was not happy with what he had because he didn't have any good house to live in. He started his life as a clerk in a government office when the salary was just Rs one hundred and fifty a month. But he called himself a *jamindar* because his ancestors had a lot of landed properties. With this status in society, he could marry a fair girl from a rich family a little distance away from his place. The girl had just passed matriculation. So she was an eligible candidate for a government clerk's job. But in those days, getting a government job was not easy. Especially with minimum qualifications. She brought along with her plenty of gold jewels and about ten acres of landed properties.

Mr Raman Nair and his people were just looking for that only. They were not very particular about the beauty or health of the bride. But still, she was not that bad to be rejected in the marriage market.

Mr Nair had a number of siblings and they all had the same share of land as he had. Being the eldest of all, he had the responsibility of looking after the well-being of those siblings and their children. In his modest home, Mr Nair was spending days happily.

By God's grace, Mr Nair became the father of three children at an interval of two-three years. After the first birth of a girl child, he felt that his income was not enough to run the house. His meagre salary drained so fast, that at the end of the month, his purse became empty. He felt that he had to secure a job for his wife. After several attempts, we succeeded in the hunt. The appointment order from the government was received immediately after the second child was born. The posting was a clerk in the nearby village office. Mr Nair's joy knew no bounds for now he has more money to spend on various wants. The demand for money was not only from his own home but also from the families of his siblings. As a big brother with a sense of responsibility, he was forced to spend for his children as well as his sibling's children.

Interestingly, none of his sisters or their husbands got any permanent job and they were all toiling in the land for a meagre income. Whatever they got from the land was never enough for the scores of expenditures. So the pocket of Mr Raman Nair got drained even before the tenth of every month and he was financially struggling.

Years rolled by.

Now both the girls got married off and they lived comfortably elsewhere. Mr Nair and Mrs Nair have both retired from service and the boy who completed the schooling could not get any job anywhere. As the marks were very low, he could go to a local college only with the influence of Mr Nair with the college authorities. Mr Balan was considered to be very intelligent by his parents and siblings for he learned to speak in small gatherings for a political party. He shined in the college also as a student leader but he gave little attention to his studies. But still, his people appreciated his oratory abilities and they held him in high esteem. He was thinking that he was still a son of *zamindar* and came from a royal family. But outside his family circle, he was looked down upon.

His needs were met by his parents. Because they thought their bright son was going to be a political leader one day or another. He outdid both his sons-in-law or for that matter all the male members of the entire family. One of his sons-in-law was recently employed in the government sector. But he had the least concern for them because he thought that his son was going to become a big political leader, and might be a Minister.

Mr Balan doing the first year of the three-year degree course was sent out of the college because of his major involvement in an assault case. He was arrested and kept in a police station but before his name appeared in FIR he was rescued by Mr Nair with his influence. But the college authorities were adamant that they would never take him back and thus his education had come to an end.

But Mr Balan was unperturbed because his aim was to be active in politics. Now he had enough time to have political activities and soon he became a popular figure among the followers of a popular party and attracted the attention of the local party leaders.

Within a span of ten years, he became secretary of the party's local committee and was authorized to collect money from the public for the party activities and thus his pocket began to swell.

When all these things were happening the other side of Mr Balan was going from bad to worse. He joined a group of friends and started drinking alcohol, and taking drugs and there were a number of incidents involving him in cases of eve-teasing. In each case, he was rescued by his fellow party men in some or another way. In spite of all those bad qualities, the locals respected him because of his hold in the party.

All this time, Mr Raman Nair was much worried. He never expected that his son would become a vagabond type. Balan's mother Amirtha who came to this family from a decent ancestry got almost mentally disturbed because of her sons' nefarious activities and the irresponsible behaviour of Mr Raman Nair and his folk.

During this time, a death occurred of an elderly lady of the family, one of the sisters of Mr Nair, who was respected and revered by all in the Mangalam family. From the death bed, she called Mr Nair and said,

"Rama, now that most of our children in the family have got jobs or got married and settled peacefully elsewhere. Only your son is wandering without any help to you or to your other children. It is time that you should find him a girl from a good family and settle him. As he had no job or any income you should give your house along with two or three acres of land to him after the marriage. I haven't seen him for the last couple of years. I learned from others that he is going to destroy the name of our family.

Mr Nair heard patiently everything, but his mind was wandering elsewhere. He said, "Don't worry sister, I will do as you said. Do you know he is a growing politician? His capabilities have surpassed everyone in our family including your children. He brings home a lot of money now and then after joining the party. Therefore, I am not worried about his future. But as you said, soon I will see a girl for him."

One among the people gathered in the room murmured, "Who is going to give him a girl in hand for marriage?"

When most of the people agreed to the comment, Nair got annoyed and hurried out of the room.

The grand old lady breathed her last in the morning hours of the next day and by noon, the relatives and the locals gathered in the vicinity. The Mangalam family members, on their own, including distant relatives, outnumbered the local panchayat population. Therefore, the entire compound outflowed with a large gathering in and around the house. The members of the Mangalam family were all proud of this, for this was the occasion rarely happened where most of them could meet and exchange pleasantries and bricks-bats.

Now the funeral was over, group by group started leaving the place and by evening most of them had left except the children and grandchildren of the old lady including Mr Nair. It was almost dark outside and some of the tired ones found their resting place wherever they could in the nook and corner of the house.

At night, everyone had enough rice porridge to their stomachs fill and was in search of a place to sleep. Available sheets, beds, mats and pillows were shared and were settling for their night.

The ancestral house was the bright point in the minds of everyone except the elder daughter "Lakshmi". The second daughter Seetha came to the portico where Mr Nair was reclining in an easy chair and looked sleepy for he had toiled the entire day doing sundry things at this age of eighty. For that matter, he had been doing the same for the last few weeks. Naturally, he was dead tired.

Looking at Mr Nair, Seetha asked, "Father, the old lady was telling about Balan's marriage, did you ever think of it seriously?"

Nair didn't like his elder sister being addressed as "old lady". He retorted, "Who was the person, who expired today?" Nair questioned Seetha angrily and said,

"She was my eldest beloved sister, your aunt. Do not address her like this, okay?"

He showed his red-tinted face to her.

Seetha thought that this was not the time to discuss the division of the ancestral home and the adjacent land. Because Nair was in a bad mood due to various reasons well known to him. She was about to go when her husband Narayanan came and squatted on the cement floor near Mr Nair and asked him,

"Uncle, now that you are getting older, we don't know how many years, months, or days you will continue like this. You should therefore write a will on this house and the other property. I have already sounded Mr Krishnan the document writer about this".

Nair looked at Narayana with a harsh note and asked Seetha to fetch a tumbler of water. After drinking the water, he said, "Time has not come."

As he was about to get up, Balan came there and shouted, "Nobody can claim this house and land! It will come automatically come to me after the demise of my parents."

On hearing these, Nair's wife Amritha yelled from inside. "We are well alive and moreover this is not the time to discuss these things. Go and sleep."

Seetha turned towards the elder sister Lakshmi and said, "Don't aspire to inherit this house. You have been given enough land just behind the house and moreover, you were also given a few farms owned by our father. Therefore, not an inch of land will be given to you from this area."

Naturally quiescent Lakshmi kept mum as usual while all this was going on and to ease this situation she asked her husband Rajasekar to get up and both started to walk towards their room. As Narayanan's take-off failed, he scolded Seetha as usual and left the scene murmuring something.

After a couple of months, Mr Nair fell ill and was rushed to the hospital where he was dragonised with stomach cancer. Within a few days of hospitalization, he breathed his last leaving all the stones unturned.

On the day of his death, all he owned as an immovable asset was a house and the piece of land near the house which came to around two acres altogether. Except for Seetha, none of his children had a good education or government job. They were not even given training for a good profession by which they could eke out a leaving. On the contrary, Seetha had a good government job with a handsome salary. The only console was that both the sisters got married in time. Neighbours always used to comment on the subject. "At least Uncle could conduct both his daughter's marriage in time."

Mr Nair had, during his later years, conducted several marriages but all these marriages were in respect of the children of his sisters. Because of his philanthropy, he used to sell many pieces of land from time to time at throwaway prices for marriage expenses. Even the land of his wife, given as dowry by her father was completely sold and sale proceeds were used for the expenses of his ever-increasing children of his siblings. Most of their wants were satiated and Mr Nair was left with only the house and a piece of land. Notably, both the other children of Nair were not ready to accept the two acres which were given to the elder one, Lakshmi, during her marriage. They still insisted that the piece of the land which was given to Lakshmi should have gone to all the children equally. That would mean that Lakshmi would get only one-third of the land already possessed by her. But the *patta* of the land was already registered in her name.

Though Lakshmi was the elder in the house among the siblings, others were not ready to accept her or obey her. Seetha would always take a lead in deciding matters relating to common matters of the home. She would poke her nose in other people's household matters, of course with the connivance of Mr Narayanan just for nothing. Even when Seetha kept quiet on some matters, Narayanan would screw her to act against anyone at any home to make some trouble, just for the sake of it!

One month after the demise of Mr Nair, on an auspicious occasion, all three children gathered at home and started discussing the "settlement" of the house and property for which their mother Amritha, was reluctant.

Yet she told, "Now you have all come here and are insisting that I should decide on the subject and if all of a sudden something happens to me, then you may fight among yourselves for this property, which I would not prefer. Therefore, let us come to some understanding."

Seetha took the lead, backed by Narayanan. She said that the entire house including the piece of land within the compound should be divided into three equal parts and distributed. Narayanan told, "What about the two acres of land near the house?"

Rajasekar intervened, "That piece of land was already given to Lakshmi. So, it is out of the question."

Immediately Seetha came yelling, "For that matter, she had already been given some cultivable land somewhere else. So should have no claim here".

Lakshmi kept mum. All others including mother Amritha didn't speak ever. It seemed that Narayan's uttering was the outcome of a pre-meeting discussion in the absence of Rajasekar and Lakshmi.

Now Lakshmi opened her mouth, "Let the house go to Balan and the nearby land within the compound of the house be divided into three."

Rajasekar had already told Lakshmi in the melee of things that there was no point in asking for any further share. He was doubtful of even getting possession of the already given two acres of land because all the agricultural produce from this land were going to others only. Amritha then asked, "Lakshmi, you don't want any share?"

"No," said Lakshmi, smiling.

Rajasekar mockingly said, "It is enough if Lakshmi gets the land already registered in her name by her father. As things are going on, I am doubtful that your children would allow Lakshmi to enjoy any agricultural produce from the land."

On hearing this Balan shouted, "Who the hell is objecting to your taking of produces?" If you have courage, you may take them!

Rajasekar didn't reply for Balan seemed to be inebriated and was in a fighting mood. His inept comment from Balan encouraged all others to keep quiet. But the schemes were brewing in all their minds including their mother, Amritha. In the heart of their hearts, she had an idea to give all the existing property to Balan as he had no job and he was her pet too.

At the end of the heated discussion, after much shouting and yelling, nothing was finalized and no tangible suggestions were put forth in the meeting. Therefore, the matter was back to square one. They dispersed with utter dissatisfaction.

After a few months at the behest of Mr Narayanan, a girl was found for Balan and the marriage took place very soon. Balan being a drunkard and vagabond, the good-natured girl could not adjust anymore because of his well-publicized activities, which resulted in a quick divorce. She left for her home with a child in hand. Balan was again blessed with his own whims and fancies and indulged in various anti-social activities, of course with the full knowledge of his people.

During these times, Lakshmi and her husband visited Amritha and asked for real possession of the land and the registered documents. But Balan, backed by others, objected to it. Therefore, Amritha said she was helpless and that she didn't know where the documents were kept. Dejected by the unusual behaviour of people, Lakshmi and Rajasekar stopped visiting home. Moreover, Rajasekar was working in a far-off place, and therefore they rarely came home. Once, Balan had told her, if she wanted to take possession of the land, she could file an affidavit in court. Therefore, as far as this land was concerned Rajasekar had almost forgotten about it. But Lakshmi had a special attachment to that land for it was her ancestral property given in writing by her father.

So, her sentiments didn't allow her to just forget the land or file an affidavit. If she went to court, the near and dears will curse her saying that just for a piece of land she had gone to the court against her mother. She was not even allowed to make a fence along the boundary in order to identify the extent of land from the neighbours.

One day Rajasekar came and constructed a temporary fence around the property, spending a fairly good sum on it. But on his next visit, he found that the fence had been destroyed and a part of the land was illegally sold to someone! All others including the mother had not objected to either destroying the fence or selling the property. Therefore, Rajasekar came to the conclusion that it was a concerted move to grab the land. Once again, a dejected Rajasekar declared that the land was a cursed one, whenever the matter popped up on some occasions. This view of Rajasekar irked everyone and they started acting against Lakshmi and her family in whatever way they could.

All of a sudden on a heavy rainy day, Amritha got ill and was hospitalized and she was declared dead after a couple of days of treatment.

The matters pertaining to sharing business were just pending and nobody dared to ask Balan about it. Because Balan was staying in the house with all his "might and glory".

As Narayanan also died due to some illness, there was nobody in the family to talk about the share.

Therefore, Balan continued his "activities" along with his friends. The once prosperous homestead became a den of a few hooligans and all kinds of illegal activities started happening there.

The neighbours dared not to speak against Balan, for he and his henchmen would harass them in whatever manner they could. Therefore, they were afraid of even informing the police. Once one of the youths in the neighbourhood complained about the anti-social activities going on in the compound to the police.

On the basis of the complaint, the police arrived and arrested a few young men from the house who were in a highly inebriated condition. But Balan escaped the arrest because of his party affiliation and no case was registered against him. Activities continued again unabated. Because of his continued anti-party activities in recent times, the higher-ups in the party gave him a warning to which he didn't pay heed. After a few days, he was removed from the party position and now it was difficult for him to survive without the support of the party or the police. All the family members one by one deserted him after a series of confrontations. Now that he did not have any income for his past time, his followers also left him. He had to ask Seetha for food and money to survive. With the connivance of the earlier acquaintance, he even prepared false documents and tried to sell a part of the land belonging to Lakshmi to someone. But that attempt was thwarted by a few neighbours who immediately alerted Rajasekar.

One day a major event happened at home, and in a drunken brawl, two of his friends stabbed him. But luckily the injury was not fatal and the neighbours intervened and got him admitted to the hospital. After his recovery, he was reluctant to go to his house. It seemed to him that the house was staring at him with dangerous consequences. The household articles were sold at throwaway prices one by one and a very meagre income got from the land belonging to Lakshmi was not even sufficient for him for the day-to-day expenses. Till his mother's death, he was enjoying the pension amount received by his mother. Now there was no income of any sort, with the empty house where nobody was ready to come forward to help him. He even tried to give it on rent, but there were no takers. On a fine day, he deserted the house and wandered visiting nearby cities. He spent his days and nights eating temple food and sleeping in *choultry* and public places. At times he used to go to public libraries and spent time, reading newspapers and periodicals. None of his friends was ready to help him in any way. In the city library, he happened to meet one Mr Mathews, who was a student in a seminary in the neighbouring district. They became library friends for some time. Because of his living in the temples and eating simple food, his interest in other things—the "activities" for which he was notorious, gradually died down. In short, he lived a monk's life.

One day Mr Mathews advised him to go back to the house and live decently by doing some work. But psychologically he was not willing to go home. Mathews even offered him to give him some sundry jobs at the seminary. As he had never done any job, not even washing his own clothes, he kept away from the offer.

Once Mathews took Balan to his Father in the church. After hearing about Balan's past, Father offered him food and accommodation and advised him to be part of the church. Though Balan was reluctant initially, after a few subsequent meetings he became inclined to listen to Father and gradually became a worker in the Church.

In the meantime, though his relatives had forgotten him, his sister Seetha came to Lakshmi's house and started talking about him and they wished to bring him home. Once when they found him at a distant relative's marriage function, Balan looked at them as a stranger and not responded to any of their offers. It seemed that his brain was badly affected due to regular substance abuse.

All these days Balan's house served as a den for the local anti-socials. With a lot of effort, the local well-wishers of the family could drive them out with the help of the police. They very often called Rajasekar to do something to the house which was already dilapidated during these two-three years and they predicted that the roof of the house might come down during the next monsoon. The prediction came true during the monsoon season and the house became the playground of less poisonous invertebrates than the previous inmates. The neighbours and the locals approached the family members to clear the shrubs and bushes from the area, but to no avail as it involved a lot of money and labour.

When the monsoon was over, on a fine day, Balan accompanied by Mr Mathew and Fr. Jones came to the place and surveyed the entire area. On hearing this, Seetha came to meet him, but Balan didn't speak. He kept aloof from the family members and he was never seen at any of their functions thereafter.

Eventually, on a sunny day, the neighbours found that bulldozers were razing the place. Within two days, the entire place was levelled and presented a look of a fair playground. The neighbour could gather information from the contractor that the place was being readied for a church to be built. The news reached Balan's siblings and they visited the spot and confirmed the activities. They immediately went to the church where he lived. Mr Balan was very stern and said that the place had been registered with the church authorities free of cost and that he has been enrolled as a student in the seminary. He asked them not to visit him anymore. Startled relatives just stood blinking at him without any words but the sublime smile on Balan's face revealed that his smile was now just like a calm lake surface after days and months of turbulence. Rajasekar, Lakshmi, Seetha and a few relatives returned home without saying a single word.

Within a year, a beautiful white church, not very big, was constructed where Balan's house stood. The cross atop the church building showered peace around the area. The neighbours remembered Balan during every chime of the church bell. As the siblings stay in faraway places, there was no chance that the chimes made any move in the minds of Lakshmi, Rajasekar, or Seetha. But their minds were highly disturbed whenever they came across any church bell anywhere.

6

The Electrician

Sathyan was a good electrician in the village. He never studied the technic from anywhere. Neither he had gone to any school or ITI, nor any such institution teaching electrical works. But since childhood, he had the ambition to become an electrician. He would visit various houses in the vicinity where the electrical work was being done for the new houses as well as the electrical repair work in the old homes. In some places, he would not be allowed to enter the premises but in some others, the electricians or the house owner wouldn't prevent him to watch the intricacies of the work. He grew up along with his apprenticeship with the qualified electricians, though unpaid, but used to get tea, snacks, etc. Thus he grew up as a well-known electrician in the area.

Now he was thirty-five years and people in the area used to call him every day for some or other work in their homes. He did not demand any fixed wages as other electricians did. If the homeowner asked him, "Sathyan, how much do you want?" He would present a large smile and say,

"What you give is enough for me." Therefore, the people used to pay him just half of the amount that they would otherwise have to pay to other qualified electricians. Here both parties are quite happy. But the people never call him for any major work as he didn't have any certificate or registration with the government as an electrician. That was really a big drawback for him. He could never take a contract for doing the whole electrical work in any new construction. But he did flawless work, sometimes better than the so-called qualified and certified electricians.

One day he went to repair a fan regulator in a house, but after a few days there was a spark inside and the wires got burned. But before some major incident happened, it was rectified by a neighbour who was also an electrician. Before leaving the house, the neighbour warned the house owner, not to call Sathyan for such a job because he was not qualified. But still, some people always called him as his charges were very low compared to others. Moreover, they pointed out that the qualified engineer's work would also get flawed sometimes. It had happened in many places.

Sathyan was very happy and not a day passed without work. Sometimes he would work in two or three homes simultaneously in one day. His parents, both of them labourers, were also happy that he got a lot of money every day. Sometimes even more than what they earned daily. As he had no personal expenses like his mentors, from whom he got trained himself, he had a lot of savings. He would never go to any tea stalls or hotels for the households where he worked gave him tea and snacks. For lunch, he visited his home where his mother kept some food. He would consume it, take a nap, and again set off for his work.

One fine morning, He was called by Mr Sankaran the Panchayat President for minor work in his Motor set installed for drawing water from the well to the overhead tank. While at work, Sankaran, the President asked him, "Sathyan, what is your age?". Sathyan said, "My father told me that I have crossed thirty-five two or three months ago."

"So now you are thirty-six, right?"

"Might be."

After a deep silence, Sathyan asked the panchayat president, "Why did you ask my age?"

"No, I just asked…" The President paused for some time and asked, "Don't you have any desire to marry?"

And continued looking at him. "Now that your parents are ageing. Your father is not in a condition to continue work. Your mother is sick with TB. I was told by a doctor at the Primary Health Centre."

Sathyan replied, "Every week, I go to the Taluk Hospital and get a lot of medicine for them."

Sankaran, "That is not enough. Now it is time for your marriage. If you marry, your wife would look after your parents and also your needs."

Sathyan looked at him, blushed, presented a sarcastic laugh and said, "Who will marry me? No girl in the area would like to marry me. I don't have two fingers in my left hand. One of my legs is affected by polio. That's why I walk this way. Some people used to call me 'lame Sathyam' and my speech is not quite audible. With all these qualifications, tell me sir, who will marry me? Then hi hi…"

He started his work.

On that night, when he went to sleep, some unknown feeling was disturbing him. The words of the Panchayat President were pounding in his ears. He sat upon the Kora grass mat at midnight and made some sounds. On hearing the sounds during the dead of the night, his mother Leela woke up and came to him. She asked, "What happened, Sathyan?"

Looking at the ceiling, he said, "Nothing."

Again, he fell down on the mat.

He never thought of getting married. He had attended several marriages of boys and girls in the homes where he had gone to work. Even during those times, he never thought that something like this should happen to him. But the Panchayat President's words gave him some points to ponder. He thought *the President was right. Who will care for me when my parents are gone? They are already sick. If something happens? But how could I say or ask my mother to find out a girl for marriage?* He thought over it lying on the mat and went to sleep.

The next morning, he remembered some work in the school teacher's house. On the way, he met the Panchayat President who was coming from the opposite direction. Sathyan expected that the President would touch upon the subject again, but he just gave him a smile and walked past him. Sathyan was disappointed.

While walking, he again started thinking of his marriage. He felt little respect for the President for at least he had a soft corner for Sathyan. Immediately, he remembered that in the evening there was a marriage reception to which he was also invited. He decided to attend the reception in the hope that at least a girl from the crowd would like him. In the afternoon, he set out for minor work at a teacher's home.

But his face became dull again, realising that the shape of his body though rustic, healthy and strong, was nowhere near handsome. There was not a single physical element for any girl to like him. He thought he was very good, well-mannered, good-hearted and never quarrelled with anybody. He was obedient to his parents as well as anyone whom he had connections with.

"Okay… leave it." He pacified himself and walked past the teacher's home.

Suddenly, he realised his mistakes. "Oh! I walked past the teacher's home!" he remembered the work at the teacher's house and turned back.

The teacher called him from a distance, "Sathya, where are you going? You forgot your work here. Are you coming?"

Sathyan came running and said, "Sorry, teacher. I was thinking of something else and forgot to enter your gate!"

The teacher said, "I saw you from a distance and thought that you are coming here only. But when you walked past the gate, I called you…"

Sathyan replied, "Sorry. What work do I have here?" he asked.

He went inside and the teacher showed him some work and he started to repair it after opening his toolkit. Throughout his working time, he couldn't concentrate on the work. It was evident from his wrong acts that, for taking a screwdriver, he would search for a hammer. Instead of the right size nail, he would take an outsized one. Watching his bewildered actions, the teacher asked him, "What happened, Sathyan? Are you not well? Something is wrong with you. I will get you a hot cup of tea."

"No madam… I am just…".

Before he could finish the sentence, the teacher went to the kitchen for making tea.

After having the tea, somehow the work was completed, satisfactorily and Sathyan was packing his tools. He went out of the house to the veranda. The teacher asked him, "Sathyan, Don't you want any money? Take this." She thrust a few currency notes into his hands.

Without looking at the money, he pushed those rupee notes into his shirt pocket and opened the gate to go out. He did not even notice Raghavan, the teacher's husband, who had just entered the compound. Raghavan looked at him, puzzled, but his wife gestured him not to ask anything.

Sathyan went back home, took his lunch and went for a nap. Since he was sleep-deprived last night, he fell asleep in no time. He woke up at six in the evening when his mother came back from work. She asked, "Sathyan, what happened? You are still sleeping. Are you not going to your Jones' marriage reception?"

He got up immediately and said, "Ah, yes! I forgot about it. I will just go now."

He freshened up, put on a new pair of clothes and walked towards the auditorium which was a kilometre away. He was not cheerful during his walk. By the time he reached the auditorium, it was already packed with a large crowd, wearing colourful dresses. He knew most of them and a few of them asked about his well-being. After having some food, he left the place. He felt as if he had lost something and went home and started watering the plantains.

Then he came to the front side and sat on the parapet wall. His father came home at around eight pm. He looked exhausted and sat on the stone step. He asked for water. When he was drinking water, Leela noticed that his feet were swollen and he was not able to walk properly and presented himself as a very tired person, breathing fast. Worried, she asked Sathyan to look after him. Sathyan suggested taking him to the hospital. Thus all three set out in an auto rickshaw to the *taluk* hospital where he was admitted immediately. After a week's treatment, he was discharged, with the doctors telling them that they had nothing more to do for him and advised Sathyan to take his father back home and treat him with the medicines given. But his condition worsened day by day and his end came a few weeks later.

Sathyan didn't go to work for two weeks. His mother also didn't go to any work. But when the reserve money was exhausted, they began to go to work again. Already a TB patient, his mother could not perform well at the work site. Therefore, Sathyan asked her not to go to work, but she would not pay heed to him. After a few months, Leela started showing signs of old age and expressed her inability to go to work.

At this juncture, Sathyan recalled what the President told him. But he was not ready to open the topic.

On a rainy day, Leela and Sathyan were sitting on the veranda, when Leela lamented that her physical condition was not good and therefore she couldn't go to work. Because of the continuous rain, nobody asked Sathyan to come to work. Except for ration items, they had no money for any purpose. Sathyan thought, *if I was married, my wife would work on behalf of my mother and bring home some money.* Helplessly, he was looking at the heavy rain drops falling from the roof tiles and the flowing water which was heading to the sandy earth below and towards the gutter on the roadside. After a brief silence, his mother spoke, "Sathyan, if you marry a girl, she would be of great help to me, don't you think so? Now, you are well past your marriage age and I am afraid no girl would be interested in you."

Sathyan asked, "Why are you saying such things, Mother?"

After observing Sathyan's physical features, she said, "Nothing, I was thinking about your father."

The silence prevailed, but the sound of wind and rain could be heard. Gradually, the rain stopped and only the heavy drops from the trees were falling.

Leela went to the kitchen and made two cups of black tea.

After having tea, both of them immersed themselves in serious thoughts. Suddenly, they were woken up from their thoughts by the thud of a coconut, which fell from the tree by the gate. It fell on a terracotta planter that had no plant in it and broke it. Looking at the broken pot, Leela said, "Soon after your father died, the roses also dried. Now, the pot itself is broken. He used to take care of all these things. I told you several times not to put pots below the coconut tree. If you marry, at least that girl would take care of these things."

Sathyan said smilingly, "Okay, Mother."

At that time, Sankaran, the Panchayat President came near the broken wooden gate, opened it and got inside the compound with a large umbrella in his hand.

He asked, "Sathyan, you didn't go to work today? I was told that your mother is also not well these days and is not going to work."

Leela stood up and said, "Yes President sir. Nowadays, I am not going to work. I am not well. Don't you see I am ageing!"

The Panchayat President laughed and agreed, "Yes, yes. That is why a few days back, I told Sathyan to think of marriage. So that the girl would be a great help to you."

After telling this the President looked at Sathyan. He was standing in reverence and did not utter a single word.

Again Sankaran asked Leela, "Shall I propose a girl for him?"

There was a ray of hope on Sathyan's face and it was evident from his body language.

His mother immediately responded, "We will be very much thankful to you, sir. Several attempts by his uncle failed. It's been more than six years now. After the demise of his father, I lost all hope."

Sankaran said, "Don't lose hope. There is a solution to every problem if you approach it in the right way. Shall I make a proposal? There is a girl in the next village, not far away. You know Mr Gopalan who was an earlier member of our Panchayat. You may not know, but Sathyan knows him well. He has a daughter named Deepa."

Immediately, Leela said, "I know. She is beautiful and married also."

"Wait and listen carefully to what I am going to say."

Leela said, "Okay, sir. If you say anything, it will be for good only."

Sankaran continued, "Of course, she was married. But the fellow was a drunkard and a rowdy. One day Gopalan kicked him out of the house and they got a divorce after a few years. Govindan and the family are much worried now. Deepa must be around thirty or thirty-two years old. If you are interested, I will talk to Gopalan."

"Sir, for this proposal, would she accept me?" Sathyan said, pointing to his polio-affected left leg.

Sankaran reassured him, "You don't worry about that. If they say okay, will you accept the proposal? I want to know the opinion of both of you."

Leela replied, "Tomorrow, I will ask my brother and tell you."

Now Sathyan got a little set back on his mind *if uncle didn't accept…?*

"Okay, sir. I am ready. I will manage my uncle. You can proceed," replied Sathyan.

Thus, on an auspicious day with a few people around, Sathyan's marriage with Deepa materialized in the small local temple. Though Sathyan was no match for Deepa, she gradually started liking him, considering his good manners and character compared to her ex-husband Babu.

Now, Leela, Sathyan and Deepa made a happy family.

Leela asked Deepa to go to work. She was beautiful and plump but had no education. The only work she knew was gardening and cooking. Leela went to several houses in search of work for Deepa, but nobody wanted her in their kitchen as she had no experience in kitchen work in any other house.

Finally, the President himself came to her rescue. One day he offered work. The teacher reluctantly accepted her as she had not had much work in the kitchen as their children were away. Anyway, Deepa started going to Sankaran's house and Deepa started getting an increased monthly allowance now and then. After a few months, she started earning more than Leela could.

But Leela had only one worry now. Sathyan-Deepa had no issues. But the couple never seemed worried about it even after four years of marriage. Once his uncle came home and cautioned them that if they continued like this they would never have children.

Sathyan thought over it for several days. One day, he told Deepa, "Why don't you deliver a child? Wherever I go, people ask me why we don't have a child yet."

Every time they asked this question, he would offer only an innocent smile and sometimes a loud laugh, crying more loudly in his heart.

Once Sankaran also asked, "Sathya, what is happening? Why can't you have a child? Tell Leela to advise Deepa."

Sathyan said, "Okay".

On that day, he returned home all the way smiling at people who wished him but cried in his heart.

Full of remorse, he came home and asked for a cup of tea. Deepa brought him tea, after having a sip, he threw the cup over the shrubs and said angrily, "Now you can't even make a cup of tea!"

Surprised to hear those angry words from Sathyan, both Leela and Deepa hurriedly came out to the veranda.

"What happened, Sathya?" Leela asked

Sathyan kept mum, throwing an angry look at Deepa he murmured, "Good for nothing!"

Deepa said, "What was wrong with the tea, Mother?"

Leela replied, "It was good, but something has happened to Sathyan. He never used to be like this."

Turning towards Sathyan, she asked, "What happened today?"

Without responding, he stood, dressed up and went to take a bath. While going out, he didn't utter a single word. But Deepa was not worried at all.

Sathyan came back home at night after watching a movie in the nearby theatre. As he was entering the veranda, Leela came running and told Sathyan the good news that the next-door nurse told her that Deepa was pregnant.

Contrary to the expectation, Sathyan didn't show any sign of happiness. He just presented his usual readymade smile to Deepa, who was sitting on a cot in the side room.

Soon, Leela started taking every precaution to have a smooth delivery. Deepa was not allowed to clean the house or do any strenuous work, the maximum she could do was water the plants using a hose connected to the tap outside the kitchen wall. As usual, Sathyan continued his daily work. Now he seemed mature as a serious worker who concentrated only on his work. He didn't engage himself in any talk with his employers because he knew that every talk began with his work and ended with an array of questions about his wife Deepa, which he didn't like. One day when one of the employer's wife was asking many questions related to Deepa, Sathyan simply asked her to give him a mug of hot rice water. After bringing the rice-water, she again started the same question to which Sathyan answered with a big smile, "Don't you have any other job in the kitchen? It is time that your husband come to lunch." She immediately went away. Thereafter, he tried this technique with everyone who questioned him about Deepa.

Then the days and months passed and on an early morning during some festival day Deepa gave birth to a beautiful and fair baby boy in the hospital.

Sathyan didn't go to the hospital, instead, he wanted to inform that news to the President and told him that Deepa would not come to work anymore.

The President and his wife had a sigh of relief when they heard the news. Sathyan left for home and was lying on the mat thinking about the future course of action. He slept for a while and got up hearing the knock at the door. He opened the door and found next door Saraswathi Amma, Leela's friend, in the hospital looking after the mother and baby. On seeing Sathyan in a sleeping mood she said, "What Sathyan, you are sleeping now? Don't you know your Deepa has delivered a child in the hospital? Deepa and Leela were anxious to see you there. All of the neighbourhood would be there to see the baby when they are shifted to the post-natal room by evening. Go immediately and take charge of the situation. The Panchayat President talked to the hospital staff to take care of everything. You go immediately!"

Sathyan without saying anything went inside, put his shirt on and got out. He told her, "Saraswathi amma, lock the door and keep the key with you."

"Okay, I am going to clean the house. Tomorrow if they come here, many people would come to see the baby. So, things should be right in their places. Go immediately," Saraswathi told and started cleaning the house.

Sathyan straight away went to Babu's eateries near the hospital and had his lunch—a *chapatti* set and tea. Sathyan thought to himself that Babu had not received the news yet. Otherwise, he would have asked him about the baby.

After finishing lunch, he entered the hospital premises. Some known faces asked him, "How are you Sathyan? How is work going on?"

Some others who knew of the episode asked, "Sathyan where were you since morning? Deepa and the baby are okay. They are in room number twenty-four. Hurry!"

Sathyan slowly walked towards room number twenty-four and saw a few neighbours standing over there. Someone scolded him for his absence since morning. Deepa's parents were also present but they didn't utter a word. That was surprising to Sathyan.

After a few days, one evening mother and child were discharged from the hospital. Deepa's parents wanted to take them to their home and would bring them back to Sathyan's after a month. Sathyan did not have anything to say.

But Leela said, "Okay, you can have them there for about two months because Deepa was here all these days after the marriage. When you requested Sathyan to take Deepa till delivery he didn't budge, so you can have them now."

Sathyan's reaction was just showing all his stained teeth. When all these things were happening there were a lot of people from the neighbourhood, mostly ladies, who visited the mother and child with and without any gifts. They were all served with tea by Saraswathi amma. Some whispers could be heard from the bunch of ladies in the garden here and there. The conspicuous absence was the President and his teacher's wife.

Before dusk, Deepa's parents started preparing to leave Sathyan's home with Deepa and the child. One of the ladies in the yard was telling people that since Sathyan came back, he hadn't touched either the baby or Deepa.

Some of the guests had already left. Now, only a few neighbours were waiting for Deepa's parents set off for their home with the child.

Saraswathi was worried, *Why didn't Sathyan take his child in his hands when Deepa offered the child to him*? She even told Sathyan, "Sathyan, take the child and give it a kiss."

Sathyan looked at the child and smiled. The child was waving his little hands towards him and seemed that it was yearning for him. But Sathyan, after touching his cheeks, gently went out giving the best of his smile to all those who were present there. An eerie silence prevailed over there. Now and then only the high pitch cry of the baby echoing in the room and Saraswathi Amma's soothing lullabies broke the silence. The ladies outside were talking among themselves about the resemblance and colour of the child. Someone in the gathering secretly told others that the child is unexpectedly fair and beautiful and also that Sathyan was lucky.

Now when the auspicious time came to leave Sathyan's home, Deepa's, mother holding the child in her hands, started to get down. Deepa followed and got into the cab waiting outside and sped away.

After dusk, Leela, Saraswathi amma and Sathyan were at home. Sathyan was busy repairing an MCB to be fitted in a neighbourhood house the next day. He seemed to be as happy as he was before marriage. Saraswathi went out to the home and Leela retired to her cot, thinking Sathyan was happy only in the world of wires, switches, appliances and tools.

7

Barn to Home

Baskaran was not a rich man but rich enough that he could rear his two children and get them decently married and settled them with comfortable jobs. Elder boy Suresh was well educated and married to a rich family. But he left the ancestral home to join a lucrative job in Dubai. His wife also joined him a couple of years later. The younger one Ramesh didn't study well but he sold his share of land and set up a thriving business and settled along with his family in a far-off city. Though he was in the country itself, he seldom visited home. He used to be busy always with his own affairs.

When Baskaran's wife Lalitha fell ill, the elder son Suresh sent his wife, Sneha, home and he continued alone in Dubai. This ancestral house inherited by Baskaran was very old but huge enough to accommodate four or five families in it. It had a sprawling backyard and a channel that had a boundary on one side. It was a very happy family till the marriage of these two children. After they left the place, the house felt silent with the old couple loitering in the house and compound. At this juncture, Sneha also came to live with them, though not willingly.

Within a short time, Lalitha's health deteriorated further and on a rainy day, she breathed her last. Now Baskaran and Sneha were alone in the house. When once Sneha's mother came to visit her, they had long hours of heated discussion and finally decided that she would go to her home to be with her mother. The reason told was that her mother was getting old and sick. As she had no one there to look after her, Sneha could go to her. As there was no other way, Baskaran had to agree to the proposal and thereby a couple of middle-aged ladies, distant relatives of Sneha, who had nobody else, were to be sent to Baskaran's house to look after him. But Baskaran came to know that Sneha was getting ready to go back to Dubai.

The same day, Suresh called Baskaran and said, "Hello, father, how are you? Hope you are happy and in good health. Sneha must have told you about some proposals regarding bringing some of her relatives to take care of you in her absence. Did they arrive? Don't you think it is better?"

It was an assertive statement from Suresh and his tone was enough for him to make out that the spoken words were Sneha's and her mother's rather than his son's.

Baskaran simply retorted, "My dear son, if you both have decided and taken this decision, I cannot have any say in this but…"

Suresh intervened, "No buts and ifs, father. This solution is more than enough."

At this end, Baskaran's hand was shivering. He was not able to hold the receiver properly.

"Suresh, listen to me. If you leave me at the mercy of some ladies, that too not our near relatives, will they perform well? There would be a lot of bad consequences. Don't you think so?"

Suresh again intervened, "I have already booked tickets for Sneha and the children. On coming Sunday, Sneha is bringing those people to our home. Those people will look after you carefully."

"Okay. But Suresh, I am…". His son had hung up the receiver at the other end. He was dumbfounded and the receiver was just about to fall. But somehow he kept it back on the stand.

So, it was all a plot hatched when Sneha was at her parents' home. That was why her mother asked Baskaran the other day, "How many days could Sneha be alone in this home with children?"

Baskaran sat on a chair and started thinking, *if children are well educated, they are sure to leave us. In the next compound, Surendran is happy with all his children married and they live together as one family in their old ancestral home. He celebrates every day as there are around fourteen members in his family, including his wife and him. He is also my age only…* His thought got wings and started flying back to his younger days seventy years back.

This home was the same one where his father, an accepted school teacher used to live here and sit on this veranda after coming from school. He would be surrounded by at least a dozen children including Baskaran as a fifth-class student, his sisters, brothers, uncles and aunties' children… *Oh, so many of them. It was not easy to remember the names of all because some children from the neighbours' houses would also come there. So much noise, quarrels, hugs, plays, sharing of food…. What a life! That type of life was never going to come in this house.* Tears rolled down his sullen cheeks with an overgrown beard. His father would give them all a lot of homemade sweets from an old lady living near the school compound, all made with palm gourd. There used to be plenty of time to play. Although the study time was very limited, it was well-disciplined. It was a happy and carefree life, with no dearth of anything-be it food, water, love, fun and what not.

He recalled a day when his uncle came with a lot of gifts, clothes, and sweets. *That uncle used to come from a very long distance and when he entered our enclave even the children from the neighbourhood also used to flock around him to have a glimpse of what he had brought. We used to help him open all the bundles-mostly the palm leaf oven boxes, tied with jute rope.*

One of the things Baskaran liked the best was a kind of edible root that was not available in the area where he lived in. His mother would boil it with salt and give them. They, all the children assembled, would share and enjoy eating it. His grandfather would yell from an easy chair in a corner, "Children, don't eat too much of it! You will get stomach-ache then you will have to take ginger juice."

There were two valid points in his advice, first was the children would get a stomach ache if they take too much of it. The second was that if they ate too much the children in the household and other members would not get their share. Then mother would go and tell him, "Don't shout father, we have enough reserve."

Grandpa would laugh it away and ask her a piece or two.

Those days were one of his finest moments which Baskaran was not going to get anymore.

Next week, Sneha brought home two ladies aged just above fifty and told Baskaran, "These are two aunties I told you about—Sudha and Sarala."

Baskaran smiled at them and asked, "How are you, people? Seeing you after a long time. The last time we met was on the day of Sneha's marriage. Remember?"

Whether they said purposely or not, but told in chorus, "We don't remember, but we know all the things about you and your family. Because time to time, Sneha's mother used to enlighten us. We also came to Sneha's marriage a few years back."

"Yeah, only a vague remembrance of you people. Anyway, now that you have come to stay here in this house... Of course, I am happy that Sneha found you out to look after me at this age."

As the conversation dragged onto many nostalgic events in their families, Sneha gestured those ladies to go inside. The two of them abruptly said okay and went inside the home. Baskaran was sitting in the veranda. He put on his spectacles and started reading the newspaper. These glasses also didn't work properly. Letters seemed to be blurred. But still, he continued to read with much strain which would lead him to mild ache at the back of his head. Therefore, he would stop reading and simply lay down on the easy chair gazing at the jackfruit tree with a lot of fresh leaves and a few ripe leaves which occasionally fell down. In no time, he would be asleep.

A week later, Suresh came from abroad with a lot of chocolates, clothes, perfumes, etc. for his father. On seeing all the things given to him, Baskaran said, "My son, why did you bring all these things for me? Don't you know I am an acute diabetic and I cannot eat chocolates though they look so tempting? Never in my life have I used any perfume, even face powder. And then these clothes. They seem to be very costly but you know I have this *khadi dhoti* and *jubba* always.

Suresh, "Sorry dad, I would take them back and give them to my friends."

Immediately Sneha intervened, "There are my friends also who can use all these things."

She grabbed everything and put them into a cardboard box.

Dejectedly, Baskaran told him, "Suresh take me to an ophthalmologist to test my eyes and buy a new pair of glasses. So that I can read properly."

"Okay, tomorrow we will go," said Suresh. Baskaran knew that tomorrow would never come in any immediate future.

He reclined on the easy chair. His eyes focussed on the new flowers sprouting in the trunk of the jackfruit tree. A convoy of red ants was marching from the ground to the tree urgently.

A couple of weeks passed. One day a car came near the gate and a few people entered the compound. Suresh ushered them to the house and was showing all around the area, inside and outside. Two men were found measuring the length and breadth of the house and were making some calculations.

Suresh was having a serious discussion with the newcomer and was found nodding his head at whatever the man was telling. They departed after having coffee, etc.

When the car left, Baskaran asked Suresh, "What was it all about?"

"Who are they, Suresh? I have never seen them here before."

Suresh replied, "They are builders and architects, Appa."

"What job do they have here, Suresh?"

"Do you remember once I told you about demolishing this house and building another one on the same ground? So they have come here for that only."

Baskaran, "Are they going to demolish the entire old structure and build a new one?"

"Yes, yes." He pulled out a broad paper from his bag and showed it to Baskaran. "This is the new plan. This covers the entire area of the house."

An awestruck Baskaran looked at the drawing and blinked at Suresh. "I never agreed on demolishing the house, just some minor repairs only were suggested."

"No, Appa, this is a very old house. In a very short time, the ceiling may come down. Some of the roof tiles have broken. That is why I decided to construct a new house before the next monsoon. I have given a contract to these people to construct the new concrete house as per plan. By next week they would come here and start the demolishing work."

Then Baskaran asked seriously, "But where will I stay?"

Suresh replied, "At the south end of the compound. You know there is a shed used by our cows previously which will be remodelled and the two ladies can stay there and our old barn at the west end which is very large enough which can be cleaned and whitewashed for you to stay temporarily.

"After the new house is built, you can come over here. Therefore, for a few months, you will have to bear with us. All facilities will be made in the barn and a few pieces of furniture will also be put there. You will have plenty of light and air. The ladies will make food in their tenement and give you from time to time. Hope it will be a fine arrangement. Okay? Are you happy?"

Sneha intervened, "If Suresh is happy, Daddy is also happy, is it not?" She hugged him for a while, unwilling to listen to any replies from him. They left hurriedly since they had to make a lot of arrangements before leaving for Dubai.

Within a few days of Suresh's departure, the few workers dispatched by the contractor came to the compound and started work on the tenement and the barn renovation.

The contractor told Baskaran, before starting the work, "Hello Appacha, we will make the barn into a new house within a few days. Then you can move over there. The tenement will be ready in two days so that the ladies can go there and start cooking."

Baskaran was not at all listening to the contractor's words but looking at the old heavy lintels made of teakwood and other design works on the wooden doors and windows. He felt all his strength was being drained down. He asked for some water and reclined on the easy chair for a nap.

The day of departure had finally arrived, and Suresh and Sneha were busy in the morning packing their stuff, etc. They were to leave in the afternoon around two pm. Suresh came to Baskaran who was waiting for them.

Soon, Sneha joined and said, "Don't worry Appa, the two aunties will look after you very well. Only next week the contractor will come and start work like removing all furniture from the farmhouse (she meant the barn which was being renovated). You can shift to that comfortable place and enjoy the natural scenery by reclining in the easy chair. You know a new toilet room is also being constructed specially for you. Within ten to twelve months, the house will be ready then you can shift back. Be happy!"

The taxi came to the gate and the luggage was loaded and both of them boarded the taxi and closed the door. Baskaran did notice the inability of Suresh to look at his father directly into his eyes. The taxi fled and the aunties came closing the gates. Without, pronouncing a single word they left to the inner rooms.

Baskaran didn't go to his cot, rather he took his nap in the easy chair itself looking at the ripened leaf falling.

A cool wind came from the west and a lot of beautiful yellow leaves and a few greens also fell. Soon the rain started. Baskaran was much tired that he even didn't feel the aerosols of the rain falling on him on his upper bare body. Such was his sleep with light snoring. The two women came out on seeing the sleeping old man. But they didn't wake him up and went inside.

The next day itself Suresh called Baskaran to tell him about their safe arrival. Baskaran just said, "Okay."

A week later, the contractor's men came and started removing all the furniture and fixtures and carried the same to the farm house. Baskaran also went to see his new abode. The walls were coated with cheap paint and the floor was very rough. He remembered the number of cows and buffaloes in that place. The smell of the barn was still around the place for him. His easy chair was also brought along with his cot and bed. His clothes, torch and medicine box everything came to the barn house.

With tears in his eyes, he sat on the easy chair with a foot stool on the veranda of the barn. The cot was put inside near a window that opened out to the west side. Coconut trees and a canal could be seen through the window. In those days all his animals were bathed in the canal, he remembered. He reclined on the chair and his thoughts flew back to his primary years.

The phantosmia of barn smell in which he played with the calves seemed to linger in the atmosphere, though the cows and calves had been gone out many years ago. He remembered how he used to run behind the cute brown calf when it was small. The calf ran all over the large compounds and played with him and the other children. The mother cow would be just looking at them. He was afraid of the mother cow for its horns were very sharp, though it was tied to a coconut tree. He never went close to it. He even drank half a cup of fresh warm milk from the milkman's pot without the knowledge of his parents. *How sweet it was*, he thought with glee in his eyes. He even remembered how his dog saved him from a big snake.

He told himself that those days would never come back. *Did the smell of the barn still linger? He took a deep breath to confirm. Yes, there it was. He looked out on the farm, and Yes, the calf was still running.*

He suddenly came to his present and decided to see how the two ladies were living there in the tenement. He stood up, took his walking stick and proceeded towards the tenement.

The asbestos door was closed but not bolted for it was moving when the wind blew. Baskaran went near the door and knocked. One of the ladies got up from the old creaking cart and opened the door. The other one was cooking something in the oven kept on the platform in the far right corner. "Coming, brother. See our place," said one of them. The other closed the pot on the oven with a steel lid and came to join her. "What brother, how is your new house?

Baskaran gave a simple laugh in reply.

He went inside and found it was warmer though there were many shades of coconut palms. The heat from the fibre sheets at the roof was coming down. They had a table fan like the one he had in his new accommodation. There was more furniture dumped in the area and therefore these people had to move about carefully lest they would hit their knees on any of the furniture. He was offered a seat but he refused and said, "Just came to see you people. Have any difficulty here? Whatever you need, you can tell me. Okay?"

In a chorus, both of them said, "We think it will at least take a year to complete the construction of the house."

In reply, Baskaran just smiled meaningfully.

He carefully got out of the tenement and walked towards his place looking at the old house, being demolished. The roof tiles had already been taken out and kept somewhere near the gate. Now, the workers were engaged in dislodging the wooden logs one by one. He was not able to bear the sight of the demolition. He never wanted to look at the house being demolished.

Most of the time, he would spend reading the newspaper, weeklies, etc. Sometimes he went to the channel side and talked to the people who came for taking bath.

One day in the afternoon, he was sitting on a tree trunk that was uprooted during a recent flood on the bank of the rivulet. After sitting for some time, because of the lack of backrest, he got tired and tried to get up with the help of his walking stick. Suddenly, the stick slipped into the clay soil beneath the undergrowth and he fell on the grassy ground. As the place was full of grass and small plants, he didn't get hurt much. The plants acted as a cushion for the body. He tried to get up but could not do so. He looked around helplessly. A few ladies who were bathing a little away downstream, saw him falling and immediately came running to him and helped him to get up. They led him up to his dwelling place and told him not to come near the channel as there were a lot of snakes roaming about. Then they asked about those people who were supposed to look after him. Baskaran said, "They must be having their regular afternoon nap." Ladies commented, "Well, very good servants."

The sarcastic comment didn't have a deep impact on Baskaran. Then the ladies threw a sympathetic glance at him and left the place saying, "Geetha, what a good man he is. He is counting his days. No one looks after him. He has a lot of money, landed property, a big house... everything. But..."

Saroja said, "Why should he suffer? At least one of his children could stay with him."

Geetha, "How can they come here since one is busy running some big business in some far away city and the other is in some other country? They also have to see their future. Why don't you think along those lines?"

Another one said, "We will also meet the same fate a few years down the line when our children will move out to some other city for work. Do we have any right to say no to them if they wish to pursue their higher education? The only choice we have is to go with them when the time comes."

Geetha, "The situation changes from time to time. Everything will not be the same as you see now."

Saroja agreed, "That is right. Things are changing day by day. So, let us leave it to fate. We will see it when the time comes."

The days and months passed by and the construction of the house was also nearing its end. Baskaran's health condition was also deteriorating day by day. The ladies who looked after Baskaran called a doctor or *vaidya* whenever he faced any health-related issues. But since he was in his early eighties, even his walking stick failed to serve the purpose. Whenever he wanted to get out of the room he had to call those ladies and wait for some time. Sometimes he asked them to help him to the gate and seat him on the garden bench. He used to sit on that bench for hours till the sun set and was brought to his room by the same ladies.

Last week when he was sitting like that in the evening, he saw his friend Govindhan Master coming down that way. He was a retired teacher but very junior to Baskaran as he could not get up from the bench he produced a loud voice calling him in. Upon hearing the voice, Govindan peeped into the gate and entered. Baskaran said, "Govinda, Govinda come and sit."

Govindan sat on the same old broken bench. Baskaran was very happy to see him after a long time and he held his hands. He asked, "Govinda, nowadays you are not to be seen in this way. What happened, unlike me you are very healthy. Then why don't you come daily or at least weekly to see me."

Govindan Master replied, "Sorry, brother, I was not here. I had gone to my daughter's house in Bangalore."

"How are they? Did they buy any property there? They are okay?"

A disgusted Govindhan lamented, "They both go to work in the morning and return by eight pm. Sometimes even later, and the children are also busy with school, tuition and the computer. They don't have time to talk to me. Throughout the day what could I do? No friends, nowhere to go. The place is very far from the city. I got fed up."

An awestruck Baskaran asked him, "Then what you used to do during day time?"

"Sometimes reading, sometimes T.V., but with my defective eyes, I found these activities were also not helping. The only solace was that if I waited near the gate I could see a lot of children going home from a nearby school. Again I returned to my canvas chair given to me on the balcony and see the tall trees dancing in the wind and some birds flocking to the trees.

Baskaran asked him, "When did you come back?"

"Only last week. Since Janaki was also alone here, it was difficult for her to manage things on her own."

Heaving a sigh Baskaran said, "You have got at least Janaki at home but look at me… I often feel life is enough."

Baskaran gently caressed his walking stick.

Inviting a small smile Govindhan replied, "I have only one Janaki but you have two ladies to look after you. Lucky brother! They are always at your command. They obey you with utmost obedience. But see my Janaki, I have to bare her rebuke at least once a day. Hotty lady!"

"Don't say like that Govindha. You will feel the importance of anything when it is not available."

Both of them talked at length about different, and mostly they reminisced on their school days. After promising that Govindhan would come and meet Baskaran at least twice a week, he left for home.

A few months passed without any major happenings except the occasional physical ailments for which he had stored plenty of medicines and oils. During the rainy season, he suffered much because of knee pain and the resultant immobility. The walking stick which was a companion for almost two decades was of no use now. It took its place in a corner of the room.

From his cot, he used to go to the toilet by holding furniture and pillars available in the room. Within this one year his health had deteriorated considerably and most of the time he was bedridden. Going to the bathroom itself was an ordeal for him. Sometimes the ladies used to help him, but he disliked it.

One day the Ayurvedic doctor came to him, on the instruction from Mr Suresh on phone. After a thorough examination, he advised Suresh to shift to a hospital, so that proper care could be given. The Vaidyar phoned up Suresh and had a conversation. "Suresh when are you coming back? Your father's condition is worsening day by day. I have arranged for a wheel chair. These ladies are taking him out of the room for some time. You should come immediately."

In reply from the other end, Suresh first asked, "Doctor, did you see my house? I was told that it would be inaugurated this month. For that function, I would come. At that time, I would see my father."

Then Vaidyar said, "Suresh I am telling you about your father, but you are more concerned about the completion of the house and its inauguration! He needs to be shifted to the hospital nearby. Therefore, come immediately."

Vaidyar didn't like the approach of Suresh in this issue. He kept the phone down and immediately told Baskaran that he was making arrangements for shifting to the nearby hospital. But Baskaran refused to go to the hospital. He vehemently told Vaidhyar, "Vidhya, my ends should come in this soil only. I am not going to any hospital. Therefore, don't shift me to any hospital."

Now, Vaidya was in a fix.

But he arranged for a wheel chair for him.

Baskaran was happy to receive the wheel chair because it was a motorized one and he could go up to the gate without the help of the ladies and see the people going here and there and talk to them. His hearing was also impaired and he was not able to talk to his people on the phone. Any information would be passed on to him by the two ladies when some phone call came.

Of late, his food intake was also very less. The neighbourhood people came to know of his condition and started visiting him very often. His so-called relatives also came to see him as if they were visiting some temple festival. Even he would not identify some of them due to damaged eyes and ears. In that week itself, the contractor came to Baskaran and told him that the house was completed and it was ready for inauguration. "We have already informed Suresh about it and he even decided the date of the inauguration of the house."

Three days before the house warming ceremony Suresh and Sneha came with the children and appreciated the contractor for the good work. His brother Ramesh could not come as he was very busy with his business affairs. New pieces of furniture were brought and placed in appropriate places. Suresh readied a room for Baskaran with a cot and all other amenities. He wanted to bring his father from that dwelling place before the inauguration.

But Sneha objected to that telling him that only after the ceremony, anybody could get inside and live.

It was decided accordingly by some elders available there. Many visitors came from far and near to see the house constructed so beautifully and they congratulated Sneha for that. Among them, very few went to the backside of the house and visited Baskaran who was in a confused state of mind.

Suresh and Sneha were well aware of his condition but they had other priorities to be looked after.

On the day of the housewarming ceremony, a lot of people assembled and the *pooja* was going on.

Everyone was standing under the shade of trees or sitting on the plastic chairs arranged in the garden.

At the same time, Baskaran was brought in front of the house where some rituals were going on. He was seated on an easy chair, and he was bluntly looking at the premises, the ceremony and the people assembled there. Many people were enquiring about his health. He replied to them with meaningful gestures and feeble smiles. Time and again he would wipe his face with a new cloth on his shoulder with trembling hands.

Now the *poojari*, after the required rituals ceremoniously opened the ornate door of the house and one by one entered the house to have a glimpse of the modern construction using marble and granites which was a new fashion in that area. Most of them were admiring Suresh and Sneha for their taste in design and colour schemes. They had never seen a such fabulous house in that area. Sweets were distributed and children ran here and there. Sneha's son, a boy of about five came to Baskaran and gave him a plate of sweets. When Baskaran couldn't hold the plate, the boy kept the plate on his lap. Because of the melee, Baskaran was not attended to by anyone. The ladies assigned to that job were busy in the kitchen. Suresh came out to bring Baskaran inside. He asked for help to lift the easy chair. He came near the chair and said, "Papa, let us go inside, your room is ready."

Baskaran's eyes were fixed on the jackfruit tree and tears were seen on his cheeks. When a couple of men came to lift the chair, Vaidya came there and took Baskaran's hands, which were cold. He examined his eyes and declared, "Baskaran sir is no more. He left us a few minutes back". On his plate, there was a ripe jackfruit leaf along with the sweets.

There was confusion and chaos. A group of fashionable ladies who were apparently Sneha's friends mumbled, "This old man should go now only?"

Then the people started doing other things related to the funeral. More and more villagers assembled. Several men and women scattered around the large compound and standing under the trees discussing many things from the good deeds of Baskaran to the state, national and international politics. Suresh and Sneha were seated on a sofa surrounded by their close associates. They were not uttering any word to anybody.

By evening the lifeless body of Baskaran Nair was cremated on the banks of the channel near the place where he used to sit during his leisure time. His wife's body was also cremated a decade back nearby. By around seven pm, a neighbourhood boy came to Suresh and handed over a smiling portrait of Baskaran. Suresh received it and asked someone assembled there to fix it on the front hall with a sandal garland on it.

Thus, in the form of the framed portrait Baskaran sir entered the new home.

8

Talisman

Georgie was hardly twelve when his father Charlie died during lightning struck his boat on the high seas while on a fishing trip. Thereafter Georgie and his mother Stella had to live by selling fish in the village market not far from their home at the sea shore. After a few days Mr Fernandez, the boat owner with whom Georgie's father was working, approached Stella and asked to spare Georgie so that he could be trained and sent to the deep sea fishing in a few years.

"Stella, hope you are recovering from the great loss to your family, but what to do? All God's will. We have to bear." Mr Fernandez sympathised.

"Georgie is going to school. If I send him with you, what about his studies? Moreover, I am alone at home." Stella expressed her helplessness.

Fernandez

"Just think over it, he will be getting income too." Fernandez again persuaded her.

"Ok, I will consult somebody and take a decision." Finally, Stella yielded to Fernanadez.

Soon after Fernandez left the house. Stella immediately went to the church to consult Fr Jones who stood as a middleman for every good or bad happening in that small fishing village in the district of Kanyakumari, the southernmost one in the country.

Stella

"Father I have come to you for an opinion from you. You know all the incidents in my family. Now Mr Fernandez of the second street is asking my son to go with him in his trawler. Should I send him?" Stella asked with remorse.

"Your son is only a little boy. He goes to school, doesn't he?" Father said.

"Yes, Father. He is studying in seventh class." Stella told with reverence.

"Then let him continue his studies…" Father simply said.

"But Fernandez said he would pay and train him to make a good fisherman." Stella again pleaded.

"Yes, I know your Georgie boy; he is bright in his studies"? He enquired.

"Yes, Father." said Stella.

"Then why do you want to stop his studies?" Father was stern that he should continue his studies.

Stella started talking about her financial issues.

"By selling fish in the market, I am hardly able to make the ends meet. If he also brings money, somehow we would be able to make it. Moreover, my health is deteriorating."

"What is the problem with your health?" Father asked.

"Look at my legs. Can I walk with these legs carrying the fish basket on my head?" she asked.

She lifted her nightie up to her knees and exposed her legs. Father Jones looked at them and exclaimed.

"Hey, your legs are swollen beyond limits. Why don't you take any medicine or go to the doctor? I strongly believe that you have severe diabetes. Visit your primary health care centre now and consult the doctor. It can be fatal." Father advised her.

'Now, tell me how can I go to market? Even I am struggling with the household chores." Stella asked.

Fr. Jones thought for a while and said, "Really your condition is terrible. But poor boy! You are pushing him to work when he should be playing with kids of his age along with studies."

"Then, kindly tell me a way out. Some days I am dead tired and I lay all the time in that cot listening to the relentless tides. From the small window, I can see the foaming tides lashing on the sand. Sometimes I see my

Charlie coming to me walking through the tides with heavy blue nets on his shoulders," her eyes welled up.

"I understand," finally, Father said. "But shouldn't he complete at least his tenth standard? Now, you go home. I will talk to Fernandez also."

Child labour was common in the fishing industry, but recently, due to strict measures by the government and firm support from some sections of society, one could witness positive outcomes. But every now and then, one might find children sneaking their way out and working on the shore to make money. These children were employed in sorting, net repairing, sea shell cleaning, etc., Most of these fishermen could never see a silver line in their life and only the big vessel owners and the large-scale fish merchants and exporters thrive well. This has been a phenomenon everywhere. But due to the awareness created by the church and government monitoring, things were getting better.

Next Sunday, after the prayers, Fr. Jones arranged a meeting with Stella, Fernandez and the boy Georgie and discussed the pros and cons of sending Georgie with Fernandez. Finally, it was decided that Georgie could go to the boats and see the studies later.

After the discussion Father told, "Stella, send Georgie with Fernandez," and turning to the boy, he said, "Georgie, be a good boy with the senior fisherman and learn to fish fast, okay? Good luck and best wishes!"

Georgie

"Father, what about my school? I need to go to school."

"No, my son. You try your luck in the sea. By the grace of God, mother sea will take care of you. Don't worry. God bless you." Father told the boy some soothing words.

While returning home from the church the boy wanted to curse his mother and Fr. Jones for sending him to Fernandez. He walked on the hot sand with his bare foot with tears in his eyes, all the way sobbing.

With brimming anger and remorse, he asked his mother, "Had my father been alive, would he send me like this?"

Stella in reply embraced him tightly. Standing in the shade of a neem tree, she waited for her friend Vimala who was approaching her.

Vimala enquired, "What happened, Stella? Why are you standing here with your son?"

Stella explained her plight to her. All the while Georgie was looking at the roaring white waves he felt as if he saw his school bag, books, instrument box and school uniform all being taken away by the tides. He stood helpless with tears rolling down his cheeks. He wanted to go home immediately and sit down in front of his father's picture and cry alone. He pestered Stella to go home. She asked him to go alone as it was only a short distance.

After hearing everything Vimala asked her. "Stella if you send him to sea, sometimes it may take one or more days to come back. Will you be able to manage on your own at home? Moreover, you are not in good health. I shall come for the night stay. when needed," she volunteered her service.

Stella got a good relief hearing Vimala's words. They departed and went home. Stella came back home and saw his son was fast asleep lying on the cot clutching a photograph of his father Charlie, which was taken on their marriage day. Dried tear lines could be seen on his tender cheeks. Stella closed the front door and she also joined him in that untimely sleep before noon.

Outside, warm wind was blowing. A few lazy lots were loitering on the beach. Some enterprising fishermen along with their family members were repairing the fishnets while some children played near the sea waves fearlessly trying to recover a few shells that tides brought.

The next day, Georgie did not go to school, where he very much wanted to go. He was so worried that he had to forget his teachers, friends, books the mid-day meal, the school playground and everything.

Even he loved that huge tamarind tree where a number of nests of parrots could be seen. He remembered picking up raw tamarind fruits that fell during strong winds. He once again wanted to 'feel' the school atmosphere. He saw his mother was busy counting the mackerels brought from the shore and was preparing for the village market. He had been told that any time after nine in the morning Fernandez's people would come and pick him up. But without waiting for anything he ran towards the school.

But alas! The school's gate was closed. Classes were in full swing. Far behind the croutons, he could see his class going on, but he couldn't see inside of the class because outside it was bright sun.

Totally disappointed, he stood there holding the iron bars of the gate for some time and remembering all the sweet things about the school with despair.

The old shopkeeper opposite the school selling some school needs, candy, biscuits, etc. crossed the street and caught Georgie's hands. "What happened? Are you not attending the classes?" Georgie who was lost in his thoughts woke up and said. "NO."

"Then go back home."

Georgie walked back silently.

When he came home, his mother had already gone. Two fishermen were sitting on the steps smoking *beedi*. On seeing Georgie one of them said, "See, he has come. Where did you go? We have been waiting here more than thirty minutes. Hurry up! Come! Fernandez has asked us to bring you. Lock the doors and come!" they walked in front and Georgie walked behind them like the lamb going to abattoir behind the butcher. Georgie gave keys to Vimala who happened to cross that way. She also stood erect looking at the helpless boy.

She thought *I would not have let my son go like this even if I had one.* She stood there till Georgie and others turned from the street towards Fernandez's house.

Mr Fernandez had some other conditions also that Stella should purchase fish for resale only from Fernandez's boat whenever it reached the shore. Moreover, she could sell only in the streets and not in the market. Though she was not in a condition to cover long distances with a heavy basket on her head, she accepted all the conditions just for her son. The very meagre remuneration to Georgie was also accepted but these conditions were not told to either Fr. Jones or Georgie because that was also a condition put forward by him. He did not want to disclose the information related to the wages.

Georgie on that day was not sent to the sea but was made to work at Fernandez's home counting fish bags which were to be put in ice boxes and sent to a fish processing centre when the van from the company arrived. After finishing his job, he came home around six pm where Stella was ready with dinner and waiting for her son.

He could not take dinner, the usual rice and fish curry, properly even though he was hungry.

After having a little, he came out and sat on the cement steps that led to the sandy ground. He started gazing at the usual stars seen in the western sky. Some people were playing cards under a dim tube light fixed on the pole. A few night birds flew silently over his head.

The next day he was scheduled to go along with a few people on a motor boat in which, as told by one of the senior boys, he could expect only harsh treatment. He also recollected several stories told by his father a few years back. He cursed his fate that he also had to choose fishing by compulsion. He turned back and saw Stella offering prayers in front of a picture of Jesus. He didn't want to join the prayer for he was annoyed with what he revered as God and he simply turned away his head and again looked at the dark sea with several waves with foaming white borders. The sky was dark with umpteen stars. Beyond the dark water with simmering foams caused by the surface waves, at the end where the sky met the sea at the horizon, he could see the lights of a ship moving from north to south. Could he also get into those ships? he thought. There were few lights of boats going for night fishing from other shores nearby. A chill went through his frail body when the thought came that he would also be in one of the boats during deadly nights, stale foods, cold winds, nauseating sea breeze, and scolding from the seniors in the boats. He would have to forego the night's sleep. Could he survive in the boat? He felt an alien feeling when all these thoughts haunted him.

Sitting on the step he leaned against the half-closed door to support his back. His body was aching heavily because of the unusually long hours of unfamiliar work he had done that day for the first time. A coast guard helicopter flew past making a loud noise. All the night birds in the trees flew helter-skelter.

Georgie was feeling dead tired and was sleepy also. After closing the door, he put on the T.V. but he could see only all the familiar faces in the school and school scenarios on the screen. Lots of faces came from his headmistress, class teachers, his friends, and the old tiled school building including Jerry, the stray dog with whom he shared his mid-day meal. "Georgie," his mother called from the adjustment room, "turn off the T.V. and come to sleep after prayer."

He turned off the T.V. and stood his front of the picture of Jesus but instead of Jesus, he could see the picture of his father, Charlie, smiling at him. He unrolled his kora grass sleeping mat spread it on the floor, turned off the lights, blew out the candles and, in no time, he was fast asleep.

The next morning Stella took him to Fernandez as he was going in the boat for the first time. He accompanied her silently but reluctantly having a hell of thought in his mind. Fernandez was very happy to receive him because he got an extra hand to work in his boat for meagre wages. He asked him to go to the blue-painted motor boat which was anchored on the shore with a direct view from his house. While walking on the wet sands, Georgie looked back several times with tears-filled eyes. He saw a blurred vision of his mother wiping her cheeks by hand.

He jumped into the boat where already a few workers stood. Fernandez gave some money to Stella and left the place while Stella was still standing like a statue looking at the boats dangerously crossing tides and speeding towards the horizon and because of the fog she lost sight of the boat. She returned tightly clutching the rupee notes given by Fernandez and wiping the unending fountain of tears. She felt as if she was doing some terrible harm by sending Georgie to the sea.

Thus Georgie started going to sea at least three days a week.

On some days, he would get a good catch and reach the shores before dawn. Sometime he would have to spend more than a couple of days because of various reasons. Stella would be worried wherever his boat would not come to the shores in time. Frantically, she would enquire about him to other fishermen who would land early in the morning. She was not at all happy when he went to the sea during the rains and inclement weather. She started watching weather reports on T.V. channels and also on the small radio which Georgie brought a couple of months back. She would carefully and regularly watch the announcement from the meteorological department. It was a regular feature to advice Georgie on the subject.

Once on a rainy day when his boat was ready to go to the sea, the mother and son quarrelled. There was even an announcement by the shore police not to venture into the sea. She rushed to the fishing jetty and asked Georgie to return home but he did not listen to her, and Fernandez and his men simply did not heed Stella's humble appeals and never bothered about the police announcements. Fernandez even asked Stella to go away from there without creating scenes, in a harsh tone. While Stella was looking on and even when some other boat owners advised him against sending his boat, he ordered his boatmen to go out into the sea.

Very few boats were seen in the sea because of the strong wind and the warming. Stella could see his boat was fiercely dancing on the rough waters braving strong winds. She cried out for Jesus and slowly walked home. On that day, she didn't go for selling fish when Vimala came to call her to the market she said she was not well, but with God's grace the boat returned early morning the next day and Stella felt relieved. Stella had a series of arguments with his son for going out in the sea during times like this she cited many examples of Catamarans and boats capsizing and people losing a life. She would say that his father also went to the sea on a day when the sky was overcast.

Years passed. Georgie was no more a trainee. He became one of the expert fishermen on that shore. Having mastered all the techniques in fishing, he became an asset to Mr Fernandez but his salary did not increase proportionately. Many times, Georgie had arguments with Mr Fernandez over his salary. On the other hand, Stella was no longer a fish seller. She sat at home, did some embroidery for a local crafts-person who used to give cloth and thread to several ladies in those parts and get the finished embroidered linen for marketing in big cities. But the income for the workers was very meagre and many of them took it as a passion or pastime which would fetch some pocket money. Stella did not go to the fish market mainly because Georgie had stopped her. Moreover, her health was also not cooperating. Nowadays, she was very much obedient to Georgie. Money brought by him was more than enough to run the home and even she had some savings in the bank.

At times she used to think about bringing a girl into marriage for Georgie, as he became a fully grown man capable of running his own family. One day she sounded him to that effect but Georgie simply objected to the proposal without telling him any reason. He simply laughed it away.

During one of those days an agent from the Kerala coast, not far from this place, visited that area to recruit young fishermen for one of the fishing companies in Quilon. He was offering double the wages and a lot of other benefits including a dormitory for stay. Many youngsters were willing to go. Georgie also asked Stella for permission.

On an evening after dinner, Georgie opened up, "Mom, you must have heard that an agent from Kerala is camping here to recruit a fisherman to work for a big fishing company. What about me going to the company? We may get a lot of benefits."

Stella, looking at Charlie's photograph said,

"Had your dad been here I would have allowed? If you go now I will be alone. See my health... how can I let you go?"

Georgie requested her again, "For a few days you may adjust here with your close friend Vimala for your company at night. I will see the situation there and if things are conducive, I shall take you also there. Many people are doing that. You know the corner house... Josico has already left with his wife!"

"Georgie, did you ask Fr. Jones?"

"If you say okay, he won't say no."

"If you think it is good for you, I will talk to Fr. Jones and Vimala and come to a decision."

The next day Stella met Fr. Jones and Vimala and discussed the matter. Fr. Jones did not say any objection. He said if the arrangement was going to fetch better life for her and Georgie, then they must go. "I will talk to Mr Fernandez and settle the accounts."

The agent Mr Peter arranged a fairly big vehicle, locally known as the minibus, and accommodated all the eighteen men recruited by him and set off for Quilon.

In Quilon, Georgie was accommodated in a billet-like dormitory where in one hall about twenty to twenty-five cots were placed. The owner of the Silva Fishers, Mr Roney De Silva, was a very rich man who came to Quilon from Goa years ago.

He owned a number of motor boats and trawlers. He also owned vast farmlands and employed hundreds of people in his fish processing and export factory. But Mr De Silva seldom visited the place because of his hectic business activities. He was headquartered in Cochin. His family was also with him in Cochin.

Georgie was introduced to the manager of the Sea-goers' division and was briefed with other new recruits. During the initial days, he was a little uncomfortable. Day by day he was familiarised with the food and air of the place. Looking at immense capacity of Georgie in handling any type of work within a short time, he was assigned the charge of a large fishing trawler. He managed that vessel skilfully and had a good catch every day.

Now his monthly salary was several times more than what he was getting from Mr Fernandez a year ago. During the last year, he used to come home once a month and gave all the money he got to Stella, keeping some for his expenses. When he brought dress materials to Stella he did not forget to take some for Vimala also, whom he considered his own aunt. Stella felt very proud of his son that the money he brought every time he came was much higher than what her husband brought for a year. Her bank balance grew fast. One evening, they went to the church together and after the evening mass, they met Fr. Jones and appraised him of matters.

Nowadays, Vimala was at home with Stella always and there was no necessity arose for Stella to go along with him to Quilon. Moreover, she didn't want to move away from the land and house purchased by Charlie with much difficulty during those days. It was more than thirty years since she came and lived with Charlie. She wanted to spend the rest of her life and end her life on that soil only.

It was a routine affair for Georgie to come periodically and bring along with him, new household items and fill the home. It became difficult for them to move around the house freely because of the new pieces of furniture. One day Vimala told Stella to buy the adjacent plot also which was lying vacant for years and construct a new terraced house and bring a suitable girl for Georgie so that Stella could be relieved of her duties. The idea of rebuilding the house was already brewing in the minds of both Stella as well as Georgie. After discussions, they decided to build a new house after the monsoon.

In Quilon, Georgie used to take food from a small hotel-cum-house, locally called a mess, run by one middle-aged woman Mrs Leela with the help of her mother Karthi aged seventy. They had been in the business for more than twenty years ever since Leela's husband deserted her and left somewhere. Her daughter Anu had also helped them in the kitchen.

Now it is more than five years since Georgie started taking food from there on regular basis on a monthly account. During the last few years due to the constant nearness of both, some kind of relationship had developed between Anu and Georgie. But neither of them revealed it to anyone or there was any doubt about this in the minds of any regulars in the mess who are familiar with Georgie and Anu. The young ones talked discretely but only with eyes, Leela liked Georgie better among all the customers because he was the only one who settled the account monthly before the fifth of every month.

But most of the other regulars used to keep a balanced amount to be carried forward to the next month and sometimes even borrowed money from the granny who gave a large amount of money as loan, of course on interest.

Several times Leela asked Georgie if he needed money for any purpose, but each time he politely refused.

One day when Georgie came for dinner a little late, Anu was alone in the hotel eagerly looking for Georgie. For the first time, they got a few minutes to talk to each other. Instantly, they both poured out to their heart's contents.

Anu asked, "Why are you late today, Georgie? All the regulars have already gone."

Georgie looked around he even peeped into the kitchen and asked, "Anu, where are your mother and grand ma?"

"They had gone to a wedding reception. Must be on their way back."

"Now it is half past nine have you got anything for me to eat."

"Why not? You can have everything that I have here," she said with a wink.

"I mean, I've already reserved your food in the hot box."

Both of them looked each other deep into their eyes which were trying to tell a lot of things.

Georgie abruptly asked Anu, "For some days, I have been thinking of asking you something. What is your age?"

Surprised by this, she said, "I am crossing twenty-five this month."

"Oh, but you look fifteen or sixteen in this skirt and blouse."

Anu liked that comment and her cheeks reddened. Without looking at his face, she asked, "How do you say?"

"Just by looks."

"Why are you asking my age all of a sudden?"

"Just wanted to know."

"That's all?"

"If you are crossing twenty-five, don't you think that this is the right time that you to marry?"

"You are older than me. Why didn't you marry?"

"My mother had been pestering me for that, but every time I just slip away."

"I know that you have told me about your people over there. I hear you got only your mother. Am I right?"

"Yes."

"Don't you think you should marry now so that your mother gets rid of all the household chores and have a peaceful life?"

"If it is otherwise?"

"What otherwise?"

"I mean if the girl I marry gives my mother more problems and makes my mother's life miserable?"

"That happens only rarely."

"No, in our place, it is rampant."

After a pause, Anu asked abruptly looking straight into his eyes with a smile, "Do you think if I am married to someone and start living with them, I would make his mother's life miserable?"

"How do I know?"

Georgie felt that she was approaching his own wavelength.

Anu quickly went out and ensured that nobody was on the road. She continued, "Georgie, if you marry a girl like me, to be specific if you marry me, do you think I would make your mother's life miserable?"

Now Georgie got the green signal and in a hushed-up voice, Georgie said, "Okay, let us have a rehearsal. If you don't make my mom's life miserable, we will continue, or else I will bring you back here. Okay?"

It took a little time for her to understand his sarcastic remark. She laughed and gave him a soft slap on his left cheek with love. In return, he pinched her cheeks with both hands but with a soft touch.

Georgie was perspiring even on that December night coupled with the damp sea wind. He took her arms voluntarily and asked for food. She pulled her hands away and ran to the kitchen for bringing the hot packs. She was shocked to see, Leela and granny sitting on a low bench outside the kitchen veranda. A startled Anu stood like a statue when they entered the kitchen. Granny told: "Hmm… Go and give food to your 'JOJI' and come back without any further romance. We will come through the front door. Don't tell him know that we were at the back!"

She quietly gave food to him and hastily returned to the kitchen. Georgie was feeling guilty and was not able to relish the food which was otherwise special for him. He just wanted to run away because he got hold of her hands.

Georgie called her again on the pretext of getting more curry. When Anu was serving curry without looking at his face, he felt something went wrong. He thought why this girl was suddenly silent and fear-stricken who minutes back talked jovially. Might be shy.

"What happened Anu? Why have you suddenly changed yourself like a garden lizard?" Again, she said, "Nothing.

Hurry up and go," in a hushed-up voice, looking out on the doorway. While Georgie was about to tell something, Leela and granny entered through the front door. Granny asked, "Why are you so late, Georgie? What happened.? When did you come?"

Wiping off sweat from their forehead, he said, "Just now, a few minutes back."

"Oh, just now only," asked Leela jovially. He doubted some sarcasm in her words.

"Smart boy!" Granny exclaimed.

Georgie smelt something fishy. He finished his food hurriedly and was about to leave. Granny asked, "Where are you running? Is anybody waiting for you? Your girlfriend?"

The unusual body language and the actions of Anu led him to think that they had listened to their talks. Anyhow, he immediately went out and had a speed walk to his dormitory. The next day morning when he came for breakfast there was the usual crowd in the restaurant. He tried to avoid eye contact with Granny and Leela. Leela came and served food but she didn't talk about anything probably because of the presence of others. Even then she threw a meaningful look at him that really pierced his heart. He finished his food very fast and walked away. But a little distance under a Mozenda tree of a house Granny was standing with a bundle of drumsticks which appeared to him as a short *lathi* and Granny looked like a headmistress, waiting to scold him.

She detailed to him about the overwhelming conversation of the romantic pair. She said that months before she could read from their gestures about it but it was confirmed only now. She told him that they did not have any objection but the only thing was that they should get married before the song spreads in the village. Moreover, there could be obstacles from the church and their community as it was going to be an inter-religious marriage. People would look in many different ways as it was a remote fishing village.

A few days later, Leela sked Georgie to bring his mother for a formal talk on the issue. As per the local custom, the boy's people should come and ask for the girl. But the news had already spread in the village. As the parties belonged to different religions, the villagers waited for many interesting developments that might happen. On Sunday, Georgie brought his mother and had a series of talks. Starting from that day, it continued for about two months. Now and then both parties visited each other's place. The news had spread widely in Anu's village that the village elders of Anu's community came to her hotel in groups and tried to stop the marriage proposal. Their argument was when there were umpteen eligible bachelors, why they were going to have a connection with other communities in another state, even though the language spoken was different? Anu was in the kitchen when the association people visited their eatery with angry faces. It was morning time and the business was brisk, therefore Leela and Granny didn't give any attention to the group.

Karthi, the grandma came out and asked them, "Why have you all started the scene in the morning? Don't you have any work? Its Friday you all must have some work in the office or somewhere. Anyway, since you all have come, have a cup of tea."

The association President Mr Narayanan retorted, "Hey sister, we have come here to discuss something important relating to your granddaughter and not to have your free tea."

Karthi stood with a serving spoon and told, "Hello, this is not the time to speak anything now. Don't you see the crowd inside? How can you expect me to leave them and come to the road and listen to you?" She gave a fiery look and told again reprovingly, "No, we don't have time now. You may come some other time when there would be a few or customers. Now, please go away!"

Somebody from the group shouted, "Hello, old lady! It is more important than your business. Come out! Bring Leela also."

Granny came out of the hotel with a ladle with which she was doing something in the kitchen. "What is bloody more important than our business here? Don't waste your time and don't spoil my morning business!"

When Granny was getting inside, Leela came out and talked to a woman, who was a member of the group. After a few seconds of discussion, the young lady told one of the seniors in the group, "Sir, we will come again tomorrow or the day after whenever they would be free. I will confirm the timings."

And thus, without much shouting, the group went away but most of them kept murmuring.

One wonky out of them even tried to peep into the kitchen window to have a glimpse of the girl Anu who was busy with some bespoke dishes for the guests, uncared of the outside thermally worded altercations.

Next Sunday it was some festival day in Anu's village and therefore Leela didn't expect any customers except the regular monthly guests.

In the village, the Georgie-Anu issue was brewing and nauseating dialogues could be heard in the mini congregations of the village square, street corners, barber shops and meetings among the hicks who lived on other's bread.

The common dialogues were, "That girl Anu is charming and fair-skinned. Why does she want to go with that dark-skinned stranger?"

"That too a fisherman…"

"He is from another religion."

"The fellow is not even rich…"

"In our village, there is a number of smart boys fit for her."

In a barber shop when these dialogues were going on, the barber stopped his scissors for some time. Balan, the barber who had seen all the strands of hair from the males of the village irrespective of caste, creed, age, colour, religion, or financial or social status. He further continued, "If the girl Anu liked and loved Georgie and if the boy had already said okay what is the hitch in marriage? Where are you and I coming in between? I know that Georgie boy. I can vouch, he is smarter, more intelligent and more sophisticated than all the so-called 'smart' boys you are talking about. I interacted with him several times."

One of the hicks on the bench looking at the pictures of the film stars printed in the magazine, for he knew little to read, told, "I don't want any dowry. Will this girl marry me?"

The barber got angry and said, "Moni, you have come without any business. Please go out! Only last week I had your hair dressed up. You still owe the fee to me. Don't waste my time."

On hearing this, two or three more persons got up, stared at Balan and left the place. Balan commented to the rest of the persons, "There are many youths here who don't go to work and simply idle away the time with *beedis* and cigarettes. You can see them everywhere in the village. Most of them are able-bodied. At least they could go and clean those uncultivated farm lands where weeds have grown. The owners are searching for unskilled workers. But these lazy lords never go for that. See the plot behind my shop that Raman Nair had several times told me to arrange someone to clean this place but none would go."

A week later on a cold morning when Granny was just sitting on the steps covered with a sheet of thick jute fabric to clean the wet feet of customers, those people from the association came. This time only three persons comprising the president, the secretary and that woman member Radha were there. Granny got up with an inviting smile and ushered them into the hotel.

Contrary to the expectation they found Granny was soft-spoken and accommodative. The trio looked at one another and seated on the benches. Leela also came from the kitchen. It was a Sunday and there were not many customers. The secretary opened up. "Karthi sister, you know why we have come here? I request you to tell your girl to forget that fisher boy and you may find somebody else from our community for which we would help. It is unthinkable that a girl from our community to marry somebody from another one. We can never approve of this." '

Granny and Leela simply stared at them without saying anything. After telling this, the secretary looked other two members. They simply nodded their heads in approval. But Radha had a wonky smile on her face and was looking for Anu inside. Anu called her inside the kitchen and they sat for some time. "Anu, Congrats! Whenever we met in the temple you never revealed this matter to me. Anyway all my best wishes." Anu, holding the hands of Radha, replied, "See, Radha, this is not the matter to be told openly to each and everyone."

"Do you think I don't know anything about the affair you have with the Vishnu Potti of the temple? You never told me about it. These things cannot be hidden for long. Tell me when is your marriage." Radha lowered her head in shame. "In my case, only my maternal uncle is the villain. He wants me for his son. And in my family, everybody is for that boy only. I don't like that vagabond Ramesh who failed in his twelfth standard several times. Now, I heard that he has completed it somehow."

Anu asked, "Is he going for some work?"

"No. You can see him always on the cement bench outside the party office with some hooligans. He drinks smokes and I don't know when he will be caught by the police for some narcotic case."

"So, you will not budge for your uncle?"

"No, never. If the pressure is too much from my family, one day you will hear the news that Vishnu Potti ran away with Radha."

They laughed at the joke and came out from the dining hall with a few cups and a jug full of tea. Anu served tea to everyone. President Narayanan asked her, "Anu, we have talked at length but failed to reach a conclusion. Now, you tell me, your genuine and definite opinion."

Anu, without wasting a single second, told firmly, "I will marry Georgie. Nothing more, nothing less. Let's not talk further."

Granny proudly announced, “That’s my girl Anu! What she thinks, she does it!”

On hearing this, the trio got up and set out to go.

Radha told Narayanan, “Now, we can congratulate her in advance.”

Everyone said, “Congratulations,” in chorus.

In the afternoon, another group of persons came. This time the group was led by Fr Williams from the local church. They talked to Karthi and Leela and about the things that need to be carried out peacefully. When they were talking about various formalities to be done for the marriage, one of the members from Anu’s community who came there the other day presented himself yelling something in a drunken state, “Let me see how you people are going to take our girl from here!”

Seeing the turmoil in front of the hotel, the wayfarers started assembling. Realising the situation, Fr Williams immediately withdrew with his men and the Verger who came along with him. A few assembled there kicked away that rowdy fellow and earnestly requested others to move away.

On hearing that the trouble was going on again in the hotel, the president came running. But by the time everyone had gone. He entered the hotel and said now that everything had been decided. “I do hope that you are preparing for other work relating to the marriage.” In a low tone, he asked Anu, “I ask you, Anu, is this your final decision?”

Anu said loudly, "I love him. He loves me. we will marry whatever may come."

Her statement was vouched by Leela and Granny ceremoniously.

The president asked, "Okay, where will you conduct the ceremony?"

Karthi said, "In our temple, where else?"

The president said, "I don't think you will get a temple for this purpose."

Then Leela said, "Then community hall."

The president replied, "I doubt that."

Leela questioned, "Why not?"

The president explained, "There would be a lot of opposition and unwanted problems."

Then Karthy said, "In that case, there is a Church hall which is bigger than the community hall where we don't need to pay any fees."

The president kept mum. "Well," while getting out of the hotel, he said, "all fate! But didn't forget to wish Anu once more."

Next week Georgie's mother came along with Vimala and a few church officials from his village. A simple ring exchange ceremony was conducted in the Church hall where a lot of fisherman folk and a very few members of Anu's community attended the ceremony.

A month later, the marriage ceremony was also conducted in the community hall which was made available by the intervention of local panchayat members. Both functions were held as per the traditional customs and practices of both communities amidst protests from many troublemakers from both sides. On the same day of the marriage itself, the bridegroom Georgie left for his village with the bride Anu along with the groom's people.

Back in the calm and serene village of Georgie, Anu felt some kind of loneliness because of the absence of her own people and the sudden change in her lifestyle. It was also amusing for her to go to church ceremonies and the village congregations in connection with religious functions that were alien to her till then.

She was longing to go to some temple nearby but Georgie hesitated fearing reprisals from the temple authorities as well as the church. While Stella was praying in front of Jesus at home, Anu was also allowed to pray in front of a small Krishna idol that she had brought from her home. When Stella was very much practising her religious functions, Georgie did not give any importance to the practices of both the ladies. He was not a staunch believer, neither had he any aversion to the practices, whether religious or traditional, unlike his mother and wife. Once when Anu expressed her desire to visit her people, Georgie took her to her village, but Georgie did not enter the temple just to avoid any kind of problems in the temple premises that could be created by some anti-social elements. After coming from the temple, Leela took both of them to some of her relatives where they could get only lukewarm reception. In the evening itself, they left for home.

A couple of years passed by, and Anu became one of the local women who participated in most of the functions in the village and other social gatherings and was gaining good popularity. Even a few people insisted that she could contest the forthcoming panchayat elections.

Now, Georgie left the fishing company in which he was working. With smart planning of Anu, they could obtain a loan from the bank for the purchase of a small motor-boat. Employing a couple of boys, Georgie started his own fishing activities. In a short time, he started earning good profits and he could repay all his loans. He renovated his home as per the design and wishes of his mother and wife. The idea of building a new house was brewing in his mind ever since he brought Anu to his old house. He was really unhappy that his father was not there to watch his growth. After a few months at the inauguration of his new house, Anu gave birth to a handsome baby boy. They named him Anoop George Charlie under the supervision and blessings of Father Jones of the local church. On the christening day, Karthi and Leela were also present and they left immediately after the function. George's fishing business was flourishing and he employed many youths in the village adding more boats and life was going on happily for them.

It was more than a year now. As it was the Christmas holidays, Stella, Anu along with Anoop went to the church in the morning for a function connected with Christmas and new year. While coming back from the church, they saw an unusual commotion on the shores and streets where people were joyously running here and there with bags and baskets full of fish. There was a great catch for everyone. They were expecting Georgie to return before noon. When they approached the shore, they were startled to see that the sea had almost withdrawn to three-hundred feet from the usual shoreline. They could see many varieties of fish, shells, crabs, clams, etc. Some of the boats had already reached the shore before the withdrawal but many were yet to come. A few were stuck on the sandy ground of the sea where water had withdrawn. Yet another few were struggling to come to shore because of the strange phenomenon which was unusual for the natives. It was a sunny day and there were no signs of any black clouds or rain. The sky was quite clear. After some time, there were announcements from the jeeps by the coastal police that everyone should go far away from the shores, but many did not bother.

Back at home, Anu saw on TV many strange things happening on other shores of Tamil Nadu and Kerala. She saw the images of powerful, giant waves engulfing and destroying bridges, houses, temples, churches, trees, etc. Everywhere the police, NGOs and other security personnel were very busy and removing people to safer places. Stella, Anu and Anoop were preparing to get away along with other people.

But suddenly when people were watching on, an enormous killer wave came at tremendous speed and monstrous force that ripped almost everything in its way along the shores of the village. Those who could go away early escaped from the waters and those who were hesitating and delaying perished. At the time of the accident, Georgie and his men were out on the sea miles away unaffected by the killer waves. The tsunami destroyed almost everything on the shore smashed buildings, uprooted trees and even broke a concrete bridge on the waters near the estuary. Hundreds of people in the village died or went missing. Among the dead were Stella and Anu whose bodies were later found kept among the dead bodies lined up in the nearby school by the authorities.

A few minutes of dreaded dancing by the waves from the sea left the village in total shambles. Some dead bodies were still hanging from the trees, a few holding the trees braving the force of the tide, and some were thrown away on the wire fencing ripping their body parts beyond recognition. A few were horribly smashed against the walls of the buildings, and tree trunks and some others simply drowned in the sand slush and mud of the sea.

The government machinery including local volunteers and fire force, community leaders, irrespective of their religion or caste, and a lot of others, everyone was engaged in the salvage operations. The sirens of the ambulances could be heard everywhere. By evening, the authorities had an approximate account of the dead, maimed, or missing.

Stella and Anu were on the list of the dead and the boy, Anoop was on the missing person list. Many boats reached in the afternoon including Georgie's. They could see some trouble from the distance itself. But it was only when they brought the boat to the shore, the facts came to be known.

Georgie ran towards his house but he could see broken pieces of concrete, bricks, twisted steel rods and a lone standing wall. Similar was the situation all along the shore. The entire scenario had changed totally. He could not believe; it was his village. He frantically asked a number of strange and unknown people who were doing cleaning work about his people. Nobody knew anything. Clothes worn by people were hanging on the trees, fences and electric poles fluttering like flags in the wind. Even in that melee, he could identify a torn red and yellow saree that he had bought for Anu for the Christmas celebrations. The saree was flying atop an undamaged electric pole just a few yards away from home. Standing on the bare red oxide floor of his house, he looked around and sat against that lone wall. Even the furniture and utensils had gone and were strewn all over the area. Everywhere filth, slush and sand could be seen. He came out and frantically inquired about his family with everyone who came across. Finally, he was led to the school building where the dead bodies were kept for identification. Among the dead there were old, young men, women, children...umpteen people trying to identify their dear ones amidst wails and cries. Some were just sitting in the corner end veranda sobbing tearfully because their loved ones' names were on the missing list. Several bodies had been claimed already and the authorities were engaged in hasty operations to bury them. The only option was the mass burial.

Georgie, already half dead in his senses, found his Anu and Stella among the lined-up dead bodies. He could not find any known persons present in the crowd except for a few children of his son's age who escaped and gathered themselves in the school as per the instructions from the police. Georgie sat beside the dead bodies of his mother and wife, numb for some time and woke up only when Father Jones shook him up to reality. But by that time, he had lost his senses out of shock and was simply searching for his son. He was not responding to any query and it seemed Georgie had already gone to the mysterious world of insanity and along with a few persons who were struck by trauma, were taken to a local hospital in the town from there a few days later, he was taken to a bigger asylum near Chennai.

Anoop was in a capsized boat near the shore and was saved. As the boat was caught between the rocks for some time and later it drifted away into the sea. Only the next day, he was rescued by the Coast Guard authorities but in an unconscious state. He was taken to the nearby medical college and admitted to the trauma care unit. Already some damage had happened to his entire body system and with continuous treatment for more than a year, he was brought to Kochi and admitted to an orphanage. The boy was physically healthy but the trauma wreaked by the tsunami had affected him mentally and left him with memory loss and after a couple of months he became normal as there was nobody to claim the child. With the help of a few philanthropists in the city, he was admitted to boarding school and continued with his studies. In the meantime, Leela and Karthi had come to the place after two days and as they couldn't find any clue about Georgie's people, they left the place in the morning. He grew into a very smart boy and came out with flying colours in all his examinations and the orphanage authorities got him admitted into the medical college where he completed his degree courses and went to higher studies in Chennai.

Many years rolled by; Georgie was still in the asylum. He had grown grey but was very healthy physically, he could read and write but he was not able to regain his memory. He was simply living in the asylum unchained and peacefully doing a lot of physical work. In fact, he was solely responsible for developing a beautifully laid out garden in the sprawling compound of the asylum. A few years back, the garden was lying unattended with overgrown weeds and bushes. Every official who came to visit the asylum including the doctors appreciated the best work that he had done to beautify the garden with flowering plants and green foliage. The doctors tried very hard to get back his memory but so far, they could find no progress in this regard.

When he was in the asylum, a second bolt from the blue struck him when several inmates were affected by the dreaded Covid. He was also one among them. Many inmates lost their lives. Due to his good behaviour and work done for the institution, the doctors had a special affection towards him. They isolated him and gave him the best available treatment in a covid speciality hospital. Within three months, the population in the asylum was reduced to almost half. Everyone was helpless. There were no enough volunteers now. Mere fate ruled most.

Georgie also went to the verge of death but a few days later, he was showing improvements and within a fortnight he was discharged from the hospital.

During his treatment in the hospital, one of the doctors in his ward looked after him with utmost care and he developed a special relationship with him. In that ward other than Georgie there were only a couple of patients were being treated for covid. After the discharge, he was taken again to the asylum. This time he was employed as a gardener temporarily on a meagre salary by the grace of a lady psychiatrist. Several times she asked him about his past. But he could never recollect.

On an evening when the first wave of covid died out and people had some relief and started to lead a near-normal life, that young doctor came to the asylum and met Georgie. When the doctor was getting out of his car Georgie was sitting on a stone slab and surveying the work in the garden that he revived after the covid.

Nowadays, he was not wearing the patient uniform but the employee uniform which matched his robust healthy looks with well-trimmed hair and beard.

But Georgie's name was registered as Xavier by mistake when he was admitted the first time to the local hospital in his village. Therefore, he was known as Mr Xavier to everyone in Chennai Hospital. Moreover, the lean clean-shaven Georgie was now presenting himself a picture of a heavily built old man with grey curled hair and beard like a Greek sailor with a thick moustache. He always lived in the present only. He always addressed a nurse or a female employee only as a daughter. The other day he caught hold of a boy in the covid hospital and told him not to go anywhere and be always with him thinking that it was his own son.

The doctor came near him and asked if he could recognise him. Georgie nodded his head positively, smiled and embraced him. The doctor said that he was happy to see him employed in the asylum. In reply, Georgie gave a large smile. The doctor had done some homework and traced his birthplace as a village devastated by the Tsunami years back from where he also hailed. When they were sitting on a slab and talking Georgie was staring at the Talisman that was hanging from the neck of the doctor. On noticing it, the doctor asked, "Dada, why are you staring at my Talisman?"

"Very nice looking," Georgie said.

"There are better ones in the market made of gold, silver, etc. Don't you think that they are better than this?" Dr asked.

Georgie again touched it and said, "Very nice."

The doctor asked, "Do you want it?"

"No!" He was constantly looking at it and murmured something inaudibly.

The doctor realised that he started to look back at his past.

The doctor asked, "Where are your people?"

Georgie looked at the sky and raised his hands. He immersed himself in deep thoughts and prostrated in front of a plant that he had trimmed almost like a cross. He got up and looked at the sky.

He again felt silent and closed his eyes. Minutes later looking at the sky Georgie cried out, "Jesus!"

The doctor got up and met the psychiatrist who was treating Georgie. The psychiatrist said that he started telling about some incident that happened long ago. He was telling things bit by bit only. We have to connect them and take a sentence in order. In that way, we can come to the conclusion that he was telling something about an incident that happened in his past.

Doctor, "Thank you, doctor. I am leaving. Please take care of him."

The psychiatrist said in a serious tone, "He is really an asset to the asylum. Many of the inmates here obey him better than they obey the doctors or staff members of this place. We have given them a separate room with free food and all the amenities."

The doctor got up and said, "That's good anyway. Incidentally I am going to his village shown in his record and find anybody out there who might identify Xavier. In that case, I can officially hand over him to them".

The psychiatrist replied, "I appreciate your good intention. Wish you good luck!"

The very next day, the doctor set out for his village identified after verifying several records in the health department. He reached the village the next day in the morning and straight away he went to the church for he knew the church authorities would keep records better than the local government offices would. He met Father Jones who had survived the brain haemorrhage but still continued in the church with faded memories of the past with a grey beard and long hair. He could not identify the visitor though Anoop knew that it was the old Father Jones. He introduced himself, "I am Dr Anoop from Chennai. I came here to know the details of a man named Mr Xavier now around fifty years of age, hailing from this village."

Father Jones asked him in a feeble voice, "Where is that Xavier now?"

"He is in Chennai," replied Anoop.

Then Father asked, "You could have well asked him about his village?"

"He is not in his senses. He lost his memory."

Father said, "Oh! I see poor guy!'

Father Jones called a boy out from the veranda and asked him to bring a long old book in which several named were written which included every individual who lived in this village under the jurisdiction of this church and that too only members of the catholic church. He ran his fingers from a particular page looking through the thick glasses for the name of Xavier. There were several Xaviers in the register. Against each name, there were remarks like dead, left, and missing, some new addresses were also there. But no Xavier of age around fifty was there in the register. Most of them were in their seventies or nineties. Lifting his head from the long book Father Jones asked, "Do you have any photograph of the person?"

Anup took out a coloured photo from his purse which was taken when Georgie was discharged from the covid Hospital. It was the photo ofw a hefty man with curled hair and beards.

Fr Jones said, "Very handsome fellow." He looked at the photo closely and gave it back. Dr said, "He is Mr Xavier from this village. But as per the church records, we couldn't match any of the Xaviers recorded in the register with this man."

Father asked again, "There could be some family names or initials?"

The doctor replied, "Nothing of that sort."

Fr Jones, calculating by the present age, said, "We can see the list of missing persons from this time backwards. If we go by that account this man might be on the missing list." He shortlisted about ten persons of which there were three Xavier Das. He read out the first name "Xavier George Charlie." Dr stopped him right there. "I think it might be the person we were looking for. Fr said, "But this Charlie was admitted for treating trauma on that day. I clearly remember that his wife and mother died and his son went missing. If his son was alive he may be of your age. The doctor said, "What was the name of his missing son?"

"In the record, it was written as Anoop son of Georgie."

"Thank you, Father," The doctor got up and was about to go when Fr jones asked him, "Where do you belong Dr?"

"I was told I belong to a place somewhere here. But I don't know the name of the correct village."

Fr Jones looked at him straight into his eyes and looked at his talisman. "Can I see the talisman Dr?"

"Why not?" Dr said.

Dr came near to the Father and removed the talisman from his neck and gave him. Fr Jones asked, "Can I open it up and see?" After a little hesitation, the Dr said, "Okay."

Fr Jones opened it and the wax-coated picture of Mary with the baby Jesus came up at the back of which it was written *Anoop George Charlie*. Father exclaimed, "It is the same copper tube in which I rolled the picture and tied it on your neck when you were still a baby!"

Fr stood up and embraced Anoop and said, "What I could understand from your conversation is that all these years you have been taking care of your own father Georgie without knowing the truth. God is great!"

Dr Anoop Georgekutty was thrilled with excitement and joy and kissed the hands of Father. "Father Jones, Did you recognise me?"

"Yes, I am Fr Jones. I was young when you were a boy here."

"Yes, Father, I recollect," he replied.

After that Anup told how he happened to land in Chennai and became a doctor. Fr Jones advised him that he could come back immediately with his father and settle in this village to serve the people.

Dr Anoop was in a hurry to go to Chennai. The same day itself he took a flight from Trivandrum and reached his father by evening. On hearing all the happening during these years Georgie was dazed and numb for some time, looking up at the sky only. Within minutes he got up cheerfully and hugged his son Anoop. The psychiatrist was awestruck in wonder to see the sudden mental transformation in Georgie who became a perfect gentleman. The emotionally charged Dr Anoop wept and a week later the father-son duo left for their home village to set up a small nursing home in the very same place where his house stood.

9

The Teacher

On a fine morning, I went on to the Medical College Hospital where my friend's daughter was admitted to the labour room. Doctors had told me that the delivery would take place around eight in the morning. But now it was twenty minutes past ten. As I could not take any food in the morning, I felt hungry. I just wanted to get away for at least some time till I meet my friend. Moreover, the stench in the area was really nauseating. I came from a distant land to take a rest at home. But here every now and then there would be some programmes connected with betrothal, marriage, child birth, death and the aftermath special programs… the list was never-ending.

After coming home, I never got two consecutive days at home for my privacy and sleep. Even if I got those days anyone of the near or distant relatives would be present to see me and then wouldn't just see me and go. They would come in the morning, take breakfast, and chat with my people at home. The subject varied from the Panchayat election and demonetization to Trump's victory and his glorious rule in the US. Unable to bear with that, I would be forced to go out. Today, I had an excuse for this hospital visit.

As I was no longer able to withstand the hospital's stench, I just asked my friend who was flanked by anxious relatives, to go out for some time. While stepping out of the premises I just remembered that many years back once when my daughter was admitted in similar circumstances, it was a terrific night. Heavy downpours with lightning and thunder and the electricity were off for hours together. I had to spend the entire night without taking food in the evening along with a herd of relatives mainly from my wife's side.

I spent all night and till eleven in the morning with much more stench than this. Anyway, this was one of my friend's daughters only. See the human level of thinking. But now there was neither rain nor darkness, but it was hot. There were a lot of gents, ladies, and children who were standing, sitting and lying on the floor. I just discreetly and slowly walked aside as if I was not going out.

I got out of the premises walked fast and reached the Indian Coffee House across the road which was not crowded. One of the tables was empty with four chairs. I sat in one of the chairs and waited for the waiter.

The waiter with a white uniform and a green coloured cap with frills walked towards the kitchen as the beauty contestant walked on the ramp. I looked around. No known person. Even if anyone was there I would not have recognised for I was away from the city for more than a decade. There were a set of boys and girls sitting around a table pulling in extra chairs. I counted, seven of them were there. They seemed to be medical students. Because they were praising some professors and cursed others occasionally using medical terms and names of medicines along with dirty and filthy words. They were in a very jovial mood and never bothered about others in the hall. I felt awkward over the scene. But helpless!

Oh! This Coffee House! It was not for a person who came to take food especially when he came with an empty stomach! It was not possible to order and get the stuff immediately. You had to wait a lot. This house was designated for the friends and groups who come to discuss business and gossip. They sit on their cup of coffee for more than an hour. I used to wonder whether this coffee house made any profit!

In Delhi when I first entered the coffee house the scene was very unfriendly. Only one seat was vacant. The reason was that the metal chair was not in the right position. Even though, I had to sit. The air was filled with cigarette smoke. Most of them were talking. The conversations were not clear. At my table, three persons with beards and peculiar attire and were seriously reading contemporary magazines. Mostly Bengalis and Malayalis could be seen. Every table had empty and half-empty cups with saucers. Cling clang noise of the cups and saucers reminded me of the ladies and children inside a crockery shop. Some speak very softly. Some are loud. Not knowing the procedure there, looking at a *kulla* wearing bearded I said, "I want a coffee."

Identifying me as a Keralite he asked me in Malayalam, "Are you alone?"

I did reply, "Yes," in Malayalam.

He left hurriedly and another fifteen minutes gone and the steaming coffee was on the table. After having coffee, I looked for the guy who gave me coffee. But he could not be identified as there were a lot of them having the same white uniforms. Each one was walking crisscross the hall filled with cigarette smoke. Understanding my helplessness, a bearded man sitting in front of me with a cold coffee told me in a soft voice in English, "You can pay at the counter without waiting for the bill if you are in a hurry."

I said, "Thank you, sir."

"Are you from Kerala?" he enquired.

"Yes."

I felt he wanted me to sit and talk with him.

But somehow at that time, I didn't want it as everything there seemed strange to me. Eventually, I came to know that the coffee house was the place over there in Delhi to get acquainted with any stranger and befriend him for good or sometimes for bad.

I got up and moved towards the counter and stood before the cashier. By the time the waiter came running to me and gave me a bill slip of thirty *paise*, I had paid in coins and left the place. Subsequently, one of my friends living in Delhi for a long time told me that the people coming to the coffee house were mostly Malayalis and they saw it as a meeting place on a daily or weekly basis. Many journalists and writers were also there.

But here it was not like that. There was not much crowd for there were a number of tea kiosks and restaurants around the medical college.

As my thoughts were flying from Delhi to Calcutta to Jaipur and so on with coffee house experiences, I noticed an old gentleman who came and sat opposite me and started staring at everyone. He was trying to hang his long postman brand umbrella on the chair. As the chair was not cooperating, I got up and helped him hang his umbrella properly. He looked at me with gratitude and wiped his face with his handkerchief taken out from the side pocket of his white *jubba*.

His finger combed his silver hair backwards surreptitiously. For his age, his looks seemed younger than anyone else of his age, present there. As I got a new subject I started analysing him. He was fair skinned and prominent green veins stood out on the back of his dry palms. His white Hitler moustache stood in contrast to the thick black eyebrows borrowed from Brezhnev. There was a black lobe just below his right ear the size of a country gooseberry. He wore a white cotton *dhoti* and *jubba*. It seemed he had a long walk in the morning sun before he stepped into the coffee house. He pulled out a purse from the right pocket of his *jubba* and counted the few rupee notes in that. A fountain pen with a golden cap was clipped just between the button holes of his *jubba*.

He had a striking resemblance with somebody I knew very close. I was not able to recollect. But the faded face was just embedded in my mind. I just asked him with a friendly respectful smile.

"Sir, where do you live in the city?"

He shot back, "Do you know me? Have you seen me before?"

"No, sir. But the very familiar face. That's why…"

"Here near and in Ulloor."

"Your good name, sir?"

"Raman Pillai."

Suddenly my memory stuck on the picture of a white, lean and tall man with *jubba* teaching Malayalam language when I was in the eighth standard in a rural government school.

Bored of my frequent questions he seemed a little annoyed, and the delay in attending to him wasn't helping either. He looked back and waved to a *kullawalah*. He came running with an apologetic smile.

"I didn't see, sir". What can I get for you, sir?"

From his gestures, I could understand that this gentleman was a frequent visitor to the coffee house. He ordered a *masala dosa*. And I also asked for the same.

Mr Raman Pillai told him to hurry up as it was already late.

After confirming that he was the same Raman Pillai, the Malayalam teacher, with respect, I told him I was a student in the same school when he was teaching during a particular year.

"What is your name?" he asked with a better gesture with a sweet smile. Perhaps the weary teacher must have spent decades to find such a situation. His mood improved with my recounting a couple of humourous incidents from the class. He seemed to really relish those old memories.

When I told him my name he could not recollect it. How could he? After all, it was more than half a century since he taught me.

"I was in eighth class at that time and was very bad at language, particularly at Malayalam grammar."

Raman Pillai replied, "Oh!"

I even remembered his several scolding over not reciting a poem. Then I reminded him that his son came to the school once for some purpose.

"You remember such things even now?" he asked. A dreamy look appeared in his eyes but his face looked disturbed.

By the time the bearer brought the stuff, we had finished it in no time and waited for the coffee to arrive.

I recollected that incident when his son came to our school.

On a sunny day when we were playing on the ground during the free period, then a boy around twelve years came to us. He was wearing some outsized old, khaki knickers with no front buttons. The knickers were tied to his waist with a sun hemp cord inserted through the loops. His thin empty stomach appeared more squeezed because of this cord. The light blue cotton shirt was on his skeleton body exposing his ribs for it had no buttons but one or two safety pins. Barefooted and with dust up to his knees, it seemed that he had walked a hell of a distance and his face was haggard with fatigue and hunger. On his arrival he was looking for water and spotted a water pot under the neem tree he drank at least four glasses of water. He came to us and hesitatingly asked in a very feeble voice, "Can you tell me where Raman Pillai sir sits?"

"Now he may be in the classroom."

One of us asked him on seeing his pitiable attire soaked in sweat, "You want to see him right now?"

"Yes."

"Where do you come from? Why do you want to see him?"

"He is my father."

"Your father!"

Our eyes blinked in surprise and wondered why this poor fellow in this shabby outfit called Raman Pillai sir, his father who was always very neat and clean with milk-white *dhoti* and *jubba*.

One of us yelled, "He cannot be his son. This dirty fellow is telling lie," he muttered, reading our minds.

"Believe me. I am Rajesh and studying in the seventh class in a government school near our home." As he was anxious to meet the teacher his pale watery eyes fluttered around all the class rooms surrounding the playground. I took pity on him and just dashed to a class room where Raman Pillai was taking lessons. I explained the matter to him in a hushed voice so as to avoid distraction in the classroom. Immediately, he came out of the classroom and gestured for Rajesh to come under a mango tree. We just kept aloof. The teacher was staring at him and they were arguing about something. As it was a distance away, I could not hear anything except their body language. After a few minutes, Raman Pillai sir took out his thin leather purse and gave him some money. It seemed as if he was scolding him and warning him not to come to this school in the future. When sir had left, Rajesh came running to us and throwing a look of gratitude doubled up out of the ground and school gate.

On another day, I chanced to see him with his mother in a city temple. When his mother was talking to her friends near the temple entrance, I called out to him and readily he came to me with a dimpled smile.

Now he looked neat and well-dressed.

"Rajesh, why did you come to school on that day and it seemed sir was scolding you?" I asked, inquisitively.

Rajesh did not reply. When I insisted, he spoke out.

"A week before my coming to school my uncle brought us to my mother's home where nobody was living. We had no money. Hence I came to get some money from my father."

"Why did you people went to that house where nobody was living".

"I don't know."

"Then?"

"On that day my father had an argument with my mother and consequently he left home along with my uncle".

Reading my mind, Raman Pillai Sir was teasingly looking at me thinking that I was lost in the pranks of school days. I suddenly recovered myself and asked about Mr Rajesh.

"Sir where is Rajesh now?"

"He is now a big officer in a bank, married and has two children."

"Wife?"

"It's been now ten years since her demise."

He told in a coarse voice, "It was her fate and mine too."

"Well, what about the children? Do they often come to meet you?"

"Yeah, sometimes."

In that reply, there was a lack of stress in the words and started drinking his coffee. It seemed he did not wish to continue to talk. I felt he was hiding something. We got out of the coffee house. I told him that I could pay the bill for both of us but he politely refused and paid his own bill.

Then he enquired about and my credentials. He said he was very happy to hear that some of his students had come up in the life. I also invited him to my home.

We departed after exchanging addresses. He was staying in an old age home near the medical college called Prarthana Mandir!

"Sir, I will drop you".

"No thanks."

"I am going to the nearby post office. You know today is Vishu. On every Vishu, I used to send some money to my grandchildren."

"Okay. Thank you."

He hurriedly walked along the footpath and vanished in the crowd. I was wondering why should he stay in an old age home. When his children were in good positions.

A couple of months later when I was driving past that area I just, out of curiosity, wanted to drop in at Prarthana Mandir where Raman Pillai sir was staying. I could find an old building having a name board.

It was run by some community trust and was a little old enough to prove its credibility. The old age home functioned in a strong terraced double-storied building with a well-laid-out garden. 'Thamasoma Jyothirgamaya' was seen written in their logo around an image of a sun and a few full-bloomed lotuses below embossed in concrete on the wall.

On seeing my car turning the gate watchman Parameswaran a tall figure with a huge twirling moustache that extended up to his ear lobes opened the gate for me. After parking the vehicle under the shade of polyalthia lined up on either side of the gate I asked for Raman Pillai Sir.

The alert watchman who still thought he was in the artillery regiment came near me and told, "Sir is not here now. He reported the leave and went to his son's house in Bangalore."

"When will he return?"

"Can't say. He visits Bangalore frequently."

"Normally, how many days he would spend over there?"

Without answering my queries, he shot back. "That is okay. Why you are asking all these questions about him? Do you know him? Are you his relative?"

"I am his student."

"Oh. Sorry, sir. Leave me your phone number. I will tell him when he is back."

I gave my phone number and turned towards the car when one gentleman of about seventy years came out of the building. With the intention of extracting some information about the inmates of the house, I gave him a friendly smile. He was one of the seniors living in the home.

"He invited me to the reception room where I was seated and he himself fetched me a glass of water from the huge mud pot."

"Hello, Parameswaran. Whose *jataka* were you telling him?"

"He asked about Raman Pillai, sir."

"Okay. You go to the kitchen and ask somebody to bring a cup of tea for sir."

Mr Varkey, one of the old inmates then asked me about my credentials and started his own version *of Raman Pillai sir*."

"Raman Pillai sir is a nice gentleman. But fate does play havoc in anybody's life. He had a boy with his first wife and was leading a happy life."

"Wait. You said, first wife?"

"Yes, first wife. After that, he had an affair with another lady and the trouble started since then. He lost his own house, a bit of landed property and a lot of money. That bitch grabbed everything from him and finally deserted him too. After a few years, he joined his first wife and till her death he was happy. Since then, he has been living alone and his son is well employed in Bangalore."

"Okay. It is sad to hear the story. Anyway, when will he come back?"

"Normally, he would set one or two weeks to stay with them. But on the third day, he would bounce back with the bag."

Mr Varkey expected a query from me. But I was silent.

He continued, "How can he stay along with his daughter-in-law? He loves them. But they? But Rajesh his son used to drop in at least quarterly. He believes everyone. He thinks that everyone is good like him. Once we were roommates. But he could not adjust to my tastes. Therefore, he changed to a single room. He reads a lot. Half of his pension goes only on books and periodicals. We inmates here have no dearth of reading materials! As a well-disciplined man even at this age he does not have any kind of diseases, like blood pressure, sugar, etc., and you know, he has been a pure vegetarian all his life."

Mr Parameshwaran intervened, "Sir, it is okay that his daughter-in-law is like that. But what about his brothers and sister? No one turns up."

Mr Varkey retorted, "Listen! you don't understand such things," and he continued, "after the demise of his wife, sir has been staying all alone in his house with a maid servant for cooking". His son also got married and settled in Bangalore.

After a pause, he continued, "But after some time, he did not approve of the strange relationship of the maid with a couple of uninvited 'useless cousins' who visited his house whenever sir went out of home! That is the reason why he came to this centre."

"Poor man," he said, looking at the lone sparrow perched on the telephone pole. "Sir has a good pension and income from rent."

Again, Parameshwaran pitied, "Just see, sir, almost all of the inmates are the same. Don't you think so, sir?

"No. No. See Mr Kuttan Pillai in room number eight. How rich he was. All his children deserted him and he landed here. And see Mr Sankarji—well educated and retired from a good position in a government office. His entire earnings and ancestral properties had been swallowed up by his own brother. Like that, so many were here. And as far as Mr Neelakantan was concerned…"

Before he could finish the sentence, I stopped him telling him that I was getting late and I would come again another day. Before leaving I gave few-rupee notes to Mr Parameshwaran who was very happy to have them. Mr Varkey yelled, "Please do come sometimes. Okay?"

I waved and drove out. Though I was driving, my thoughts flew back to the school again.

Sir would be present daily sharp at nine am. Although the distance could easily be covered by bus he used to come on foot while his colleagues always used the town bus service.

At least once a week he used to deliver a personnel lecture to us. "My dear children you should study well. I have studied a little and this is why I crawled into this job at least. Otherwise, I would have gone to rear some body's cattle or do some other sundry work. I have only two pairs of *dhoti* and *jubbas.* Every alternative day I wash them with blue-contained soap and wear them. Because a teacher does not get a good salary. But you guys should study well and go to higher jobs. Understood?" Then he would strike his split-end cane on the table to make a noise to bring silence in the class.

Days and months passed. A kind of ill feeling started to pop up in my mind time and again that I was not able to see him so far. What a busy life! Again, on a Sunday I left for the abode of the deserted ones. I drove with a determination to meet him somehow or other. In between these days, I had attempted several times but was wasted by a hell of affairs both physical as well as mental.

I selected this day because it was the same day last year in Vishu that I met him in the coffee house.

When I reached the gate, I found there was no watchman. I got out and pushed the gate apart. The housekeeper came running and saluted me.

"Where is the watchman Parameshwaran?"

"He has gone to the medical college hospital. Oh! Can I see Raman Nair?"

"No, sir. He is bed ridden in the hospital. Only Parameshwaran is there. He is critically ill."

"How did it happen? He was hale and healthy when I met last year at the same time."

"They were saying that he had a stroke or something like that."

I dashed to that hospital, which was ten minutes away.

He was in the general ward. Mr Varkey and Parameshwaran and a nurse were around his cot. Raman Pillai sir was on his back with unmoved open pale eyes. He was not recognizing anyone. Mr Varkey called me out on the veranda and told me, "The doctors have lost hope and yesterday they asked me to take him home as there was nothing to do on him. I phoned Rajesh's house several times after admission to the hospital. Every time his wife responded that Rajesh was on a tour. Just at that time when we were talking, Rajesh came running and also the nurse along with Parameshwaran to say that sir was no more. There was nobody else to mourn except Rajesh. Unexplained tears rolled down his cheeks. We also stood there keeping mum for a few moments with watery eyes. I did not know why my goading conscience was haunting me. I actively participated with the team till Rajesh left after having all the socially required rituals at the crematorium. While driving home I felt my conscience was pricking my mind for whatever reason.

10

Turmeric and Jasmine

One day when I was busy at my desk in the city post office, the postmaster called me to his chamber and told me about my promotion orders and that I had to go and take charge of a small branch office in an interior village on the banks of the most time dry river. Looking at the emotions on my face he said, "This is a promotion-cum-transfer and therefore you have to join within ten days. Are you happy?"

"I am happy… but this place you are telling me is very interior…". Postmaster said with a smile, "Hello my dear boy. you are lucky to have this post at an early age. You should be very happy."

"But, sir."

"What but… why do you bother about interior or city centres? You don't have your parents or relatives with you, neither you have any property here and you are well past your marriage age. But still don't lose hope. Who knows somebody might be waiting for you in the new place of posting. "

"Sir, I don't think I would ever get a girl there because even in this city where thousands of girls are there, I could not find one. Then…».

"Don't get disheartened, my boy. You will soon get one. I hear that your father came all the way from his hometown with several proposals nothing worked. Anyway this time my blessings are with you."

Back in the hall, other colleagues congratulated me and some were even jealous of me. Mr Ramesh who had a small stint in that village post office very recently once told me that it was a fine village with loving people all around. He told me patting my back, "Sundar, you are lucky as you can be king over there. Not like this bloody city with lots of problems."

As this fellow Ramesh had served in that village for some time I requested him to give me first-hand knowledge about everything. In the evening we went to the dining room and he narrated his experiences in the village with a positive note on everything. I asked him, "Nothing bad about it? Am I fit for that village?"

"Why do you want me to speak the other side of it? Ok, hear me. You cannot have many good friends like you are having here. Then, most of the village elders and youth of the area come to the banks of the river and sit under trees for gossip. When you go to the village and settle you will have to join those groups and take part in, mostly, useless discussions. Sometimes it ends in quarrels.

"Age is not a criterion. The more money you shell out, the more respect you get. The extra money you spent in the evenings for snacks coffee, etc. would fetch you more friends." Whether the water in the river flows or not the country liquor is perennial. "You will be taken care of by the experienced lot in the group. And you get a bonus also."

"Bonus?" I asked enthusiastically. The curiosity wars only in my mind and I carefully avoided that to reflect in my face. He continued, "Yes, bonus. That is very interesting. After weekly revelling is over at the riverside you will be taken to a tea shop at the entrance to the village from the main road near the bus stops. There is only one bus which runs twice a day, morning at nine am and evening at seven pm obviously to carry people to the nearby town around ten kilometre away and back."

He took a long breath and was emotionally charged and a bit restless.

I gave him a glass of water and asked, "Shall we go to the canteen for a cup of tea?" In no time we reached the canteen at the rear side of the building and sat on a dancing bench. I asked, "Tea or coffee?" He wanted coffee with *bonda*. I thought that the price for the information he was going to give me was damn cheap. We started enjoying the coffee and *bonda*. Ramesh was not talking about anything. He was in a pensive mood looking at the textures of the green banana leaf on which his bonda was served. I woke him up.

"Ramesh, where are you? Lost in the village?"

He hurriedly finished his snacks and coffee and looked around.

I said, "Continue."

"No, let us go to the dining."

By the time we reached, the office time was over and many people were coming out of the office except a few cash handlers who were still busy in the respective counters. We entered the dining room and again took positions near a desk.

Ramesh continued, "Ok. I will tell you. Here there are no over hearers! Where did I stop?"

I said, "Tea shop."

"Yes, the tea shop," he started, "the tea shop was a small one with a thatched roof devouring a little of the road.

You have to enter the place with your head ducked to save your forehead from the bamboo beams supporting the woven coconut leaves. Once you enter, a few sets of age-old benches and desks invite you to sit. It is a rectangular type of place with a concrete floor and built-in platform for tea making place, which was set on the far end of the place. You could see Saroja in her early thirties busy boiling water in the copper boiler, straining tea bags, adding milk and sugar, etc... She did everything in a very professional manner and occasionally came to the desk with a basin full of *snacks*.

People coming for tea only take one or two *dal vada* not wanting to eat but to see the white beautiful array of her gleaming teeth and enjoy some hearty talks. She knew the customers by name and used to call them by name with the suffix *anna*, meaning elder brother. She would take a few banana leaves cut into small pieces to keep *vada* on the leaf and would start some small talks and new happenings in the village. She had that magnetic way of talking that many men would sit for hours together and order more *vadas* and tea. She was also adept at controlling the crowd.

During evenings when the crowd overflows her small place, she would stop talking and clear out the customers so that the waiting ones on the road side get seats inside. This act of clearing the place led to clashes among the customers. Then she would intervene and keep the peace. At any cost, she would not take sides with anyone for the only motto was more sales."

"Ok. Ok. Ramesh."

I intervened, "Now, it is high time that you come out of the tea shop. It is boring. What is there to describe so much about a tea shop? Just skip the tea shop and go further."

"Alright, I will tell you briefly," Ramesh continued, "On a particular day when we entered the tea shop there were very few people inside sipping tea and were unusually silent. A small girl of about ten years was cleaning the tea glasses in cold water and then in hot water. As we sat on an empty bench the girl ran inside yelling, 'Amma, new customers'. In a few moments, Saroja, the tea shop owner came out from the ante room, draping a cotton saree and a blouse made of voile cloth with a ball of jasmine flowers at the top of her plaited black thick hair length. The smell of fragrant turmeric from her face revealed that he had taken bath just now only.

"When she came near us the smell of jasmine, that fragrant turmeric added with the smell from the sandal incense sticks provided some kind of inviting aura in that shop. It was seven in the evening and outside there was only one tube light provided in the pole by the panchayat. But inside the room, it was sufficiently lit by a few high-watt bulbs."

He looked at my face for a few moments.

I said, "Ramesh. Enough, you are going on telling irrelevant things. You may be getting late. Your regular bus would have gone. Your wife and children must be looking for you. I have no problem. If you have to continue your story let us make it tomorrow."

"Listen. Listen. I am not in a hurry. My family is away at her parents' home. They will reach late at night only. I have plenty of time. Moreover, I would like to have dinner with you today! Promotion- transfer-dinner!" Ramesh calmly told this with extra patience.

I was impatient. He was going on with the same thing and not coming to the bonus point. I attempted to get up.

But he caught my hand and forced me to sit and listen! I said, "Ok. Be precise." Ramesh started again.

"While checking the boiling milk in the brass pot kept on the hearth, adjusting firewood to low flames Saroja asked us, 'Tea or coffee?' showing her shining teeth

The village elder who took me there looked at my face.

I said, 'Anything.'

He asked for coffee. Saroja asked him staring at me, "Who is this new boy?"

"He is our new postmaster, sir."

She gave a big *vanakkam* and commented, "Very young postmaster!". I personally felt a little elated by her remarks. She did not know that I was basically a clerk only. During those days I ran the office with one ED staff only. Now the same has been elevated."

"Ramesh. Okay. I know all these official things. Now come to the tea shop."

Now I showed interest in knowing the details related to the tea shop.

After the tasty coffee and *vada* the elderly man started a conversation with her.

"Saroja, nowadays, we don't usually see you in the daily market in the morning."

She replied with a smile, “Oh, Anna, I am getting things on a weekly basis from that chettiyar boy. He brings everything in a vehicle every Sunday.”

“Oh, yes. I saw that handsome boy taking bath in the river the other day”.

She rushed to tell them his name. “He is Seenu.»

But how come he took bath in the river on that day early morning? Saroja did not like his questioning. “I don’t know,” she said indifferently.

“If I am right, he is the only son of Raghuraman of Radhapuram.”

On this question, she was startled and I saw Saroja’s face blushing. Suddenly, she changed her facial expressions and tone and went inside throwing an angry and suspicious glance at the elderly man and uttering some feeble words.

I felt the air was somewhat disturbing and wanted to get back. Understanding the mood of the elderly man, she called him in. When I was about to get out of the shop he came out and said she had prepared dinner for me and I could finish it and return to my room.

I asked the man, “Why should I take dinner here? As usual, I’ll have it in my room.”

But without telling me anything that man left me in the hotel and while going out, he said, “We will meet tomorrow. Good night.”

Now, I felt smelling something foul over there. I could not understand what was going to happen to me there."

Ramesh took a long breath and sat relaxed. This time I didn't rush up. I wanted to know what happened next. I grew impatient. As it was time to close the office we got out and started walking along the footpath enjoying the usual cacophony of the busy road in the city with occasional body dashes with the window shoppers.

The speed walking over takers always hit us. The broken walkway was another obstacle for the free walk, coupled with the pavement encroachers compelled the walkers to get down on the busy road. Many a time, the bikers came in for a close encounter. The slightest carelessness could lead the walkers to the hospital. And in some stretches, the acidic stench emanating from the broken gutter lids forced us to hold our breath for a very long time.

I often felt that an hour of a walk along the foot path in the city equals two hours of physical and breathing exercises. In some places, the platform was eighteen or more inches in height forcing the pedestrians to climb down or climb up. Enjoying all the musings we walked carefully. In the midst of all these, he was narrating the story amidst panting and I was listening. This time word by word.

He continued, "No customers were in the shop and Saroja suddenly took my hand and pulled me inside. I could not resist the smell of jasmine, turmeric and sandal but I wanted to get myself free. I felt all my strength was draining out."

I said. "Let me go. It is getting late."

She threw a harsh look at me and asked, "Where are you going? Is your wife waiting for you? Idiot!"

I, using my full strength loosened myself from her grip and prepared myself to go out. Angrily she questioned me, "Then why the hell did you come here for?"

"For coffee and *vada*," I said calmly. Again she caught my hand. Her hands were rough enough to squeeze my soft palms. I looked outside. It was dark and no one was to be seen on the road. When again I pulled my hand she yelled at me, "Coward, get lost!"

And she was murmuring something which I could not decode. My only aim was to get out of the murky place. At this point, a little girl in a frock came running and informed her that she was going to bed. The unusual situation there did not seem to bother her and she left. I kept moving a little towards the door and trembling like a lamb in front of a hungry tiger.

Saroja was all in white as she could realise my temperament by watching my facial convulsions. Still holding my hand, she moved towards the door and loosened her grip. As I pulled myself away, I could hear her uttering, "I haven't come across such a nerveless fellow like this. That too at this age." She showed me the door for me to get out. I wanted to run away in the darkness. But still, I turned back and saw she was looking at me showing her jasmine teeth. The low fixed bulb was glowing on her turmeric-coloured face which was overflowing with all the navarasas! She called out 'Come again, sir.'

Ramesh heaved a sigh and told, "This was the only muddling experience for me over there. Or otherwise, the village and its people were very nice and enjoyable."

I asked him, "So that was the gift that the elder man gave you? Can I believe your story?"

We laughed aloud standing near his bus stop and departed soon when his bus approached.

A week later, I came to the office and spent the whole day clearing my desk as I was taking leave from my colleagues the next day. Today was my final day in this office. Vasantha who occupied my next table commented, "At last, you could escape from the hustle and bustle of city life. I wish you all the best". Some young bachelors were envious of my posting. "Lucky fellow!" "Heartfelt congratulations!" came from my immediate friend.

Ramesh wished me good luck with a sparkle in his eyes and with a crooked smile reminding me of that turmeric and jasmine. He looked as if he lost something!

Back in my room, I started cleaning and packing my paraphernalia for I had to leave the room key to the landlord that night itself and board the night train. It is an eight-hour night journey to the nearest city to the village I was heading to. After finishing all the work, I met the landlord and handed over the key.

I reached the railway station one hour early and the train's departure time was at ten pm. The only job left for me was to have dinner. I went to the nearby Udupi restaurant where the bachelors working in the vicinity flock around for dinner. Even some husbands of lazy housewives come and took heavy parcels for the entire family. Some bachelors opted for the monthly system in which they could devour as much as they wished. I finished my dinner and started walking towards the station. Still, there was a lot of time left for the departure of the train. As my luggage was already safe in the clock room, I was free with a handbag only. I wanted to experience the long walk once again on the foot paths having all the obstacles, which I might surely miss in my host village. While walking, I enjoyed the familiar shops, buildings, evening scenes and the stench.

I felt as if I was losing all these things. What to lose. They were never mine! More than ten years I spent in the city made me feel that all these familiar objects were mine. Strange. My mind got lost in a lot of happenings during my long association with the city. My thoughts ramified into several happenings both happy and sad. In between, that jasmine and turmeric smell also came. Was it? No! It was only a sandal smell coming from some shops, burning sandal incense sticks. Suddenly the smell of the railway station overtook the others and I came to reality and I went straight to the clock room and received my luggage. An unusually pleasing-mannered porter, who seemed as if an old-time friend, enquired me with polished politeness, my well beings and where I was going…etc. I could not make out whether it was an acting or trade trick or anything else. Any how I liked him for his sophisticated lip services. With my permission, he lifted my luggage and started to walk to the designated platform. He left, telling me to take care of the luggage. He also told me that he would come back as soon as the train arrived and by that time he would look for some other Sahib like me. I knew that these porters simultaneously engaged three or four passengers at a time to earn more. He was walking hastily to spot other passengers.

I looked around the place to sit but there was no suitable place to sit. Most of the chairs on the platform were either shabby or broken, but still occupied by passengers, non-passengers, night dwellers, and even beggars and street urchins.

Therefore, I started to loiter along the platform observing the untidy up keep of the place. In some places, a nostril-piercing stench was felt, emanating from the tracks for which both passengers and authorities were responsible. While I was just strolling, my eyes were always on my luggage. Because when the train arrived there would be a sudden rush and some of the unattended boxes might vanish.

Mostly the luggage lifters targeted luggage of families or groups who travelled to attend marriages and other family functions.

As I was alone with old and shabby trunks and beddings, the robbers would not be attracted. But still, I had to be careful not to lose my things whatever I could say my own. The train arrived with a new diesel engine. It was talk of the town that Railways were replacing all the stream engines with the new diesel ones. Our porter came in doubles through the jostling crowd. He had already with him a set of two large suitcases on his turbaned head, three shoulder bags which seemed anytime they would zip out and also a number of cloth carry bags bulging like some people with the enormous fatty body. He was followed by the owners of these luggage bags, a fat and short man of around sixty and an equally sized lady. They were sure to board my bogie as the porter was pushing through the crowd to the same compartment where my birth was booked. I wondered whether the three-seater could accommodate these two and all their luggage. I prayed to let them not go to my cabin and watched eagerly.

But to my dismay, my prayers did not work and they had already occupied the spaces in my cabin. But somehow the porter had kept all our luggage everywhere under the seat, over the berths on the hangers and side walkways which I expected, would cause a sure tussle amongst us and also other passengers who were about to come.

As expected, the other three persons also came. They had black steel boxes, one each, not very big, with their name written. I learnt that they were Army personnel going to join some field units. They did not speak a word about the space. Instead, they murmured something and found some other places in adjacent compartments.

The porter settled coolie with the couple after having some arguments. He received the amount given by them and turned to me.

"How much do you want?"

"Whatever you give me," he humbly said.

"A porter in the city talking like this?" Anyway, I gave him a reasonable amount. He accepted it and while leaving he said, "Sir, I am Murugan. My number is eighteen. When you come again please look for me. Bye."

I said, "Sure."

He smiled and walked away contented.

In the compartment that lady was scolding her husband.

"Why did you give him that two rupees extra? He did not deserve it."

Her husband contested, " Why not? He deserved more. We should have given more than what he demanded. Because he carried all these boxes single-handedly and kept them safe and secure."

"Did he carry all the pieces," the lady got annoyed.

"I carried my handbag and you carried your handbag. Do you know how much this bag weighs? It contains *idli* for both of us, chutney and your bunch of bananas and this whisky bottle containing water." The fatty husband looked at all of us and his gesture requested the rest of us to kindly bear with her.

The train started thirty minutes later than the scheduled time as usual. Our three army boys opened their dinner packets and immediately the air filled with the aroma of masala. They had purchased biryani from the nearby hotel. Our couple did not like the pungent smell of biryani specially the women started making faces. The man asked her, "Shall we also start?" "No. No. Not now. Let them finish and settle." She told looking out through the window.

The train had already passed the city limits and was moving fast. In the other compartments also people were busy eating and some were preparing their beds.

The man threw a friendly gaze at me and asked, "Where are you, sir? Up to Tirunelveli?"

I said, "No, Trichy.

Without asking he revealed, "We are going to Tirunelveli. We are returning from our daughter's home in Madras."

"What is your son-in-law doing in the city?" out of curiosity I asked.

"He is doing business". His wife looked at him. From her looks, he understood that he could not reveal anything further about himself or his family. Again she turned towards the window. Contesting her warning look again he asked, "Where do you work?"

I said, "Post office."

"Oh, very nice. What service they are doing! Just imagine if there is no post office functioning in the country we can never communicate with our relatives and friends". In a low voice, he told me, "Her brother is also in the post office in Avadi."

I appreciated him, "Very nice". His wife did not like our conversation.

But again he started, "Where are you going?"

"Trichy."

"Yes. Yes. You told me."

"You stay in Trichy or in Madras?"

"I am on the way to my new place of posting as a village postmaster."

"Oh very nice."

Turning towards his wife, he said, "See, Marathakam, he is going to join as postmaster. Your brother is also in the post office working as ED for so many years." He started greying, "Still he is ED only."

I could see the chubby face of Marathakam turning hues. She gave him a powerful jerk with her knee on him. She thought with the metre gauge train's jerks on the tracks her jerk would go unnoticed. But that proved wrong when the army boys had a veiled laugh on seeing this. She immediately asked him to go and wash his hands. When he reached out of the compartment, she took the bottle of water and washed her hands splashing droplets all around.

By the time Mr Paramanand came washing his hands and sat with a thud on the wooden train seat. He asked me, "Aren't you taking food?"

"Thank you. I have already taken from Udupi."

After thrusting a bit of *idli* into her mouth she looked at me and asked, "So where is your family? Why did you take your dinner in the hotel?"

Paramanand intervened, "Marathakam, do not ask such stupid questions. He might have started early from his residence and hence he might have taken food from the hotel. These are to be asked to a stranger?"

His reasoning did not solve her quest.

"Then he could have brought a packet from home. His wife did not care for him properly". Turning towards me again, she asked, "What about your children? How many kids do you have? "

I said, "Not yet married."

"Not yet married! Why? You have a good job. Not bad to look at and healthy also. Then what happened? You must have crossed thirty?"

Looking deep into my eyes she said, "Get married soon, okay? Being single does not help anybody".

This time Paramanand gave a stronger jerk on the knee of Marakatham gesturing her to stop her queries.

Having delved deep into my personal affairs, I felt that it was not fair if I did not ask anything about their family.

"How many children do you have? All are married?"

It seemed they did not expect such a question from me. They lapsed into silence for some time and gestured to me that they would tell me later after finishing their *idlis.* But during the course of dinner, he said, "Only one daughter got after years of medical tests and visiting most of the temples in south India. It was a late issue and only recently did my daughter got married! Anyhow God's grace!" They finished dinner and were looking for their berths.

When the T.T.E. came and finished his job and left our compartment, the poor couple realised that they had an upper and middle berth. In any way, neither of them could climb on to the upper berth. I had a lower berth and one of the trio had also the opposite lower. Mrs Marakatham stood up and looked at me as if she as pleading. As I had already decided that I could climb, one of the trio also offered the lower berth. We saw a great amount of relief on the faces of the couple and they profusely thanked us. When we all settled for sleep it was nearly eleven pm.

Around six am. the train pulled into the Trichy junction. As I was readying to take out my luggage, an aged TB patient like a porter came inside and demanded a certain amount to keep the luggage in a taxi outside the station. The amount he demanded was lesser than what the porter at Madras demanded. I immediately consented and after bidding goodbye to my fellow passengers who were still in bed I walked to the taxi stand. The taxi driver along with his cleaner took me to the bus stand at fairly low charges.

The bus station was very much smelly and totally nauseating combined with the dirt and marsh caused by the previous night's rain the uneven surface of the bus stand floor had a number of pot holes and the stray dogs had their morning contributions everywhere.

The usual fight for the morning food between the crows and the dogs had its heyday on the waste dump heaped along the border of the bus station. The waste dump was the main source of stench as rodents, flies, and mosquitoes had their own contributions along with the crows and dogs. In addition to this, there were a number of persons from children to the old aged and differently-abled persons selling their wares like snacks, sweets, cut fruits, and even some items like needles, combs naphthalene balls, etc… while doing services to the passengers they also were a nuisance in the bus and the bus station.

Having seen and experienced all these, I thought I should not have come here for the bus. Instead, I could have taken a cab from the railway station straight away to reach my destination. Now it is seven in the morning and I approached a person sitting on a three-legged steel chair resting his elbow on the rusted small table in front of him, who seemed to be a timekeeper of the bus stand. I asked him for the bus going to Kumbakonam via Maruthoor. He said it would take another hour. Looking at me and my luggage pieces he advised me to take a taxi.

Because I would not be able to manage in the bus which would be over crowded. With a smile, he said, "You may get a place to stand on the bus but your luggage has to be loaded on top of the bus. Here some porter would be available but in the village, you would have to climb and get them landed on the roadside. Can you?"

"Not possible. Therefore, you may look for a taxi," he himself replied.

He turned away to attend to an old couple. Having heard his sermon on reality I decided to hire a taxi. On seeing my helplessness, the time keeper asked a boy standing nearby to take me to the taxi waiting outside of the bus stand.

There were a few taxi drivers having morning tea and chatting away. An eagle-eyed one had spotted me and said, "Sir, where do you want to go?"

"Maruthoor."

"How many are you?"

"Only me."

"Any luggage?"

"Yes. A steel trunk and bedding and tell me how much you would charge?"

"Why do you worry about the charges? Where is your luggage?" He said as if he was taking me for free.

"No. First, tell me how much you want?"

"Okay."

He discussed with his fellow drivers and told me, "Twenty rupees."

I explained it is only fifteen km.

"Yes, sir, I know but you have to go a long winding way from the main road." With a grim face, I turned away from him and looked at the bus stand.

The boy who came with me recommended, "Sir, just accept it. You won't get lesser than this amount."

Again I kept quiet for some time.

Other taxi drivers also sang in chorus with the boy.

"Sir, accept it."

The boy ran towards the bus stand and victoriously brought the luggage and kept it on top of the black and yellow taxi.

I said, "Keep it in the boots."

The driver apologized saying, "The dicky door is in repair. Don't worry. I will tie them with ropes on the carrier."

As the boy was sticking on to me for some time and looking at my face only to make me realise that he wanted coolie for the work he had done. I gave him one rupee which he accepted with brimming gratitude. I was asked to sit inside. The cleaner cleaned the backseat with a shabby torn towel that was black due to oil and dust.

After two or three attempts the old land master roared to a start and then only I sat in the rear seat, which was found punctured in several places. The cleaner occupied the front seat near the driver and we left the place sent off by the happy boy.

I did not want to comfort myself in the cab for the shabby interior was really annoying. Also, the incense stick which was burning on the dashboard made me sneeze several times. The only solace was a thick garland of fresh Jasmine flowers hanging from the rear view mirror. The Jasmine once again reminded me of my friend's cafeteria in the village.

To break the silence and to divert the attention of my ears from the cling - cling metal sound of the old vehicle and the roaring engine noise I asked.

"Driver, what is your name?"

He said, "Habeeb, and my cleaner is Alex."

On looking at the stone-carved Ganesh statue with sandal paste on the forehead, I asked him, “Who owns the vehicle?”

“Sir, this vehicle is owned by Shanmugham, who owns another six vehicles also. He owns a theatre also in the heart of the town.”

I exclaimed, “Oh, very nice!”

Alex commented, “Very rich guy,” he continued, “sir, our master owns six houses and six paddy fields.”

I said, “Strange. Everything is in six.”

“Sir, he is a staunch devotee of Lord Murugan. You know Murugan has six faces?”

Alex added, “You know, sir, he has six fingers on both of his hands?”

Then I asked, “How many wives does he have?”

“Only one sir, but he has six children! And he says before he dies he wants to have a total of six theatres!” Alex told with great admiration to Mr Shanmugham.

When we reached a small junction the driver said, “Now we have to turn left for the village. It is more than five km. The road is not black toped but gravelled with a lot of pot holes. No much vehicular traffic on this side. Occasionally a bullet motorcycle owned by some rich farmers runs apart from the regular bullock carts.”

We stopped at the junction in front of a small tea shop on the roadside and had tea. I was really hungry as I had not even taken a drop of water since morning. I took a pair of small bananas also. When sipping tea, Alex shouted, "See our master is going". A sky-blue Chevrolet was going at normal speed. The man at the wheel was Mr Shanmugham Chettiar.

I asked, "He is your master?"

"Yes, he must be going to Kumbakonam where his elder son is living with family. He never allows anybody else to drive his vehicle. Always self-drive only. Even he won't allow his children to drive. He used to say that he purchased this vehicle from some film star living in Chennai."

Habeeb said, "The car is nice to look at. But the performance is not up to the mark. Every month we could see it in Ganeshan's workshop."

We continued on the bumpy gravelled road. So many bullock carts could be seen with a heavy load of agricultural commodities heading towards the markets in Trichy and Kumbakonam.

On the left of the road, I saw newly planted paddy fields, and on the right side ploughed farm land with marsh where a flock of ducks was feeding. Those ducks were attempting to cross the road but the duck owner never bothered to shoo them away from the road. He was simply standing with the long slender pole with a white cloth tied as a flag to regulate the traffic of ducks. After honking several times, he slowly started yelling at those ducks in some peculiar whistling sound and with this somehow these ducks were driven out of our way.

After some time again another left turn came where it was written "Welcome to Maruthoor panchayat". From a distance, the village looked beautiful with green fields, orchids and the blue mountains as a backdrop spotted with a lot of terracotta tiled houses in between. From this place, we could even see the small Gopuram of the temple standing majestically. We stopped near a man standing in front of a tea shop with a thatched shed and a tiled roof at the back which appeared like a small house. I thought this could be the place vividly described by my friend back in the city. I asked him for the village post office. He suspiciously looked at us and said to go straight and turn left.

After entering the village, we turned left and immediately we could see the red and white board of the post office at the far end of the street on a corner plot. We went past an array of small tiled houses without compounds with broad verandas and reached in front of the post office. This building was also tiled but had an upstairs also. A large hall designated for the stay of the postmaster was upstairs. The hall had four numbers of small windows opening out to the street and also, and we could see several windows on all other sides.

We got down from the car and were about to enter the premises which had also no compound wall on the front side. The peon had already arrived and there was rangoli in front of the steps leading to the door. The peon came out and took my luggage which was brought down by the cleaner from the car. I paid the amount agreed with the driver and an extra five rupees to the cleaner who was very happy to receive it. The car left and I entered the post office premises. There was a board painted red which showed working hours from nine am to five pm without any break!

A quick survey of the building revealed that the building was at least a hundred years old but heavily built with thick walls and pillars. The wood used was so thick that the two central pillars bearing the structure had almost fifteen inches in diameter and solid teak wood! Similarly, the door and window frames were made of almost five inches-thick logs of teak wood.

I could see a lot of people peeping out of the doors and windows towards the post office. Their inquisitive glances provided a way for other bystanders and household ladies to come out openly to see who had come over to the post office.

As I entered the main hall a few children, most of them without any upper garments were looking inside through the windows. I thought probably they were looking for a friendly post master. The peon Mr Ramaswamy was simply chasing the children and said.

"As it is a local holiday today these children have no classes. So they pass their time roaming in the village.

Today they got a subject to ponder over!" "Sir," the peon continued, "as there is no piped water in the village you have to use the well water drawn and stored in that cement tub. This water is used for all purposes including drinking and cooking. You may go upstairs where all arrangements were made for your stay. There is a kitchen facility also done at the far corner of the hall."

I went to the backyard and surveyed. The well was neatly maintained with steel mesh as the top cover. There were some hibiscus, *tulsi* and jasmine plants that were seen uncared.

"Ramaswamy, you don't water the plants?" "No, sir who cares? Moreover, nobody wants these flowers. And those children are regular visitors here because of the Jamun tree over there. It was a well-grown tree having a lot of fruits. But not ripe at present."

"During the season, these children would play havoc. Previous postmasters have befriended these children and therefore they think it is their right to play inside the compound. But I don't allow them to do so."

"Where do you stay?" I asked Ramaswamy.

"My home is at Paloor, just a few minutes' walk across the fields. Or you can go by cycle also in a roundabout via Main Road. Paloor village is also under Marathoor Panchayat only."

"Are you married?"

"Yes sir".

"Children?"

"Two. A boy and a girl aged ten and seven years."

"What is your wife doing?"

"She is looking after a set of buffaloes and she sells milk to a few houses."

"You don't mix water in the milk?"

"No, sir. It will be pure. You can see the milk I brought already… it is kept upstairs. Very pure. From tomorrow, my wife would be bringing milk to you and to a few houses in the opposite lane."

Though I said I was going to cook I was not in the mood to do so. I told him to go and come before office time. I finished my morning ablutions. Though the tub was filled up I tried my hand at drawing water from the well. The rhythmic creek of the pulley reminded me of some music notes.

I thought of sending one proposal for an overhead tank and motor with tap connections. But I was not sure when the sanction would come. By the time sanction came, I would have been transferred or even retired. If I do it, someone else could enjoy it if not me. Many people enjoyed the fruits of the trees planted by a few people.

I surveyed the village by walking mainly the four streets centred by the Shiva temple. The temple seemed to be very old. Signs of renovations done over centuries were loudly visible. The four walls built with heavy stones attracted me. On close examination, I found there were no plasters in between the stone blocks. Later, I learned that the walls were built using the pit and rod technique to keep the blocks in position. The wall had survived many floods and storms through the ages and it was still intact. In the middle of the compound was the Sanctum Sanctorum with a small tower on top of it built using bricks and lime mortar. The tower seemed to be relatively built at a later stage.

I loved the place, specially the open areas between the walls and the shrine. For it was all fresh river sand with a narrow granite walkway. Along the wall there were a variety of plants like *tulsi* of different types, jasmine, hibiscus, *parijathas*, *pavizhamalli* and a tall banyan also could be seen with a few *vilva* trees. Whoever might be the gardener all these plants were well groomed and maintained.

I learned from an elderly devotee that the temple was run by the village trustee. These trustee members used to meet just before the annual festival and after the celebration, the temple was left in the lurch. Sometimes, there wouldn't be enough money even to purchase *pooja* materials.

It was revealed that the Panchayat gave some money. The daily *pooja* was being done by Mr Ramanatha Iyer who was a clerk in some government office in the city.

"Is he getting any money for doing these *poojas*?" I asked the elderly man.

"No, sir. He has been doing it on his own, spending sometimes his own little money."

I thought I should meet that great Iyer who was in service to God.

"No contribution from the villagers?"

"No, sir. During festivals, the landlords of the village give money to show their might."

"Where is that Iyer staying?"

"On the east street just outside the temple compound."

I said thanks and was about to leave the place when he asked me, "I have never seen you in this village. What brought you here?"

"Oh. Sorry, I forgot to tell you. I am the new postmaster here. I came only today."

"Very nice. Glad that I met you here."

He left after promising to meet me at the post office. His short-paced steps and the little bend on his vertebrae spoke his age. Thereafter I made a habit to visit the temple every day in the morning and evening.

I stepped out of the temple and immediately on the right was the house of Iyer, a very old tiled structure with an open veranda, facing the street. I made it a point to meet him in the evening. As I was feeling much hungry. I remembered my friend's fragrant tea shop.

That was the only tea shop in the village which I saw in the early morning when we asked for the location of the post office. The very thought of the teashop brought me the imaginary smell of turmeric, jasmine and sandal.

As I approached the shop, I saw a lady clad in a yellow Madurai *Sungadi* saree with a blood-red *voil* blouse which presented a veiled revelation of her rich contours. She was cleaning some glasses and occasionally stirring the milk vessel with a ladle. I stepped inside and sat on a bench. She approached me with a strange look. "Come, sir. New to the village? Any relatives? Would you like to have *idli* and *vada*?"

I said, "Yes."

She called her daughter and asked her to bring *idli* and *vada* on a piece of plantain leaf. The little girl of around twelve years brought me a glass of water along with *idli* and *vada*, which were of course tasty. The lady asked me, "Coffee or tea?"

I said, "Coffee."

By then a few others had also got in to have breakfast. They seemed to be the Paddy field workers. They also looked at me curiously.

My coffee was served and the lady went to the kitchen side. She was taking hot *idli* into an aluminium bowl.

The place was just an extension from the front door of her house which was previously used to be an open veranda. A pounding stone with a pestle, a grinding stone, a dry grinder made of stone, etc., were neatly kept along the wall of the house on the polished cement floor. It seemed there were no other workers on the premises.

The lady looked more charming than my friend had described. She must have celebrated her thirty-fifth birthday recently. But she looked much younger and was very active. But the only thing missing from what Ramesh detailed to me was there was no turmeric or jasmine only the sandal *agarbatti* was burning. I looked all around but I could find only a thin last night's small garland on a large picture of Lord Ganesh with a small brass oil lamp. I thought she might have abandoned the habit of using jasmine and turmeric.

The food was much cheaper than at Madras hotels. Moreover, it was fresh and very tasty also. It seemed she wanted to ask more queries but when she found more and more people coming in, she told me to come again and turned to others.

By the time I reached the post office, though it was a Sunday I saw Ramaswamy was doing a cleaning job. Here the job of ED clerk or peon was multitasking—cleaning, sorting, sealing, collecting mail from the two mailboxes in the villages, vending stamps and stationery when the master was not there, etc., were all part of the job specification for them. The best of it was that they did all this with utmost sincerity, unlike city guys.

After having surveyed the different areas within the office, I occupied the chair the postmaster was supposed to sit, which had visible signs of old age and one of the legs was broken and was joined with a piece of wood by an unskilled carpenter, probably one of the staff members of the post office. The cane weaving at the chair back had been torn in more than one place. I decided to have a new chair. If I was asked permission from my controlling officer, I might not get it during my service period. Therefore, I decided to buy one chair with my funds and use it. Again, if some strict auditor came, I might be in trouble for using personal property in the office!

When I told this Ramaswamy, he said that the proposal for the new furniture was pending in the controlling office for more than eight years. He promised me that by evening, he would arrange to have a new chair from the town. I finished my lunch and dinner also from Kanakas.

On the next day also, I did not do any kitchen work simply because of laziness. The people started to pour in for various postal needs. Most important of all was the urgency for a trunk call. I learned that none of the households had any telephone connection, even the rich farm owners did not have it!

All of them heavily relied on the post office. Most of them come for the trunk call only to their people in different cities.

Ramaswamy came with the day's mailbag collected for the day and started sorting. In just an afternoon he would go on his bicycle with the mailbag and return by four pm as he had to go two-three other villages. But he had to clear the mailboxes in all the villages whether rain or shine. Before going, Ramaswamy asked me about lunch. He said, "You haven't had anything since morning. What about lunch?" I said with a hidden smile, "Ramaswamy, in the morning, I went to Kanaka's tea shop."

"You went to Kanaka's!" exclaimed Ramaswamy. "Sir, if it's okay for you, then I would send some food for you. Home-cooked lunch today."

Reluctantly, I agreed. Ramaswamy took his old cycle and came back in half an hour with a brass tiffin carrier and a plantain leaf. He kept them in the rear room where a bench and desk were provided. A bottle of boiled water was also brought to him. I felt guilty when I was taking Ramasamy's lunch. I could have gone to Saroja's tea shop. In the evening, he carried a flask full of coffee from home.

I said, "Look, Ramaswamy. It is fine today. Thank you for your hospitality. But from tomorrow onwards, I will do it. Okay?"

"Yes sir, "

"Bring me some kerosene oil and arrange for milk every day."

"Done, sir". He left on his cycle as the day's work was over and it was well past six in the evening.

I opened up my steel box and took out the newly purchased kerosene stove and a few stainless steel kitchen wares. I set up the kitchen in an hour. But as kerosene was to come only the next day I sat quietly thinking about what was to be done. When the *agarbatti*'s smell came along with the wind from the neighbour's house my thoughts hovered over Kanaka's tea shop. I also felt that imaginary smell of jasmine and turmeric. I felt I missed lunch in the teashop. After a lot of analysis, I decided to have dinner at Kanaka's tea shop.

When I locked the side entrance and stepped out, the lady from the adjacent house came and told me, "I came to know that you have joined this post office yesterday. I am Janaki, a teacher in that school… you can see out there. It seems you are going out for dinner."

I said, "Yes."

"But there is only one hotel in this village. But that won't be suitable for you."

I did not know what made her say that. Anyway, I just presented a smile and left the place. I walked straight to Kanaka's. Inside, a few people were having a variety of food items, like *idli*, *dosa*, *vada*, *bajjies*. Saroja and her daughter were busy serving food.

I sat on the edge of a bench for there was no other space. The girl came running and told the other man to move a little more so that I could sit properly. She placed a plantain leaf and served me *dosa* and *vada* which I asked for, with a generous serving of *sambar*. The girl said, "Hold the leaf, sir, or else your *dhothi* would be smeared with *sambhar*!"

I was more on observing Saroja. She was very busy making tea and coffee. Now, I noticed that she had that turmeric and jasmine. Really, the space was full of fragrance more so when she came close to the customers for serving coffee or tea. It seemed she was fond of wearing colourful dresses. Now, she was draped in a pink *voile* saree with a maroon-coloured *voile* blouse—of course, in her own bewitching style.

I looked around and realized that most of them were drunk. Their body language clearly told that. I felt sorry for this lady and her daughter that they were destined to serve these drunkards. While taking cash from me for the food she gave me a clue that either I could visit the teashop before seven or after nine pm when these drunkards won't be there.

While returning, Sethuraman, the headmaster of the school, accompanied me. He talked about many things about the village and was staying alone for the last couple of years. He was on a 'punishment transfer' from Madurai. He said he was simply punished by the government because of some irregularities found in the milk powder by CARE, a programme of the US government to eradicate malnutrition among Indian school children. Apparently, he was made a scapegoat for the corruption done by the local politicians and higher officials of the department! His wife and children were in Madurai. He used to visit them on weekends.

He accompanied me up to the post office and left. The next day, while discharging my duties, I had a chance to meet Mr Ramanatha Iyer, in the post office. I respectfully wished him. He invited me to his house. I always wanted to visit his house, and a formal invitation confirmed the same. That day, after dinner, I went to meet him.

I knew that he would be free only after seven-thirty pm when the temple was closed for the day. Iyer was sitting on the granite block of the veranda. Upon seeing me, he stood up and invited me into the hall where some old, simple furniture could be seen. He led me to an old chair and gestured for me to sit. We had some chats at the temple and the village. Iyer was a very pious gentleman, on the verge of retirement. Neither did he have any side business to supplement his income nor did he have any substantial savings.

By that time, a lady of about thirty years old came with two brass tumblers with coffee. He introduced her, "She is Ganga, my only daughter."

I asked her, "What are you doing?"

"Nothing particular."

"Then? Not working?

Iyer intervened,

"Sir, she has finished her B.Sc. But for several years she could not get any job. Finally, she got one but that was somewhere in north India, in a government corporation. Everywhere they needed experience, moreover, the cast marked in the certificate stood as a disqualification in several places. What to do? We have to bear with this complex socio-political system." After a pause, he continued, "Look here, sir. I am not blaming anybody. Now, my only wish is to give her hand to a responsible man in marriage. In a matter of two years, I will retire. Then I would be doing full-time service to Lord Mahadeva."

I left the place with some kind of distraught and that night I could not sleep well. Many thoughts had repeatedly banged my head.

After seeing that girl Ganga, I had a feeling which was unexplainable. The very thought of turmeric and jasmine getting faded out from my mind instead I started seeing Ganga in my mind screen.

I did not know when I went to sleep. I woke up only when Ramaswamy's wife yelled through the window, "Sir, milk! Sir, milk!" It was six in the morning and I opened the door for her. She straightaway went to the kitchen and kept the milk vessel and asked, "Shall I heat the milk"? "No. You may go. But still, I thought I should have asked her to make tea for me! I felt I am becoming lazier and lazier in kitchen work. By then Ramaswamy came and he made coffee for me and suddenly he asked me, "Don't be annoyed, sir. It is high time at least now you should find some girl for marriage. Shall I help you, sir? See, I have two children and I am just five years younger than you! Please think of it."

Many people have asked me and advised me previously but this time I felt I should see for myself instead of my parents looking for a daughter-in-law with lots of dowries. The entire day I was pondering over Ramaswamy's words. In the evening, before the post office closes, Ganga came there for some postal stationery along with a few children, to whom she was taking tuition classes.

I was happy to see her near the window, so I asked her, "Hi, Ganga! What brought you here?"

"Just a few items I wanted to buy from you, postcards and inland letters and some ten paisa stamps."

"Why so many stamps?"

"My father had brought me a lot of plain envelopes. I would send job applications using them!"

After she left I asked Ramaswamy, "Does she come here often?"

"No, sir… very rarely… mostly Iyer comes".

My thoughts went wild. Immediately after meeting her the previous day why did she come? Moreover, I noticed Ramaswamy carefully watching us while she was at the window. Could it be the handiwork of Mr Ramaswamy?

Throughout the next week, I was thinking about my marriage and I felt as if it was coming closer. I started feeling a sense of attraction towards Ganga, the slender and well-mannered girl. In the evenings, when the women of that age walked around I saw Ganga in everyone! I started thinking about her very often.

A few days later, Ramaswamy and his wife came to me in the evening.

"Sir, we have come to you with a purpose."

I asked, "Any financial help?"

"No, I am coming to the matter directly.

"His wife said, "Ganga would be a good match for you… I mean for marriage."

She looked at Ramaswamy.

Ramaswamy bending his head said, "Yes sir, we could judge from her walks and talks since you met her the other day".

I paused for a while and said, "What do you say? Ramanatha Iyer is an orthodox Iyer and I am a non-Brahmin. How can it be?"

"Sir, just tell me your opinion, rest we would see."

I kept quiet for some time. Then I told them that I would tell them the next day. They left on a positive note. That day I contacted my parents by trunk call and told them everything. Without any objection they readily accepted and the next day morning they reached the post office.

Ramaswamy had arranged a meeting between us and Iyer. During the discussion, the talks of Brahmin and non-Brahmin did not come from anybody. I had already explained the financial status of Ganga to my parents but I was surprised to see that they didn't have any such expectations!

Everything followed in haste. Both sides had informed the near and dear ones and the marriage was solemnised in the Ekambareswaran temple. But I noticed my parents kept a grim face with reticence. I doubted it was because of "loss of dowry".

I became one among the villagers and I shifted all my belongings to Ganga's house. We spent more than about five years in the village and we had a baby boy also. Now the aroma of *Kanakas* never excited me. One day I got a letter posting me back to Madras on a higher post. My mind told me at least once, once again I should experience the fragrance of turmeric, jasmine and sandal. I took Ganga on a Sunday and visited the place, Kasturi, daughter of Saroja, came running to Ganga's teacher. Ganga told her that she should study well and get a good job.

She said, "Teacher, you studied well and taught a lot of students. But never got a job. Then how can I?"

I prayed in my mind Kasturi should not make another Saroja.

I simply laughed and commented, "Smart girl!"

I really wished them good luck. Saroja, clad in a new silk saree and had a bunch of jasmine on her hair. Her face glowed due to the fragrant turmeric. I could really experience the combined smell of turmeric, jasmine and sandal, because of our close proximity. Saroja asked Kasturi to get ready for the temple. Turning towards us, Saroja said, "Today is Kasturi's fifteenth birthday."

"Oh. Very nice, Kasturi, come here," Ganga called her and gave her a few rupees and said, "Keep it as my birthday gift to you, and remember what I said regarding your future."

"Ok, teacher."

We told them that we were leaving the village.

A few years rolled by. We were almost settled in Madras and my son had already completed high school. At this time, I chanced upon visiting Maruthoor village post office on an inspection tour. One fine morning, I landed once again in the village. Not many changes could be seen. Before entering the village, the first thing I looked for was Kanakas. Yes, it was there but with a lot of changes.

Approaching the hotel, I found it was improved well in frontal appearance. The thatched roof was no more there. In its place, a *pucca* residential cum-commercial building with bright paints could be seen. A couple of shops selling daily need items were also attached on both sides of the hotel's entrance. The shops were managed by some men. Probably rented out to them by Saroja. It was just past ten in the morning. I hesitated to enter the hotel. The newly painted multi-coloured board seemed to be shouting—Saroja Café. At the bottom right it was written, 'Prop. Kasturi'. The road to the village had been black-toped. I just walked past the hotel and reached the post office.

The post office building was the same and the Master was a person from a nearby town. The peon was the same, Ramaswamy, who was on the verge of retirement. Apart from the two, there was a female clerk also available. He was very glad to meet me. After my work, lunch was arranged at the Saroja Cafe.

I came to know from Ramaswamy that Kasturi became the owner of the hotel after Saroja's sudden demise following a short illness. Ganga's advice and tutoring did not have any impact on Kasturi and she was simply following her mother's footsteps. Other than the newcomers in the village almost all others who frequent the place were the youngsters of the village.

My friend Ramesh's description of the place was totally erased.

The unmarried Kasturi was not alone; she was assisted by a young and smart well-built man working as a tea master, server, cleaner, bodyguard and an illegal husband to Kasturi. A girl of around seventeen years and a boy of fifteen years were also doing menials in the hotel.

Before leaving the office Ramaswamy told that his father-in-law was waiting for him at his home. "I did not inform him about my visit for I wanted to have a taste of Saroja Café's lunch."

"But I told Ramaswamy that I did not want to bother my father-in-law although the reason was different. Then I went to Ganga's house and had a chat with him for some time and left the village with the satisfaction of tasting once again the aroma of *Kanakas*. But I was also sad about the untimely demise of Saroja. When I passed again on the road I had a slight desire to get into the hotel but my inner mind rebuked me and I had a speed walk as a stranger in the village and I reached the bus stop which was now an improved one."

www.ingramcontent.com/pod-product-compliance
Lightning Source LLC
LaVergne TN
LVHW091254150826
845673LV00006B/1421

* 9 7 9 8 8 8 8 0 5 4 4 1 3 *